Her Perfect Murder

Tanya Stone FBI K9 Mystery Thriller

Tikiri Herath

Rebel Diva
ACADEMY PRESS

Her Perfect Murder

Tanya Stone FBI K9 Mystery Thriller Series

www.TikiriHerath.com

Copyright © Tikiri Herath 2024

Library & Archives Canada Cataloging in Publication

E-book ISBN: 9781990234309

Paperback ISBN: 9781990234293

Hardback ISBN: 9781990234286

Paperback Large Print ISBN: 9781990234484

Hardback Large Print ISBN: 9781990234583

Audio book ISBN: 9781990234279

Author: Tikiri Herath

Publisher Imprint: Rebel Diva Academy Press

Copy Editor: Stephanie Parent

Back Cover Headshot: Aura McKay

Tikiri

The Red Heeled Rebels Universe

The Red Heeled Rebels universe of mystery thrillers, featuring your favorite kick-ass female characters.

Tanya Stone FBI K9 Mystery Thrillers

Thriller series starring Red Heeled Rebel and FBI Special Agent Tanya Stone, and her loyal German Shepherd K9, Max. These are serial killer thrillers set in Black Rock, a small upscale resort town on the coast of Washington state.

Her Deadly End
Her Cold Blood
Her Last Lie

Her Secret Crime
Her Perfect Murder
Her Grisly Grave
www.TikiriHerath.com/Thrillers

⬦——⬥

Asha Kade Private Detective Murder Mysteries

Murder mystery thrillers, featuring the Red Heeled Rebels, Asha Kade and Katy McCafferty. Asha and Katy receive one million dollars for their favorite children's charity from a secret benefactor's estate every time they solve a cold case.

Merciless Legacy
Merciless Games
Merciless Crimes
Merciless Lies
Merciless Past
Merciless Deaths
www.TikiriHerath.com/Mysteries

⬦——⬥

Red Heeled Rebels International Mystery & Crime - The Origin Story

The award-winning origin story of the Red Heeled Rebels characters. Learn how a rag-tag group of trafficked orphans from different places united to fight for their freedom and their lives and became a found family.

The Girl Who Crossed the Line
The Girl Who Ran Away
The Girl Who Made Them Pay
The Girl Who Fought to Kill

The Girl Who Broke Free
The Girl Who Knew Their Names
The Girl Who Never Forgot
www.TikiriHerath.com/RedHeeledRebels

Tikiri's novels and nonfiction books are available in e-book, paperback, and hardback editions, on all good bookstores around the world. These books are also available in libraries everywhere. Just ask your friendly local librarian or your local bookstore to order a copy for you.

www.TikiriHerath.com

Happy reading.

A Gift for You

Dear reader friend,

Thank you for picking up my book.

I write twisty thrillers that feature feisty female detectives who hunt villains and make them pay.

In my books, justice always prevails.

My stories are for smart readers who love pulse-pounding thrills and nail-biting twists. There is no explicit sex, graphic violence, or heavy cursing in my books, and no dog is ever harmed.

I'm not a marketing company or a branding firm that employs ghost writers or artificial engines. I don't hide behind a pen name or a fake avatar. I write my own books.

I'm also a reader, just like you, and I'm delighted to meet you.

Enjoy the read!

Best wishes,

Tikiri

Vancouver, Canada

PS/ There's a bonus story for this novel. You'll find the secret link to your story gift at the end of this book.

PPS/ All my books use American spelling because most of my readers live in North America. But I am a Canadian who went to international schools all over the world, so I write in mostly British English. (I know. I'm a mixed up gal.) As soon as I finish writing a book, I run a US English spell checker, and after that, my wonderful (American) editor double checks any remaining errors. But words are insidious. And sneaky. If you see a funny-looking word, please report it. Rest assured, they will be given a sound talk to and banished from my books.

<hr />

Tropes you'll find in this mystery thriller series include: female protagonists, women sleuths, police officers, police procedurals, detectives, serial killers, small towns, dark secrets, family lies & deceptions, plot twists, shocking endings, missing people, creepy cabins, fast-paced action, vigilante justice, crime, murder, kidnappings, revenge, intrigue, and psychological suspense.

<hr />

There is no explicit sex, heavy cursing, or graphic violence in my books. There is, however, a closed circle of suspects, twists and turns, and nail-biting suspense. NO DOG IS EVER HARMED IN MY BOOKS. But the villains always are....

Her Perfect Murder

FBI Special Agent Tanya Stone doesn't know she has stepped into a deathly gilded trap.

The tranquil halls of Black Rock's luxurious senior residence hide dark secrets and a devious serial killer. The killer comes at night. Their touch leaves no trace, only the chill of death.

Tanya has forty-eight hours to unmask the murderer before another precious life is taken, but the killer's whispers echo through this seaside retirement home.

"You can't outrun the past."

The residents of this resort harbor more than lifelong memories. They hide skeletons deep in their closets.

As Tanya fights to unravel the threads of betrayal and long-buried vendettas, the violent murder of her own mother haunts her troubled mind. With help from Max, her loyal K9, she is determined to uncover the twisted truth before the next victim takes their final breath.

Will Tanya survive the storm of lies?
Or will the killer claim her too?

The Night Killer

T he killer treaded softly toward the lavish bedroom.

He stood by the threshold, waiting for his eyes to adjust to the darkness. In his gloved hands was a butcher knife, clutched close to his chest.

A gust of ocean breeze blew across the grounds and wafted through the open French windows. The curtains fluttered and shivered, like they knew what was about to transpire next.

For one mesmerizing moment, the moonlight shone on the beautiful, gray-haired woman on the king-sized poster bed. Her eyes were closed. Her chest rose and fell to her steady breathing.

Good, thought the killer, as he gazed at the sleeping woman. *The pills have knocked her out.*

She looked so serene, but he knew shadows lurked behind that troubled mind, haunted by dark memories from long ago.

She's still good-looking though, after all she's gone through in life.

An ancient grandfather clock stirred from deep within the building. Its clangs echoed through the hushed corridors of this ritzy retirement home. No one spoke about it openly, but this was where the uber rich came to die.

The killer counted the chimes silently.

Eleven.

A raspy breath came from the woman on the bed. The clock had interrupted her deep slumber.

Time to finish the job.

The killer slipped inside and closed the door gently. His feet sank into the lush rug. The carpet absorbed sound well. Perfect for the night's mission.

The sleeping woman's fingers twitched, but her eyes remained closed, oblivious to her imminent fate.

The sweet aroma of lavender hung in the air. The killer recognized the brand. It was the perfume she used to hawk on television for years until she was ruthlessly replaced by a younger face.

He hovered over the victim, breathing in her smell, before placing the cleaver next to her stomach.

There's a faster way.

He slipped one hand under the woman's cheek and gently turned her head. Using the other hand, he pried the pillow out.

The woman stirred.

The killer's heart raced.

She's waking up!

Her eyes snapped open. A shocked gasp escaped her lips.

Now.

The killer jammed the pillow on her face. She gargled, fighting to breathe, but the drugs had made her weak.

The killer pressed down with both hands.

And soon, the beautiful, gray-haired woman went completely still.

The Unwanted Witness

A smile broke across the killer's face.

He pushed the pillow off the woman and picked up the cleaver.

With every kill, it got easier. It was almost addictive. Every kill had also been different. The knife hadn't even been necessary this time.

A sudden movement caught the killer's eye. He jerked his head back and peered into the darkness.

Who's that?

Someone was asleep on the velvet chaise lounge in the corner of the room. By the unlit fireplace.

The killer's heart skipped a beat.

No one was supposed to be here tonight.

Outsiders weren't permitted to stay over without permission, and permission was rarely given. No one was allowed in another's room after ten at night, either.

The residents at this exclusive retreat respected its strict rules. It was why they paid the hefty fees. The Silver Serenity retirement home gave them the privacy and peace of mind denied to them by the world outside.

The silhouette on the lounge moved and kicked the blanket briefly, before falling still again.

The killer held his breath.

As if realizing something was wrong, the figure on the lounge stirred. The blanket slipped to the floor. A young woman sat up and rubbed her drowsy eyes.

The killer clenched his jaws.

What's she doing here?

The girl gasped out loud. She had spotted the stranger in the room.

"Who... who... who are you?"

The killer remained in place, staring at the unwanted witness. Even through the darkness, he could make out the teenager's face.

What a pretty girl. Just like her grandmother is.... Was.

"Who... What... what's going on?" The girl picked up her blanket with trembling hands and covered her chest, like that would protect her.

"Who are you?"

The killer didn't speak.

I know who you are, but you don't know who I am.

The girl turned to the bed.

"G... G.... Grandma?" She stood up, clutching her blanket. "Grandma?"

The killer straightened up. It was time to finish this charade before someone heard her.

He approached her silently. Her eyes widened as the moonlight glinted off the butcher knife.

"What... what did you do to G... Grandma?"

He stepped closer, his eyes on her. She wilted under his glare.

"Who... who... are you...?" She trembled.

He put a finger to his lips.

"Hush."

The killer leaned in close, grimacing as the pungent odor of cheap cologne hit his nose.

Teenagers.

"You weren't supposed to be here, little girl."

She opened her mouth to scream.

But the killer was faster.

One strong hand wrapped around the teen's dainty neck, while the other clamped down on her mouth.

"Relax, sweetheart," he whispered. "This will be over soon."

Day One - Early Morning

FBI SPECIAL AGENT TANYA STONE & K9 MAX

Chapter One

"**H**elp me!"

The frightened yell came from Lulu's café.

Special Agent Tanya Stone jumped out of her Jeep, one hand on her holster. In the backseat, Max started to bark.

Lulu's panic-stricken cry had rung through the café's open kitchen window.

"Stop it!" cried Lulu. "Give that back!"

Tanya pulled out her Glock.

Is she being robbed?

She glanced around the parking lot, her heart ticking fast. In the corner, as usual, was Lulu's green Mini Cooper with her café logo. Next to it was a beat-up truck with the tailgate almost falling off.

Tanya narrowed her eyes. She didn't recognize the rusty pickup, but the driver was inside, attacking her friend. Whoever it was didn't know an undercover FBI agent and her K9 had just arrived for an earlier than usual coffee run.

Max was twirling around the backseat, barking his head off. Tanya pulled his door open. He leaped out of the Jeep and dashed across the parking lot toward the café's back door.

"Stop it!" cried Lulu from inside. "Why are you doing this to me?"

A ball of fury rushed through Tanya to hear her friend's high-pitched screams. She raced after Max and vaulted up the steps toward the kitchen door. She yanked the screen door open and tugged the doorknob.

Locked.

Max rose on his hind legs and scratched the wood, ready to tear through it.

Her German Shepherd knew Lulu well. She was one of his favorite humans. The café owner always offered him a frothy puppuccino every time they visited.

Tanya was thankful she hadn't had time to remove his K9 bulletproof vest and her Kevlar armor before coming on this coffee run.

A loud crash came from inside the café.

Tanya took stock, her heart pounding.

She had no idea how many assailants were inside, if they were armed, or what state of mind they were in. She also didn't know if innocent patrons were trapped inside the small shop. The hardest part of her job was to subdue the culprits with the least amount of collateral damage.

"Stand back, Max," she said.

Max shuffled back on his hind legs. His shackles were up and his eyes were beady. He growled at the door, as if to ask, *Why haven't we rammed this down already?*

Tanya slammed the screen back with her elbow and kicked the door.

That was when a gunshot blasted inside the café.

"Lulu!"

Chapter Two

T anya gave another swift kick at the café door.

The door buckled but held.

She aimed her sidearm at the lock and fired. The bolt snapped. She slammed the door open and tumbled in with Max.

Inside the bakery, Lulu whirled around, her eyes wide. "Tanya!"

A skinny young man was by a bread rack, his back flattened against the wall, his arms up, and sweat trickling down the sides of his face.

Tanya stepped toward the lone offender, her eyes targeted on him like laser beams.

"Stay where you are!" she hollered.

"Wasn't me! I didn't do nothing!" he cried.

The aroma of freshly baked donuts hung in the air, and the kitchen windows were steamed up, like Lulu had just opened the oven.

Tanya kept the barrel of her gun aimed at the intruder's head.

At first glance, he had looked like a twenty-something male. On closer look, she realized he was a teenager, tall for his age. He seemed more terrified of the growling canine than the Glock staring him in the face.

Where's his weapon?

She did a cursory check of Lulu.

No blood. Still standing. That's good news.

"You okay, hun?" she said.

That was when she spotted the pistol in Lulu's shaking hands.

"*You* fired the shot?"

"It was a warning," said Lulu, her face reddening. "This is an airsoft gun."

Max's growls turned into barks. Tanya swiveled around to see the culprit had moved, ready to run away.

Before she could say anything, he dashed toward the open doorway that led to the main seating area of the café. Max vaulted over the counter and sank his teeth into his thigh, bringing him crashing to the floor. The teen let out a shrill wail that sent a shiver down Tanya's back.

"Lemme go! Help me!"

Max didn't let go. Growling like an angry wolf, he shook the young man's leg violently. The kid screamed like he was being butchered alive.

Tanya stomped toward them and yanked Max's collar.

"Stand down."

Her dog let go of the kid's leg, but sat on his haunches, his jaws inches from the young man's stomach, ready to attack on command.

"P... please don't b... bite me," stammered the teen. He turned his terror-filled eyes toward Tanya. "Get this monster away from me. He's gonna kill me!"

Tanya squatted next to him, her eyes boring into his.

"What were you doing here? I heard Lulu's screams from the parking lot."

"Nothing. I didn't do anything."

Tanya holstered her weapon and brought out a pair of handcuffs from her utility belt.

"If you did nothing, why did you try to run away?"

She yanked his hands toward his back and locked the cuffs, before glancing around the café. Thankfully, there were no patrons inside like she had feared.

"I didn't hurt anyone," cried the kid, writhing in her grasp. "I swear I only came for a blueberry muffin."

"A blueberry muffin? My foot!" spat Lulu from behind the counter.

Tanya looked up at her friend. Lulu was pointing her gun at the young man on the ground.

"Drop your weapon," called out Tanya. "Now!"

Lulu turned the barrel away, but kept it in her hand. "You were rifling through my cash register. You were about to steal all my money." She turned and glared at Tanya. "Check his pockets."

"I didn't take anything!" cried the kid.

"Let's see about that, shall we?" said Tanya, as she rummaged through his pockets.

She drew out a handful of one-hundred-dollar bills and stacked them on the nearest coffee table, while Max kept a sharp eye on the perpetrator.

"You call this nothing?"

"I swear I didn't know she had a gun," whimpered the teen. "I'd never have dunnit if I knew."

"So, if she didn't have a weapon on her, you'd have just robbed her blind?"

12

"No! I swear... I was just...just...." He dropped to the floor and his warbles got muffled.

Tanya shook her head.

Most common criminals weren't the sharpest of knives. Driven by short-sighted gains, they made stupid mistakes and filled up prisons everywhere.

Until ten minutes ago, all Tanya had wanted was to grab a dozen chocolate donuts to celebrate Katy's new job as the precinct's office manager. She'd been out of town on training all week and hadn't had the chance to give her friend a proper welcome.

But now, she was stuck dealing with a petty criminal and the accompanying paperwork that would fill her morning.

Great way to start the day.

"You should have known better than to rob a coffee shop right next to a police station," said Tanya as she pulled another tightly rolled wad of bills from his pant pocket.

"That's my entire weekend's cash!" cried Lulu. She whirled around to the kid on the floor, frothing at the mouth.

"How could you do this to me? I changed your nappies when you were a baby. What would your mother say if she knew where you were now? Answer me, Troy West!"

Tanya spun around to the café owner.

"You know him?"

Chapter Three

"Lemme go! I'll never do this again. I promise, Officer."

The teen struggled to wiggle out of Tanya's grasp. She tightened her grip.

"Not until I know what's going on here."

"The... the cash wasn't for me," he whined. "It was for my mom. Honest. My mom.... my mom has cancer—"

"That's a lie!" shouted Lulu, emerging from behind the counter, waving her small pistol in the air. "How dare you bring your mother into this? She kicked you out weeks ago. She had enough of your lies and games. That goes for me too. I'm done with you!"

Tanya glared at her.

"Didn't I tell you to put that thing away?"

Lulu glanced down at her hand like she had completely forgotten she was carrying a gun.

"It's perfectly legal. Besides, it's not real."

"It looks like a weapon and sounds like a weapon." Tanya swallowed a ball of frustration. "You can't swing it around in public like that. You know better."

"But I'd never hurt him. I only wanted to teach him a lesson, once and for all. Shock therapy. You know?"

Tanya pinched her lips together and glowered at her friend. *Shock therapy?*

Lulu blinked. "You won't write me up, would you? You're a contractor. You don't have to report anything, do you?"

Tanya sighed.

She was no contractor. She was a federal agent on an intelligence-gathering mission on a notorious West Coast crime ring. But she couldn't tell Lulu that.

Even Black Rock's police chief, Jack Bold, thought he had hired a combat veteran who happened to show up just when he was severely short staffed and desperate for help.

The FBI director in Seattle, Susan Cross, knew the region's precincts inside and out. And she played her cards well. No one knew who was working undercover where or with whom. Not even the agents in the field.

Tanya gritted her teeth. "Put that down. I'll be confiscating that."

With a resigned sigh, Lulu placed the pistol next to the cash on the table.

Tanya pulled the kid to his feet. "Troy West, you're under arrest for attempted robbery—"

"Help me, Aunt Lulu!" cried Troy.

His eyes welled with tears, but Tanya knew better than to fall for such tricks. She pushed him toward the back door.

"A couple of hours as our guest will do you some good."

Tanya felt a tug. She looked down to see Lulu pulling on her arm.

"Don't you think jail's a bit much for the boy?"

Tanya stared at the café owner.

"You pulled a *gun* on him."

"A pretend gun. I just wanted to warn him. He got mixed in with a bad crowd and needed a slap on the head. His mother couldn't do it, so it was up to me."

Tanya narrowed her eyes. "What do you mean, it was up to you?"

"We simply wanted to educate him. His mother's heart would break if she learned he got arrested."

Tanya scoffed in disbelief. "You and his mother *planned* this?"

"It worked, didn't it? He's learned his lesson. He'll never do this again."

"I won't!" cried the teen, tears flowing down his cheeks. "I'm sorry, Aunt Lulu."

Tanya turned to him. "How old are you, kid?"

"Seventeen."

"See? He's just a minor," said Lulu, still holding on to Tanya's arm. "Let him go—"

A loud buzz in Tanya's cargo pant pocket made her stop.

Tanya reached in with her free hand and pulled her phone out.

She carried two cell phones, one public and one burner mobile that had been issued by the federal bureau. It was her secret FBI phone that was buzzing. The screen said *Unknown Number*, but Tanya knew this wasn't a call she could ignore.

She pushed the handcuffed Troy into a kitchen chair and stepped away from him. She clicked on the call icon and placed the phone to her ear.

"Agent Stone?" came a cold voice from the other end.

It was a voice that was all business, the kind of business that meant the difference between keeping a job or getting fired. Everyone was deathly scared of the director, for good reason.

Though FBI Director Susan Cross couldn't see her, Tanya instinctively straightened her back and stood at attention.

"Stone, here."

"Were you aware of a potential serial killer in Black Rock?"

Chapter Four

"Three deaths were reported over a period of twelve months."

The FBI director got to the point as usual.

"They were attributed to natural causes, but they might be targeted. We expect more to come, hence the urgency."

Tanya swallowed a grumble.

Can she at least ask if I'm in the middle of something before she barks out instructions?

With a glare at Lulu and Troy to let them know she wasn't done with them, Tanya stepped through the open doorway toward the café's front area.

"This isn't your average senior home," continued Cross in a clipped tone, like she was in a hurry. "This is an exclusive five-star hotel for the retired. Residents pay a truckload of cash to get pampered. Privacy is their middle name. They don't like outsiders, so getting in won't be easy."

Tanya frowned.

A retirement home?

She lowered her voice. "Could these incidents be the result of simple aging?"

"If they were, would I be calling you to take on a job, Agent?"

Cross's voice was as dry as it was cold.

Tanya's mind whirled with the pension home case histories she had studied during her training at FBI's Quantico training center.

Are these mercy killings? Inheritance murders?

She darted a quick glance through the open doorway at the handcuffed Troy. He was watching Lulu put the cash back in the register, his shoulders drooped and a forlorn expression on his face. She knew that look. He was sorry not for what he did, but that he got caught.

Max had taken position a few feet from him, and was watching him with beady eyes. Tanya turned and stepped toward the café's front doors. This wasn't a conversation she wanted anyone to overhear.

She slipped outside. The main street was empty. It was still too early for commuters or shoppers.

"What about the Grimwood case?" she said. "Is that no longer a priority?"

On the other end, the director took a deep breath in and let it out, like she was summoning all her patience to respond.

"Get this case off my desk, Stone, and you can focus on the real reason why you're in Black Rock."

Tanya recognized her big boss's idiosyncrasies now. Cross didn't believe in this case, but someone was pulling her strings, and Tanya was the lowly gofer who would be expected to clear things up quickly and quietly.

"I have neither the time nor the budget," Cross was saying, "to inquire into every death in this darned state. I can tell you this file is at the bottom of the pile. Help me get rid of it, Agent."

Tanya clenched her jaws.

She's sending me on a baseless mission.

"Yes, ma'am."

"We have a contact inside the residence."

"May I ask who that is?"

"You'll find out when you visit Silver Serenity."

So much for serenity, thought Tanya.

"Tell your police chief...what's his name...Bolt?"

"Jack Bold."

"Tell him you're visiting an old relative at the venue, check it out, and report back. You have three days."

Three days to investigate a potential serial killer at an upscale retirement home?

Tanya swallowed a curse. "Will do my best, ma'am."

"No one can know the bureau is sniffing around. This might not amount to anything."

Before Tanya could reply, the line went dead. She stood in her spot, staring at her phone for a few seconds.

Why didn't Ray Jackson call me?

It was rare for the director to contact a field agent directly, especially one who was new to the bureau. Ray was her intermediary, who transferred instructions and gave her details on new cases.

She dialed Ray's number, but he didn't answer.

Something stirred in Tanya's gut.

If her former combat experience in Ukraine had taught her anything, it was to trust her instincts. For Susan Cross to call her like this, even though she sounded irritated by this case, meant there was smoke in the air.

And where there was smoke, there would be fire.

Tanya tried Ray's number again, but she got radio silence. She slipped her burner phone in her pocket when Max started barking.

She yanked the café door open and sprang inside. Her dog's angry barks were coming from the kitchen.

Tanya raced to the back. Troy and Lulu were nowhere to be seen. Max was barking at the closed back door. On the floor, by his paws, was a half-crumbled cookie.

Tanya peered out the back window. Lulu and Troy were in the parking lot, next to the rusty pickup truck.

Troy was out of his handcuffs.

Chapter Five

With an exasperated roar, Tanya kicked the back door open.

Max leaped down the steps. With a frightened yelp, Troy jumped into his pickup truck and slammed the door shut.

Tanya and Max raced across the parking lot.

"Troy!" hollered Tanya. "Get out of your vehicle now!"

Max circled the truck, barking, but Troy was already pulling out. Max chased the car as it gathered speed along the back alley and disappeared around the corner.

"Come back, Max!"

Tanya whipped around and glared at Lulu, who was now huddled by her Mini, red-faced. In her hands were the unlocked handcuffs and a hair pin. She blinked rapidly as Tanya approached her.

With an apologetic bow, she handed over the cuffs and the pin to Tanya.

"He's just a kid. I couldn't bear to see him locked up."

Tanya stared at the woman who had been a friend, one of the few who had welcomed her into this new town. She had a soft spot for the café owner, who had the kindest, if not the most misguided heart, in Black Rock.

"Troy's family," said Lulu in a soft voice, eyes averted like she was too embarrassed to make eye contact. "He won't steal again. If he does, he'll have to deal with me and his mother."

"There are laws about this sort of thing, Lulu."

Lulu offered her hands. "Go ahead. Arrest me, then."

Tanya shook her head. "Troy should be the one answering to his criminal activities. You have too much faith in people sometimes. What I can't believe is you procured a weapon and schemed this whole thing."

"I got it off eBay. It's a toy. I swear it wouldn't hurt anyone."

Max came trotting across the parking lot, his tongue lolling, panting from his brief but failed car chase.

Tanya stepped away from her friend with a resigned sigh. Now wasn't the time for this conversation, because any words that would come out of her mouth would be ones she'd regret later.

Ever since Tanya's mother was assassinated, she had a tendency to adopt kindhearted older women as surrogate aunts. Or, at least good friends, who filled a small part of the hole in her heart from the loss of her entire family.

"Bring that toy to the precinct and we'll dispose of it," she said, striding toward her Jeep. "Don't ever do this again. When you're in trouble, dial nine-one-one or call me."

"I didn't want to bother you because you're busy with important cases. All I wanted to do was scare the boy, so he'd change. Next time—"

"There had better not be a next time." Tanya turned to her pup and snapped her fingers. "Let's go, Max. We have a new job."

A buzz in her pocket made her stop. It was her public phone this time, the number she gave to the local police precinct, and anyone in Black Rock who didn't know her true identity.

She let Max in the back of the Jeep and jumped in the driver's seat before plucking the phone out. She put it on speaker mode.

"Yes?" she snapped as she started her engine.

"Are you back in town, Stone? I've been trying to reach you." *Chief Jack Bold.*

Normally, Tanya would have been happy to hear his voice. Not today.

"I was occupied with a small altercation at Lulu's."

"Is she all right?"

"All taken care of." Tanya sighed. "Hope you're having fun at the summit, Jack. Have the bigwigs figured out how we're going to fight crime yet?"

Lulu waved at her as she pulled out of the café parking lot, but Tanya didn't respond, still stewing over what she'd done.

"I have bad news," said Jack.

Tanya rolled the Jeep into the back alley and headed toward the precinct.

"You're on a swan trip in Emerald City. You get to stay at a five-star hotel with free gourmet meals and hang out with the big boys and girls. How can that be bad?"

On the other end, Jack let out a heavy sigh.

"I take that back," said Tanya. "You couldn't pay me a million dollars to hang out with state bureaucrats. That would be torture."

"It's worse than torture," came Jack's voice, more somber. "The mayor plans to privatize Black Rock's police force as a cost-saving measure."

Tanya sat up. *"What?"*

In the backseat, Max's ears pricked up at her tone.

"We might all be out of jobs soon, but that's not what concerns me." Jack's voice was glum. "The mayor's proposing a private paramilitary firm to replace us. Thing is, everybody thinks they'd be fast, cheap, and good for the town, but I know the guys he has in mind. They've done some shady dealings."

"How shady?"

"The kind of gangsters you used to fight overseas," said Jack. "We're talking blood diamond traders, war mercenaries, and killers for hire."

Tanya stared at the phone, wondering if she'd heard him correctly.

"He can't get away with that."

"They operate under a legitimate business front. It will take years to unravel the maze and round them up. If you ask me, the mayor's only concern is hiding his own shady businesses."

Jack sighed again.

"If the mayor has his way, Black Rock will be run by international gangsters next month."

Chapter Six

"Hey, Stone?"

Tanya slammed on the Jeep's brakes and opened the back door for Max to jump out.

She recognized the friendly voice calling out to her from across the precinct's parking lot, but was too upset to speak to anyone at the moment.

Her real boss at the bureau was sending her on an unsubstantiated goose chase of a case that had to be solved in three days. And her other boss was having an existential crisis that could mean serious repercussions for this little town.

Max whined and wagged his tail happily as the officer approached the Jeep.

"So nice to see you, big boy," said Deputy Fox, bending over to pet him. "I bet you were top dog in class. We missed you, buddy."

Tanya had been training at an FBI off-site camp all week, but Chief Jack Bold and everyone in Black Rock thought she'd taken Max to a special doggy school in Oregon.

"He made us all proud," said Tanya, jumping out of the car. "I just heard from Jack. Sounds like he's got his hands full."

Fox looked up, his forehead creasing. "Our jobs are on the line, aren't they?"

Tanya put her hands on her hips and let out a sigh.

She and Max were already employed by the federal government. The mayor's decision would impact the lives of her colleagues more than her.

Having a bunch of war mercenaries running around pretending to be cops would only increase her workload. It wouldn't be easy to handle the Grimwood Case as well. She made a mental note to ask Susan Cross for extra resources if it came to that.

"Jack will figure things out," she said, putting on a sympathetic face for Fox. "Let's not jump to conclusions yet—"

"Hey, Stone? Fox?"

A familiar female voice called out from the direction of the precinct building.

"Brace yourself," whispered Deputy Fox, making a face.

Tanya peeked over the Jeep to see Deputy Lopez standing at the entrance of the squat concrete building where the town's emergency services were located.

Lopez jumped down the steps and walked over to them.

Her uniform was usually pressed perfectly, her shoes were always polished to a shine, and her shirt was typically as sharp as she was. But Lopez looked different that day. Her clothes were crumpled, her shoulders were slumped, and her eyes were covered in dark wraparound shades.

Lopez stopped to take a call, gesticulating wildly as she spoke. Her high-strung, nervous voice rang through the parking lot.

Tanya had seen her colleague angry and frustrated, but never flustered. She wondered what had agitated her.

"Is she okay?" said Tanya.

"She got back from vacation a week ago," said Fox in a low voice. "She's been looking like a train wreck since. Katy tried to ask what happened, but got yelled at."

"That doesn't sound like the Lopez I know."

Fox lowered his voice further.

"If you ask me, something really bad happened to her in San Diego."

Chapter Seven

"She's been wearing those shades inside," whispered Fox. "She's covering up something."

Tanya shrugged. "Jet lag, maybe?"

"From a trip to San Diego?"

Good point.

"Whatever happened to her, it's driven her to drink," said Fox. "I caught her sipping from a bottle in her office. The hard stuff." He grimaced. "Guess who's acting boss this week?"

Tanya looked at him. "Jack didn't say he left her in charge."

"You were away in doggy school with Max and I had a few things to take care of at home, so Lopez was it. She promised to finish the paperwork on his desk. He told her to get on with it and that's that."

Tanya groaned. "Who in their right mind offers to do paperwork all week?"

"I told you," whispered Fox. "Something's not right with Lopez."

Lopez stomped over to them. Even with those darkened shades, Tanya could see the stress lines on her face. She looked like she had aged a decade during her time away.

Tanya leaned back as the smell of alcohol wafted to her nose. *My goodness. Fox is right.*

"Hey, how was your holiday?" she said, keeping her voice casual.

Lopez gave her a dismissive wave. "We don't have time for chitchat. We've got a truckload of files to go through."

Fox raised his hands.

"I'm really sorry, but I need a couple of days off. I already put in my request through Katy."

Lopez spun around to him, the sunlight glinting off her shades. "You want to take a vacation *now?*"

Fox rubbed the back of his neck.

"There's just... er, some personal stuff I've got to deal with."

"Personal stuff can wait," snapped Lopez. "It's all hands on deck right now. Chief's back on Friday, so time's running out."

Tanya raised a brow. Lopez wasn't the friendliest of colleagues, but she had never been this sharp with them.

Fox blinked a few times and looked down, his face turning a shade pale.

"What's up, Fox?" said Tanya, softening her voice. "Everything okay at home?"

His shoulders drooped. He glanced down at his feet and sighed.

"It's Zoe. She was in remission, but it's back."

Tanya inhaled sharply.

"The brain tumor?"

Chapter Eight

"We're taking it day by day," said Fox, not looking up.

A pang of sorrow cut through Tanya. "I'm so sorry."

"I didn't know," said Lopez, sounding normal for once.

"It's fine," said Fox in a broken voice. "Zoe's at Dr. Chen's clinic right now. The doctor found a cancer specialist in Seattle and pulled some strings. We have an appointment tomorrow in the city, so that's good."

He looked up, his forehead lined with worry.

"Sorry guys, but I've got to take care of my family."

Lopez and Tanya watched silently as he got into his car and drove off with a half-hearted wave. Tanya's chest tightened. All of a sudden, the petty annoyances of that morning seemed insignificant.

"Please let Zoe be okay," she whispered to herself.

"I guess it's just the two of us and the new girl," said Lopez. She spun on her heels. "You coming?"

Tanya watched the deputy march into the precinct building, her heart heavy and her mind elsewhere. She wanted nothing more than to talk to Zoe, ask if she needed anything, but two urgencies were pulling her apart. One of them, she couldn't ignore.

I need to figure out how to get into the Silver Serenity retirement home.

Tanya locked the Jeep and turned around, searching for her dog.

Max had been chasing a gray squirrel around the parking lot. The fluffy-tailed rodent was now perched on top of the precinct's chain-link fence, chirping, taunting the German Shepherd.

"Max," called out Tanya.

He wagged his tail unenthusiastically, but kept his snout pointed firmly at his immortal enemy.

"Leave that animal alone—"

Her smartphone buzzed in her pants pocket. She reached in, wondering what fresh hell was coming her way now. She pressed her finger on the mobile to unlock it.

First Lulu, then Susan Cross, then Jack, and now Zoe. What's next, universe?

A red dot on the messenger icon stared at her, daring her. She clicked on it, feeling a peculiar sense of dread.

The text had no subject line or sender name. Her heart skipped a beat.

I don't have time for this. Not today.

Her heart ramped up as she read the note.

"WHY AR U ignoring us? Your bro's alive, bitch. Wanna see him? ANON."

Tanya swallowed hard.

These anonymous messages always followed a pattern. They were brief, vague, and threatening. Tanya dug her fingers into the phone, like she wanted to crush the device.

Who are you ANON?

"Everything okay?"

Tanya jerked her head up so quickly, she almost dropped her cell. Katy was ambling over to her across the parking lot.

Katy and her husband, Peace, had moved from Manhattan to the West Coast three months ago, saying the fresh ocean air and small-town atmosphere would be better for their nine-year-old daughter, Chantal.

Short-staffed and overworked, Chief Jack Bold had jumped at the chance to hire Katy. The precinct now had a new civilian office manager with experience in private investigations. Though Tanya never said it out loud, she was also glad she had a good friend in Black Rock.

She rustled up a weak smile as Katy approached her.

"Lopez asked me to get you—" Katy stopped. "You look like you just saw a phantom."

Tanya waved her cell in the air.

Katy's shoulders dropped. "Don't tell me ANON is harassing you again."

Tanya nodded wordlessly.

"It's a prank, hun. A mean and nasty one, but it's probably just a sick kid hiding in his mother's basement."

"What if it's true?"

"That's what scammers do." Katy shot a cross look at the phone. "They troll for personal info on social media and attack where you're the weakest. I'll bet you next week, this idiot will ask for money in return for fake info about your brother."

"What if he's really alive?"

Katy put a hand on Tanya's arm.

"Your brother was killed in Russia, hun. They took him away. You went to that camp. You have to believe your own eyes, ears, and memory, not some scummy weirdo in a basement."

Tanya blinked a tear away.

"I never saw his body."

Day One - Later that evening...

Chapter Nine

T anya squinted in the dark.

Max was sniffing a bush by the corner of her house. His ears were up and his shoulders were tensed, like he had caught a scent.

She took a quick look around the front yard of her cottage. They were alone, except for the low hum of nocturnal insects coming from the underbrush.

Tanya squinched her eyes to stop the painful throb in her head. She hadn't known Lopez was a taskmaster, but the migraine had saved her. She had said goodnight to Lopez and Katy, leaving them at the precinct, still sorting out Jack's case files.

But for Tanya, there would be no rest.

It wouldn't be easy to infiltrate an upscale retirement residence known for strict privacy. Her plan was to research the area around the pension home before staking it out, that night.

It was half-past nine, and she had parked the Jeep in front of her rental cottage. Max had darted out as soon as she'd opened his door, like something had called out to him.

Tanya watched him with a wary eye. He was trotting toward the back of the house, his nose to the ground, following an invisible trail. He turned around and barked, as if to ask why she wasn't following him.

She retrieved her Glock and snuck up to her front door. She yanked the doorknob. *Still locked.*

She scanned her one-story, two-bedroom cottage for signs of a break-in, then peered through the windows, but nothing seemed amiss. The house was empty.

Her FBI intermediary, Ray Jackson, had found this property for her. This was her temporary home for the time she would remain in Black Rock as an undercover agent. It was isolated from the rest of town, in a place where locals seldom dared to tread.

Tanya glanced up.

She was at the foot of the hill where the town's psychiatric hospital was located.

The asylum.

While it stoked fear and mistrust among the locals, the hospital was really a private medical institution for those who could afford its exclusive rates. Its compound consisted of a handful of fancy log cabins built in a circle, surrounded by tall evergreens. She never spotted the grounds from below, as it was always hidden in an eerie cloud of fog.

Another bark made Tanya turn, just in time to see a furry brown tail disappear in between two tall hemlock trees.

He's found something.

FBI Director Susan Cross had yanked Max out of K9 school before he finished his certification, so he could help Tanya with her undercover mission. By then, he knew how to locate missing children and concealed cadavers.

Tanya scurried after her dog, her heart racing.

What is it? A lost kid or a dead body?

He had surprised her before. Max had led her to an underground drug den, to stashes of cash in the back of a car, and even to a jail-breaker hiding in an abandoned building.

She turned on her flashlight and followed him into the woods, instantly feeling the wet and damp atmosphere of the rain forest.

She wished she had brought her night vision goggles so she could move more stealthily. Then again, she was in a small-town, USA, not in the trenches of a violent war zone in Ukraine anymore.

She caught sight of Max's silhouette a few yards ahead of her. He was meandering around a clump of trees, his nose glued to the forest floor.

The ocean wasn't far away, but the earthy smells of oak and pine pushed out the briny odor that breezed from the sea below.

Giant evergreens loomed over, frowning like they were upset at her encroaching on their land. But a deathly quiet had fallen around her. All she could hear was the thud of her own heart and the occasional rustle of Max as he wound his way deeper into the woods, determined to show her something.

Breathing deeply to ease her nerves, she followed her dog up the hill.

Suddenly, Tanya felt a prickle in the back of her neck, like someone was watching them. She stopped and swiveled around.

Through the spiky branches, she spotted the pale lights on top of the hill, blinking in and out as the trees swayed to the breeze.

The asylum is closer than I thought.

Chapter Ten

F rom somewhere deep in the woods, Max barked.

Tanya recognized that bark. He had encountered the object of his search.

She slinked through the trees toward him. Max was standing alone in a small clearing, wagging his tail, as if to say *Look what I found, Mom.*

She gritted her teeth, hoping it wasn't a dead squirrel. Max shook his tail faster as she got closer. It was only when she was a couple of yards from him that she realized he was on a brown patch on the periphery of the clearing.

Someone was digging here.

Max barked, as if to say, *Come closer.*

With a chill, she realized the patch he was on was the shape and size of an adult grave.

She turned slowly in a circle, her gun aimed in front of her, her keen eyes peering through the trees. But the woods remained silent.

Max trotted over to her and bumped her thigh with his nose, as if to say, *No one's around.*

Tanya patted his head. "Good boy," she whispered.

She kneeled next to the grave, picked a handful of earth and let it fall through her fingers in a waterfall of dust.

Fresh soil.

This grave had been dug in the last twenty-four hours.

A shiver went down Tanya's back.

She reached up and touched the sunflower pendant that hung around her neck. The necklace had been her mother's once. That was before she was brutally gunned down by the Russian militia.

This small piece of jewelry was now Tanya's talisman, a precious connection to her mother which always calmed her nerves.

There's only one reason someone would bury a body in the most inaccessible spot on the hill.

To hide a murder.

Chapter Eleven

"Female. Mixed heritage. I'd say fifteen years old, at the most."

Dr. Chen hovered over the corpse, her flashlight shining on the pallid face of the dead girl.

"From a preliminary glance, I'd say death occurred approximately forty-eight hours ago."

Tanya kneeled next to the body and wrinkled her nose as the smell of a popular teen fragrance wafted toward her. She was thankful for the perfume as it masked the more unpleasant smells of a human corpse.

She stared at the pretty young face, now a deathly gray.

"Is it just me or does she look oddly familiar?"

A chorus of voices answered.

"Never seen her," said a young officer leaning against his shovel.

"Nope," said another. "She's not from around here."

Katy let out a heavy sigh. "Why would anyone bury an out-of-town kid in such a lonely place like this?"

"To hide the evidence," said Tanya.

"Kill and dump," said another officer.

Tanya surveyed the small group of uniformed officers standing around the open pit. The area looked like a crowded bus stop now. The clearing had appeared a lot more sinister a couple of hours ago when she was alone in the dark with Max.

Katy had driven Dr. Chen over when she had called. Soon after, the sheriff from the next county over had sent a team of junior members to secure the crime scene and conduct door-to-door checks in town.

It was a good thing Black Rock's police chief had amiable relationships with his colleagues in the area. One call from Tanya was all it took to get extra hands, but she knew they would be indebted to them now.

Dr. Chen touched the dead girl's face and gently moved it to the side.

"Multiple ligature marks around the throat area. Barring contradictory findings, I'd say she succumbed to asphyxiation as a result of strangulation."

"Oh, my.... poor girl....," whispered Katy, a hand on her heart.

She staggered back, whirled around, and threw up in a bush nearby.

Max, who had been sitting at Tanya's feet, trotted over. Katy rested one hand on his back while she held on to a tree trunk with her other hand as she threw up.

Tanya stepped up to her friend.

"You don't have to be here. You're the office manager. No one would say a word if you go home."

"I'm okay." Katy wiped her mouth. "I've seen dead bodies before, but it's always hard to see a child. Makes me want to grab Chantal and never let her go."

Tanya reached over to squeeze her shoulder.

By the dug-out grave, Dr. Chen gently laid the girl's head back on the ground.

"All right, people. Let's get her to the morgue. I can tell you more after the autopsy."

"The killer was pretty smart," said one of the junior officers, who had been watching from a safe distance. "No one comes to these parts, ever, especially with the asylum up there."

Tanya didn't blink.

Little did the killer know an undercover federal agent and her K9 were staying in the cottage at the bottom of the hill.

"All credit goes to Max," she said. "If he hadn't sniffed something unusual, the grass would have grown and by fall, no one would have guessed anyone was buried here."

Dr. Chen glanced around the clearing, a frown on her face.

"Where's Lopez? Isn't she on acting duty? She should be here."

Tanya nodded. "Called her several times. She didn't pick up, so I left a message."

"She's at home," said Katy. "I got in touch with her just before we left. She said she had some urgent things to take care of."

Dr. Chen shook her head. "What's more urgent than a dead girl buried halfway on the hill?"

"Ma'am?" came a youthful voice from inside the forest.

Tanya spun around.

"What is it, Officer?"

"You need to see this."

Chapter Twelve

Tanya hurried into the woods with Max at her heels.

It was the junior officer she'd charged with putting barricade tape around the surrounding area.

"Something happened here," said the officer, pointing at the trampled foliage next to a yew tree.

Tanya shone her flashlight at the foliage. Max circled the tree, sniffing it intently.

"Good job finding it, in the dark too," said Tanya.

The officer smiled shyly.

"I have a theory, ma'am."

Tanya didn't reply, knowing how overly eager cops in small towns got when they realized they had a real murder investigation on their hands.

"The vic was killed up there and dragged here," he said.

Tanya shone her flashlight around. "Did you see drag marks?"

"Nope, but I'd bet the killer's from the nuthouse."

Tanya lifted her head and glanced at the yellow lights that shimmered through the trees on top of the hill.

"It was probably a totally crazed dude," said the officer. "He forgot to take his meds, went ballistic, and killed the girl. He panicked, carried her down here, and buried her to hide his crime."

"The manner and the place in which the body was buried tells me the killer was methodical," said Tanya, speaking slowly.

"I'd bet there's a sex offender locked up at the crazy house." The officer's face brightened. "He escaped from his room, hunted this girl down, and raped her. She fought back, and he strangled her deader than a doornail."

"I phoned the hospital soon after I called your sheriff," said Tanya. "According to the night manager, nothing's been out of the ordinary tonight. And they have no record of a young girl staying there either."

He shrugged. "Who knows what's going on over there with a bunch of locked-up nut cases."

Tanya shone her flashlight up the incline and back.

"Whoever did this wasn't impulsive. They cleaned up the scene and left nothing behind." She paused. "We need to cordon off this area. I'll come back in the morning to get a better look. Until then, don't touch—"

A strange cry stopped her.

Tanya spun around.

"That came from the gravesite," whispered the officer.

Max twirled around and scampered down the hill. Tanya and the officer followed at a slower pace, making sure to not trample on any evidence.

They emerged from the woods to see Deputy Lopez swaying on her feet at the edge of the clearing.

She was in civilian clothes and looked like she had deteriorated even further. Her hands trembled uncontrollably, her hair was askew, and her face was puffy like she had been crying.

Katy walked over to her. "You okay, hun? You look awful."

Deputy Lopez turned her wild eyes to Katy, then Tanya. Before either of them could say anything, she spun around and fled down the hill.

"Lopez!" Dr. Chen got to her feet. "Carmen Lopez, get back here. You're acting chief, for heavens' sake. Act like one."

But Deputy Lopez crashed through the woods, heading straight down toward Tanya's cottage. Soon, the sound of a vehicle screeching down the road came from below.

"Oh, man," snickered a junior officer. "She's not seen a dead body before?"

"She's so pissed, she can hardly stand straight," scoffed another officer.

"And I thought Johny was bad when he got drunk. Haha."

Katy whirled around to them. "She's had a bad week. Give her a break."

Dr. Chen glared. "She just came from a week-long vacation. There's no excuse for this unprofessional behavior." She shook her head. "Jack goes to Seattle and this place goes to the dogs."

"She wasn't on holiday!" cried Katy. "There's a good reason she's super stressed out. She just admitted her parents to an assisted living center in San Diego. Both are suffering from dementia. Could we all be a little more empathetic, please?"

Tanya frowned.

"That's strange. Lopez told me her parents died in a car crash when she was seven."

Day Two

Chapter Thirteen

A war siren screeched through the air.

Tanya sat up and stared into the darkness, her heart pounding.

She had gone to bed at three in the morning, after helping Dr. Chen transport the dead girl's body to the morgue. Lopez had barricaded herself in her office and had pretended not to hear Katy and her knocking, but no one could ignore the strong smell of gin in the air.

In the end, they had given up and returned home. Tanya had a few hours to rest her tired mind before heading off to Silver Serenity to look into her other case.

Her ears rang from the cacophony inside her room. Her headache was back in full force.

What is that noise?

Temazepam was the only reason she slept at all.

Without those pills, a hurricane of bloodied images swirled through her head, refusing to let her sleep. Collages of mass graves in Ukraine spun like a kaleidoscope, night after night. The ear-splitting blasts of bombs raining from the jets that soared above collided with the heartbreaking cries of injured soldiers, all too young to die.

The air raid had turned into an incessant ring now.

Tanya turned her head.

Max was standing by her bed, his head cocked to the side. He turned and wagged his tail when he saw her glance his way, and licked her face. Tanya squinted to see what he had been gazing at.

My phone!

Her FBI-issued burner cell was lit up and vibrating at maximum volume, hopping on the table like a bizarre creature come to life. She threw the coverlet to the side and placed her feet on the rug, before fumbling to pick up her mobile.

What time is it?

She clicked to take the call.

"Stone," she warbled.

"I've been trying to reach you for the past ten minutes."

Tanya sat up and shook her head to clear the cobwebs of sleep.

Only Director Susan Cross would call at five AM.

"Good morning, ma'am—"

"There was another death in the past forty-eight hours. Were you aware of it?"

Tanya's heart ticked faster. The pale face of the girl in the shallow grave flashed into her mind.

"I was at the crime scene last night. It was a teenage girl. Most likely a homicide. The autopsy is being—"

"What girl?" Susan Cross's voice was sharp. "I'm referring to Silver Serenity. The deceased was in her late forties or early fifties and supposedly suffered from serious addiction issues."

Tanya furrowed her brow.

There was another death in Black Rock?

She scrunched her eyes to collect her thoughts.

"Forty or fifty is a tad young for a retirement home."

"My thoughts exactly," said Cross.

"Was it a staff member?"

"A resident." Cross paused briefly. "Or a patient of sorts. That's what I was told, but I need you to double-check that."

Of course. Your secret yet unreliable source.

"The funeral is scheduled for this morning," said Cross. "Find a way in and see what the heck's going on over there. Hopefully nothing, and I can wash this off my plate."

Tanya frowned.

"A funeral that quickly is unusually fast." She paused. "Unless someone's trying to hide cause of death."

Chapter Fourteen

The rustle of paper mixed with urgent murmurs came through the speakerphone.

Tanya rubbed her weary eyes.

The director's assistant must have come into her office. Boy, they work early.

She got to her feet but swayed on her wobbly legs. She grabbed the headboard to balance herself, wondering if she'd even had an hour's worth of sleep.

Max looked up from the oversized armchair he had taken over and thumped his tail. He yawned, making her want to do the same, but she stifled it in time.

"The deceased," came Cross's voice again, "was a Hollywood actor who starred in B-rated movies."

A Hollywood actor?

"She was known more for her alcoholic antics than her acting, so her death might be of interest to lowbrow celebrity media." More ruffling of paper came from Cross's end. "Once the tabloids hear about this, they'll be swarming that place like insects."

"And the killer, if there is one," said Tanya, the fog slowly lifting from her brain, "will go underground."

"Exactly."

What Tanya really wanted was to find out what happened to the dead girl on the hill. Her pale young face kept swimming into her mind, as if calling her for help, begging her to find her killer.

"The young girl," said Tanya, swallowing hard. "The victim we found buried was also killed about forty-eight hours ago. I'd like to finish—"

"The locals can take care of it," snapped Cross. "Last time I checked, Black Rock had a law enforcement team."

Tanya sighed.

Good luck with that. The police chief was fighting to keep the team alive, while the acting chief was hiding in her office, dead drunk.

"Single homicides are within their bailiwick," Cross was saying. "A sequential or serial killer with multiple victims is in *our* jurisdiction. This is your job, Agent, unless you no longer want your job."

Tanya's heart lost a beat. She was about to reply when Max leaped out of his armchair and rushed to the window, barking.

She whirled around to see a peculiar face staring at her through her window.

Daylight was just breaking. That was enough for her to notice the deep scar on the man's cheek. It wasn't a face she would forget easily, but he disappeared the second she glanced his way.

Tanya jumped toward the window, apologizing for Max's yapping. She yanked the curtain back and looked out. Whoever it had been had vanished.

"Report back in twenty-four hours."

Tanya brought the phone back to her ear, her heart racing.

"Yes, ma'am. I'm on it."

But only half her mind was on Susan Cross's command.

Who was watching me just now?

Chapter Fifteen

"**D**id a man come this way, a half hour ago?" said Tanya.

The junior officer guarding the crime scene on the hill turned around. He was the same officer who had shared his murder theories with her.

"Haven't seen a thing. Been here all night."

He slurped from his paper cup.

The forest floor was covered in dew, and the nighttime bugs had turned silent. Sparrows and robins sang on the branches above, welcoming the sun rising over the misty ocean below.

Tanya pointed at the steaming cup in the officer's hands.

"How did you get your coffee?"

"My partner. He was here with me, except for the donut and coffee run he made an hour ago. He didn't go far, just to Lulu's."

"There was always one of you up here?"

"Just like you asked, ma'am."

"Where's your partner now?"

The officer's face flushed.

"He's, um.... taking a... a...."

He pointed at something over her shoulder. Tanya turned around to hear a stream of liquid hit the soil.

She rubbed her tired eyes.

You'd better not be contaminating any evidence.

She spun around to the officer with the coffee cup.

"I'm looking for a middle-aged male. Deep scar on his right cheek. He was hanging near my cottage this morning."

The officer's eyes widened. "No one I know like that. What was he doing near your house? Was it a creep or what?"

Tanya shrugged.

"If you see him, find out who he is, and report back."

"Morning, ma'am," came a voice from behind her. "Did you find the killer yet?"

Max twirled around and barked, wagging his tail. Tanya turned to the second officer, who was strolling toward her.

"Appreciate you guys coming over at short notice," she said. "Keep an eye out for a man with a scarred face. And make sure there's always one of you up here."

The officers grinned.

"We'll be here twenty-four-seven, if you wish. It's all overtime."

Tanya stared at them in surprise. She had been bracing for complaints for giving them an all-night job.

"We've been planning a Vegas trip for months," said the first officer. "A few more days of this and we can pay for it in cash."

They slapped each other's shoulders and bumped their elbows, as if in a secret victory sign. Then, they turned and offered their hands to Tanya.

"Thank you for the job, ma'am."

Tanya tried not to grimace.

Did they wash their hands at all?

"You're welcome, boys." She turned around to leave, glad she had extra resources, but worried their inexperience could hinder the investigation.

"Forensics will be here in a few hours, so be careful where you step. And where you pee."

"Yes, ma'am," they chorused.

Calling Max to come with her, she made her way back down the hill to the cottage.

After Susan Cross had hung up, Tanya had searched the woods around her house. Max had rambled through the yard, sniffing every bush and tree stump, but whatever trail he picked up seemed to disappear as quickly as he discovered them.

Whoever the scarred man was, he had been careful to leave no trace. Just like the girl's killer.

Tanya bent down and scratched Max's ears.

"I don't care what Cross says. We're going to work on both cases."

Max wagged his tail like he agreed with her.

Katy had said it best. It was hardest when the victim was young and their life had been cut so brutally short. Tanya gritted her teeth.

I'm going to find out what happened to that girl.

Max trotted over to the Jeep and pawed the ground. He knew they were supposed to drive somewhere that morning, and a car ride was one of his favorite activities.

With a sigh, Tanya plucked her phone from her pocket and swiped to the research she had done that morning.

Where's Silver Serenity located now?

She squinted to read the address.

1 Silver Serenity Drive, Black Rock.

Susan Cross's words came to her as she clicked on the map.

"A private five-star spa and hotel for the retired. Residents pay a truckload of cash to get pampered in an environment of utmost privacy. Getting inside won't be easy."

The map flickered to life, and a small red dot appeared in the middle of the screen.

Tanya zoomed in and took a sharp breath in.

Silver Serenity was located on the very hill she was standing next to. The retirement residence and the psychiatric hospital were neighbors. An unpaved path wound through the woods above, connecting the two institutions.

Her mind whirled. Something strange was happening up on the hill.

Two people died within the last two days, right in my backyard. Are they connected?

Chapter Sixteen

Tanya had just jumped inside the Jeep when Katy called.

She sounded breathless, like she had been running.

"We have a weird visitor. He came in a helicopter."

"A helicopter?"

"You heard me," came Katy's voice, low and quiet like she didn't want to be overheard. "It landed in our parking lot."

Tanya put the Jeep in gear. "Is this a joke, hun? Because I'm running late—"

She stopped in mid-sentence as the whine of a helicopter came through the phone's speaker. Tanya braked the car and turned her head back to her mobile.

"Where are you, Katy?"

"At the station. I've been babysitting Lopez all morning. She's really in bad shape. Then this man came over to talk to her. He's with her right now."

Tanya's frown deepened. "Who's this man? Is he armed?"

"What? No. And I've never seen him before."

"Does he have a scar on his right cheek?"

"No....I don't think so. Why do you ask?"

Tanya turned the Jeep's engine off and leaned in to her phone. "What's going on, Katy?"

The machine in the background had gone silent. Tanya had flown helicopters in combat missions and for private buyers before, so her ears were attuned to different aircraft. This sounded like a light, single-engine....

Her heart sank.

Is that a news chopper?

Susan Cross had warned her about paparazzi swarming the retirement residence when they discovered who had died. Her job was about to turn twice as hard.

"I came in this morning to open the front counter as usual," said Katy. "Lopez was in her office, sleeping with her head on her desk. I think she spent all night in here, can you imagine? I got her a glass of water, made her a cup of coffee, and put the empty bottles away."

"Is she safe?" said Tanya, wishing she'd get to the point. "What about the visitor?"

"Whatever happened in San Diego is killing her. She's a complete mess—"

"Tell me about the chopper."

"I was about to drive her home when this helicopter landed right next to my car. It could have scratched it. I didn't know aircraft could land here. Is that even legal? Am I allowed to ticket it?"

The sound of an unfamiliar female voice came from somewhere.

"Hold on," said Katy.

"Who's that?" asked Tanya.

"The masked man's assistant."

"The what?"

"Gotta go."

Katy hung up.

Tanya stared at her mobile for two full seconds before glancing back at Max, who had been patiently waiting for his ride.

"Change of plans," she said, turning the engine on and taking her foot off the brake.

With a loud sigh, Max lay down on the backseat.

It took Tanya ten minutes to get to the precinct, driving as fast as she could. She had barely parked in front of the station's entrance, when Max jumped to his feet and started to growl. He had sensed the strangers in the vicinity.

Tanya got out with him and treaded along the exterior of the precinct building, heading toward the back parking lot.

When she got to the corner, Tanya stopped and gaped.

It wasn't every day she saw a helicopter in a city parking lot.

Chapter Seventeen

The single-rotor black chopper was sitting in the middle of the lot.

Katy's car was parked at an angle not too far from the machine, like she had come to a screeching stop.

The helicopter had no identifying decals, but a man in a pilot's uniform was leaning against the front panel, his nose buried in his phone.

Pacing frantically behind the aircraft was a woman in a sharp navy skirt, her phone to her ear. She was shouting at someone about rescheduling a meeting and didn't seem too happy about it.

Max cocked his head and looked up at Tanya as if to ask, *Should I get 'em?*

"Heel, bud."

Gesturing him to follow her, she stepped around the corner and walked toward the helicopter. The woman was so engrossed in her call, she didn't even notice Tanya and Max approach.

Tanya stepped up to the pilot. "Hey, how's it going?"

He looked up startled, glanced down at Max and back at Tanya, before checking his wristwatch.

"He wants to head back already?"

"He's still occupied." Tanya pointed at the chopper. "I flew a Robinson R22 from Brussels once."

The pilot raised his eyebrows. "Brussels? Wow."

"EU and NATO delegates." Tanya shrugged. "Bigwigs with funny accents from all over Europe. They were polite, and the gig paid well."

"I bet." He straightened up and slipped his phone into his pocket. "I'd kill to get a job like that."

Wrong choice of words, mister.

"How did you snag the gig?" He stepped closer, his face keen. "Is there lots of competition for that sort of thing?"

"Personal contacts. Guess I got lucky." Tanya pointed her chin at the machine behind him. "So, does your boss own only this one, or does he let you play with bigger birds?"

"He's not my boss. I work for a charter company."

The pilot shot a quick glance at the woman in the suit. She was balancing her phone between her shoulder and ear, while scrolling through something on her tablet.

"She called last minute, so I was the only one available. She gave me twenty minutes to collect her boss from a hotel in Seattle and bring him to this gawdforsaken backwoods...." He gave Tanya a sheepish look. "Sorry."

"No offense taken." Tanya smiled. "So, who's your well-heeled client?"

"All I know is he offered double for this last-minute flight. But I get paid the same, so what do I care?"

"I can tell you they do things differently in Europe," said Tanya. "They give good benefits, dental too. It was sweet."

His eyes widened. "Hey, can you... um... hook me up to your Brussels contact, by any chance? I have good references."

Tanya held out her hand. "Got a card?"

He rummaged through his pockets and brought out a business card that was bent at the corners. Tanya took it.

"I'll see what I can do."

"I'd appreciate that."

"Let's go, bud." Tanya snapped her fingers at Max, who had been sniffing the helicopter with interest. "Break's over."

She marched back toward the main entrance to the precinct and slipped through the front sliding doors. She stepped up to the secure entrance that led to the offices, the bull pen, and the jail cells in the back.

She swiped her badge on the electronic pad and opened the inside door just as a man stepped out of an office. Tanya stared at the apparition standing in front of Lopez's closed office door.

Katy hadn't been making things up.

The masked man.

Chapter Eighteen

The gold Rolex on the man's wrist glittered under the somber office light.

He was wearing dark glasses, a brown hat, a tan suit, and a scarf around his neck, despite the warm spring weather.

But it was the light blue polypropylene mask that covered the lower half of his face that caught Tanya's attention. The pandemic was over. She frowned, wondering why anyone would wear a disposable mask unless they had serious respiratory health issues.

He's trying to hide his face.

Her eyes flew to Lopez's office. The door was shut and there was no sound from within.

"Hello there," she said, wondering what he had been doing with her. "May I help you?"

He didn't answer.

"Sir?" came a female voice from the bullpen. "Is everything all right?"

Katy was at her desk next to the chief's empty office. The man gave a start as if he had just noticed her.

"Everything's perfectly fine," he said. "Just having a chat with an old friend."

As if a sudden thought struck him, the man turned and strolled over to Katy.

Tanya couldn't help but wonder if he was trying to avoid her by the entrance. Katy always looked friendly. Tanya never did. Plus, she was accompanied by a German Shepherd wearing a K9 ballistic vest.

"I didn't see you when I came in." The man offered Katy his hand in a grand gesture and bowed like a nineteenth-century aristocrat. "I normally notice beautiful women."

Katy's face flushed. She pushed her hair back, like she didn't know what to do with herself.

Tanya was used to seeing men ogle her friend. If Katy had lived during the Marilyn Monroe era, she would have been on the cover of Vanity Fair. Some missed the intelligence and empathy that lay behind the surface of this pretty woman with red hair.

But the man wasn't done.

He leaned across Katy's desk, and for a second, Tanya wondered if he was going to remove that mask and try to kiss her.

Good thing Peace isn't here, she thought, thankful Katy's husband of ten years was busy finalizing a lease for his new law practice in town.

"I like curvy girls," the man was saying, his eyes traveling down Katy's figure.

Tanya grimaced.

She's a woman, not a girl. And you're a creep.

"I'm... I'm... married," stammered Katy, taking a step back, her smile frozen.

"Does it matter?"

Katy winced, but he didn't seem to notice.

"I'm having a party at my beach house on July fourth. It would be great if you could come. Stay for the entire weekend."

He laughed a hollow laugh.

"You can't say no to me. No one can say no to me."

Tanya furrowed her brow.

A man with a mask. A beach home. A helicopter. How did our Deputy Lopez get involved with him?

Katy smiled awkwardly. "That sounds... er, lovely. Thank you."

"Sir? Sir! We've got to get back."

The sound of frantic heels clicking on the concrete floor came from the precinct's reception area. Tanya kicked the secure door back to see who it was.

It was the woman in the navy suit.

Chapter Nineteen

The woman in the suit was juggling two phones, a tablet, and a notebook, which all looked like they'd slip out of her hands at any moment.

She hurried up to the open door and poked her head in.

"I'm so...so sorry to bother you, sir, but your meeting's in an hour. We really have to return like, like, er...right now."

Tanya noticed her swallow hard.

She's scared of him.

Without answering her, the man turned back to Katy. Before Katy could protest, he grabbed her hand and kissed it. Tanya's stomach turned to see her friend's discomfort.

The man spun on his heels and brushed past Tanya as he stepped out, barely acknowledging her. He stomped toward the front entrance with his assistant scurrying after him.

Tanya turned to Katy, who was staring back at her.

"What just happened?" said Tanya.

Katy pointed at Lopez's office. "They were having a huge argument."

"About what?"

"No idea. They were screaming at each other in Spanish."

"Do you know his name?" said Tanya, walking over to Lopez's office and grabbing the door handle.

Locked.

Katy shook her head. "His assistant came running over saying, 'He's here!' like he's the King of England or something, but I've never seen him before."

"Lopez knew him, though?"

"They seem to have some history," said Katy. "Lopez shouted at him to get out in English at the end. She opened the door and pushed him out. I saw her face before she slammed the door. She looked furious."

As if on cue, something heavy crashed against Lopez's door.

Katy gasped out loud, and Max started to bark. Tanya banged her fist on the door.

"Are you all right in there?"

Lopez didn't answer.

"Wait, I have keys," said Katy, scrambling around to an office cabinet. She plucked a large key ring and picked the one she was looking for.

"We're coming in," called out Tanya as Katy unlocked the door. Tanya pushed the door open.

Katy grabbed her arm. "Watch out!"

Tanya stopped mid-stride and stared at the broken glass shards on the floor. The odor of strong alcohol filled the small office, mixing with the musty smells prevalent in any county building. But Lopez was nowhere to be seen.

Katy craned her neck. "Carmen? Where are you?"

"Stay back," said Tanya as she stepped over the broken bottle and walked toward the desk. She peered over it and her eyes widened.

Carmen Lopez was crouched on the floor, leaning against her desk, sobbing silently.

Chapter Twenty

Tanya circled around the desk.

"What in heaven's name happened here, hun?"

Lopez swallowed a sob and covered her face.

"Oh, sweetie, you're in such bad shape." Katy came over and kneeled next to her. "I'm taking you home. We're going to get you in the shower, then you're changing into your pajamas."

Lopez shook her head.

"That wasn't a question, sweetie. We're not staying here another minute." Katy reached over and tugged on her arm. "Come on. Get up. I'll make you a warm cup of tea and tuck you into bed."

"Hold on," said Tanya, putting a hand up. "I'd like to know what's going on here, first. Lopez, who was that man?"

"It's none of your business," said Lopez in a hoarse voice, like she had been shouting for hours.

"It is when you're acting chief and we have a murder investigation underway."

"It's a personal matter." The deputy turned to her. Her eyes were bloodshot and the lines on her face were deep. "Leave me alone."

"We're only trying to help you, sweetie." Katy wrapped an arm around Lopez's shoulders. "We want to know if you're okay."

The deputy looked away and blinked rapidly. Then, she let her hands fall to the floor and groaned like she was in pain.

Tanya softened her voice. "Did that man threaten you?"

Lopez clenched her jaws, but kept her face away from their gaze. Tanya and Katy waited for her to speak.

"No," said Lopez, after what seemed like forever. "I threatened *him*. I told him if I ever see him in this town again, he's a dead man."

She turned to Tanya, her eyes flashing in fury.

"I swear if he comes back, I'll shoot him dead, so help me."

Lopez wiped her nose with the back of her hand. Katy reached over to the tissue box on the desk and plucked one out for her.

"We've all been there, sweetie," said Katy in her soothing voice. "Sometimes a man can trip you up and piss you off, right?"

Lopez took the tissue but remained silent.

"What did he want from you?" asked Tanya. "If he's bothering you, I can have a talk with him. I can make sure he never comes near you again."

Lopez blew her nose but didn't answer.

"Is he a member of the Mafia? A biker gang? Was he someone you put behind bars when you were working in Cali? Did he come back for revenge?"

Lopez wiped her face and turned to her.

"Are those the only kind of men you think I meet?"

71

Tanya straightened up and looked into her eyes. "The hat, the sunglasses, and the mask told me he didn't want to show his face. So, who is he?"

"It's a personal issue and I'll resolve it myself." Lopez turned away from her. "I'm fine."

Tanya and Katy exchanged quick glances over her head. The deputy wasn't fine by any stretch of the imagination.

Lopez put a hand on the floor and pushed herself up. She got to her feet, swaying. Katy jumped up and grabbed her by the arm.

Tanya's public phone vibrated in her pocket. She stepped away from them and returned to the bullpen.

"Almost done with the autopsy," came Dr. Chen's crisp voice on the phone.

"That was quick," said Tanya.

"There's something you need to see. Come alone. Don't tell Lopez."

"What? Why?"

"Because I need to confirm the details legitimately."

Legitimately?

"What details?" said Tanya.

But the physician had already hung up.

Chapter Twenty-one

The small corpse lay cut open, her internal organs on display for the world to see.

The harsh smell of ammonia mixed with the odor of putrid flesh.

Tanya wrapped her hand over her mouth, trying not to gag. Even after experiencing the horrors of war, she could never get used to seeing a mutilated child. Not now. Not ever.

"Hope you didn't have breakfast, Detective," said an intern in a white lab coat, brandishing a bloodied scalpel in her gloved hand. Her eyes were bloodshot and lined, like she had been working all night.

Tanya swallowed her nausea and gave her a weak smile. "I'm good."

"Every cop who's come in here has vomited at one point or the other," Dr. Chen said from the other end of the autopsy table. "If you people can't handle blood and guts, why do you get into this profession at all?"

Ignoring the doctor's snide jab, Tanya turned to the cadaver on the table.

Dr. Chen had no idea her reaction was precisely due to her witnessing the senseless blood and guts spilled in war. But this wasn't the time for that conversation.

The girl's body was petite and slender. She had worn her brown hair at shoulder length. Her face was pallid and tinged in a purplish hue, but her eyes were closed like she was sleeping.

That is, if Tanya could ignore what had happened to the rest of her body.

Folded neatly next to the gurney was what looked like the girl's pink sweats or pajamas. Rows of steel trays holding sharp and frightful instruments lay neatly next to the corpse. The kitchen scale on the side table contained something small and bloody. Tanya didn't even want to know what it was.

The noise of doggy claws pawing on the door of the morgue came from the other side.

Trust me, you don't want to be in here, Max, thought Tanya, as she stepped gingerly toward the autopsy table.

"What's her name?" said one of the interns.

"Jane Doe," said Tanya with a sigh. "We found no identification on her."

"The killer was careful," said Dr. Chen, picking up the container from the scale. "But we may have some clues."

Tanya covered her nose to stop the foul odor that emanated from it.

"Do share," she croaked through her hands.

"Her last meal," said the doctor, "consisted of a rare steak. We also found remnants of walnuts and cashew nuts, most probably from an accompanying side dish. This isn't something you'd find in a local diner."

Tanya frowned. "I doubt they serve gourmet steak at the psychiatric hospital either."

"Given the rate of digestion, I presume she died three or four hours after that dinner. That means her time of death was approximately between seven and ten, Saturday evening."

"Can you tell me anything else to help identify her?"

"She had healthy teeth," said the physician. "Her dental work indicates she came from a well-off family. She was in good health, athletic even. I would hazard a guess she played sports in school. Given her meal that evening, I'd say she could have been at a fancy dinner with her family the night she died."

"We have two officers scouring the town with her picture," said Tanya. "So far, nothing, but maybe they'll dig up something at the local school."

Dr. Chen pointed at the dead girl's neck. Tanya took another step closer.

"The ligature marks," said the doctor, leaning over the corpse. "I can now confirm this was a homicide by asphyxiation."

Tanya stared at the brown bruises that circled the victim's dainty neck, her stomach sinking.

"Was she sexually assaulted as well?" she whispered.

Dr. Chen shook her head. "That's the only good news I have today, I'm afraid."

"These bruises on her shoulder tell me someone grabbed her, and she fought back," continued the doctor in her crisp, formal voice. "I can only assume she struggled because we couldn't find anything under her nails. No skin or pieces of fabric. Nothing. That's a conundrum for you to figure out, Detective."

Tanya looked at her, her brow furrowed.

"Perhaps the killer washed her after they finished the job?"

Dr. Chen nodded.

"A valid hypothesis. There were also no finger marks on her, which meant the killer was wearing gloves or some form of protection. They were prepared, and they knew what they were doing."

"So, we're looking for someone with enough knowledge to remove as much evidence as possible." Tanya's frown deepened. "But if that was their goal, wouldn't they have chosen a different technique, one that would conceal the cause of death?"

"You mean like a hard-to-detect poison or something like that?" said an intern.

"That's what I'm thinking," said Tanya. "Have you checked the stomach contents yet?"

"On it," said the intern. "I'll be doing the toxicology tests next."

Dr. Chen glanced down at the body.

"My assumption is this wasn't premeditated. She could have been in the wrong place at the wrong time. She could have stood up to an attacker who jumped on her and choked her."

A deep feeling of sadness crawled into Tanya's heart. She hardly knew the girl, but she knew what she had to do.

I'm not going to stop till I find who did this.

"It would really help to know her identity," said Tanya, speaking to herself more than the others. "Did she have a family? Did she live in Black Rock? Was she visiting town? Who is she?"

The interns exchanged a glance and a smug look came over Dr. Chen's face.

Tanya stared at the medical trio gawking at her from the other side of the gurney. A chill of realization went through her.

"You know her name, don't you?"

Chapter Twenty-two

"Why did you ask me for her name if you knew it already?"

Tanya glared at the physician and her interns.

"Who said we knew her name?" said Dr. Chen in a cool voice.

"But you know who she is, don't you?"

"I'm aware Jack hired you as a contractor," said the doctor, "but you have become a valuable member of the team that everyone trusts. I'm glad we have you in Black Rock."

Tanya narrowed her eyes.

That wasn't an answer to my question.

Besides, Dr. Chen rarely said anything nice about anybody. Everyone in town was scared of this diminutive woman and her sharp tongue, even Chief Jack Bold.

"Why are you telling me this?"

"You were there when my father died," said the doctor, ignoring her impatient glare. "You're a straight shooter, which I like. Honesty is a good and rare trait, not one I'd normally associate with a murderer attempting to hide their tracks."

Tanya's heart ticked faster.

"What are you saying, Doctor?"

Dr. Chen took a deep breath in.

"I believe someone from your team is involved in this homicide."

Tanya gave her a startled look. That was when she recalled the odd call she got from the doctor at the precinct.

Come alone. Don't tell Lopez.

Her mouth went dry.

"Are you telling me Lopez is involved?"

Dr. Chen turned to one of the interns.

The young woman in the lab coat stepped forward. "We did a series of rapid DNA tests. We checked the victim's DNA with the samples we had in the lab...."

She gave a side glance at her boss, but Dr. Chen's face remained expressionless.

After clearing her throat, the intern continued. "It took us all night, but we found a familial match. A very close one."

That explains the team's exhausted faces.

Tanya stepped up to the intern.

"Tell me what you found."

"On one condition," said Dr. Chen, raising a finger. "That you do not share this information with anyone."

"Why?"

"These tests are controversial. This particular one wasn't authorized, and I'm not getting my team into trouble."

Tanya stared at her.

"You broke the law."

Dr. Chen didn't answer.

Tanya spread her arms wide. "Can you tell me *anything*?"

"It will be completely off the record."

Tanya nodded, struggling not to show the exasperation she was feeling with every passing second. She pushed an errant hair off her forehead and collected her thoughts.

Okay, I'll play.

"I understand. You were trying to expedite the investigation to get justice for this girl. I'd have probably done the same in your shoes." She paused. "So, tell me. *Who is this girl?*"

"She's Deputy Lopez's daughter."

Chapter Twenty-three

Tanya gaped at the doctor.

"Deputy Carmen Lopez?"

"The only one we know," said Dr. Chen.

"You had her DNA on file?"

The interns shuffled their feet and looked away.

"Wait." Tanya frowned. *Why* do you have her DNA on file?"

"You people leave your genetic code everywhere you go," said the doctor, unfazed. "I merely pick up a hair or two from your office chairs."

"You've collected all of our DNA?" Tanya spluttered. "Is that even *legal*?"

The doctor pursed her lips, which usually meant she wasn't open to a debate.

"It's risk management. I like having complete records of everyone I work with, just in case one of you lot washes up on the beach, dead and decomposed or something. I can identify your corpse within an hour at best."

Tanya glared at her. "How reassuring."

The doctor put her hands up. "Don't get too excited, now. What we did last night was only a rapid test."

Tanya filed away the medical examiner's unusual and unethical practices in the back of her head. It had to be addressed, but not now. She had more urgent matters to consider.

"A rapid DNA test isn't conclusive evidence."

Dr. Chen nodded. "I realize you cannot take these results to court, and anyone can contest our findings. That's exactly why this is off the record."

"So, why not do a complete analysis?" said Tanya, leaning over to her. "*Legally*, this time?"

"For that, we'll need Lopez to provide express consent, but if she's in the state we saw her last night, I highly doubt she will."

"If she knew what you knew, she'd comply."

"I didn't take you to be gullible, Stone." Dr. Chen narrowed her eyes. "I'm only a physician, but if you ask me, I would start my detective work on her."

"She's a disciplined officer. A straight-laced cop. If anyone works by the book, it's her."

Dr. Chen made a face. "Did you *see* that woman last night?"

Tanya looked away, a sinking feeling coming to her stomach.

"That wasn't her."

The doctor raised an eyebrow.

"You cannot ignore the probability she murdered her own child."

"She told me she didn't have a family—"

"Red flag."

Tanya stared at the doctor.

"But where was the girl all along? In Black Rock? Or did she bring her back from San Diego?"

"My money is on the latter."

Tanya turned her gaze at the girl on the table.

"It was dark on the hill, but I thought she looked familiar." She spoke slowly, trying to recall memories from the night before. "If this is really her daughter, that would explain why she ran off like she'd seen a phantom."

"It's hard to believe your trusted colleague would be involved, but you have to accept it," said the doctor in a clipped tone.

"Hang on. She ran off because she recognized her child. Her shocked reaction indicates she hadn't known of her death." Tanya paused. "What we witnessed was a grief-stricken mother, not a killer."

"When Fox came in with Zoe yesterday, he was worried about taking time off with Jack being away and Lopez out of commission. Even Katy, your new office manager, asked me to check up on Lopez. Everyone noticed she'd been seriously off for the last week. Not just me."

Tanya scrunched her eyes, trying to reconcile the battle raging in her. Her brain was scolding her about doubting a good colleague, but her gut was telling her the doctor's logic had a lot of truth to it.

"If Lopez was innocent," she said, thinking out aloud, "she wouldn't have run off. She would be fighting for us to find the killer. That means, she knew of the events that led to the incident. She may even know the identity of the killer."

Dr. Chen nodded. "I see you're getting your sensibilities back, Detective."

Tanya turned to leave, her mind buzzing.

She put her hand on the door, her heart heavy, but glad to know that Max was waiting for her on the other side. He always had a calming effect, and what she needed right now was a clear head to think.

"Stone?"

Tanya turned around.

"There's something else you need to see," said Dr. Chen. "It wasn't the cause of the victim's death, but it will give you more information."

The doctor nodded to her interns. "Roll her over."

Her employees stepped up to the autopsy table. Using their gloved hands, they turned the corpse to the side so the girl's naked back was exposed.

Dr. Chen pointed at the body.

"What's your opinion of Lopez now?"

Chapter Twenty-four

Tanya stared at the deep scars on the girl's back.

"Someone beat this poor kid," said Dr. Chen. "Pelted her over a period of years when she was quite young."

A chill went through Tanya. She swallowed the ball of fury rising inside of her.

"So, these are old injuries?"

"Incurred seven or more years ago. Whoever abused her, stopped, or didn't have access to her anymore."

Tanya's stomach churned.

What's going on, Lopez?

"Seems like you've got your work cut out for you," said Dr. Chen. She nodded to the interns who gently laid the girl's body back down. "You may not like my methods, Stone, but we do good work here."

Tanya couldn't disagree with that statement.

She turned to the doctor.

"Do you do autopsies for all suspicious deaths in Black Rock?"

"We're not *CSI New York*. You're looking at my entire team in this room. I prioritize the requests that come in and do what we can, where and when warranted."

"What about Silver Serenity? Have you examined any of their deaths over the past few years?"

"People drop like flies in pension homes all the time. If I have to investigate every old age death, I wouldn't have time to sleep, let alone assist with your cases."

"Do they have a medical team at the residence?"

"A high-priced, private physician flies in from Seattle regularly. I believe he signs off on their death certificates." Dr. Chen shrugged. "They certainly don't contact me. I'm a mere small-town doc. Not exclusive enough for them."

One of the interns turned to Tanya.

"My family tried to get Grandma in when she was diagnosed with severe onset Alzheimer's. She was seventy, so she met the age criteria, but they didn't even want to talk to us. They said we weren't the right fit."

"Right fit?"

"It was a humiliating experience."

Tanya frowned. "Why do they have an age restriction?"

"Most upscale residences do," said Dr. Chen. "Publicly, it's a marketing ploy. But if you ask me, it's just one way to keep operational costs down. They charge sky-high rates for a short time to a small demographic with similar issues and needs and voila, their profit margin goes up."

"Who's the decision-maker at the Silver Serenity?"

"Carolyn Pennett-Staresinic, the residence director," said the second intern. "If you don't have the money or the right connections, she chases you off like a dirty rat."

Dr. Chen scoffed. "That woman is an affront to common decency."

Tanya turned to her.

"Do you know the director?"

"Sat next to her at a business luncheon when she started her position." The doctor's mouth curled into a sneer. "I've never met a more prideful, surly, impudent.... Let's just say we don't see eye-to-eye on many things. Whoever hired her committed a travesty."

"That's what Mom said, too." The first intern nodded. "How she got that job is a total mystery."

Dr. Chen's eyes narrowed.

"Why the sudden interest in Silver Serenity, Stone?"

"Just a hunch, Doctor."

Tanya spun around and grabbed the door handle, then stopped as she remembered the incident that morning by her cottage. She twisted around.

"Have any of you come across a man with a prominent scar down his right cheek?"

Chapter Twenty-five

"Do you know this girl?"

Tanya displayed the headshot she got from Dr. Chen at the morgue.

Max was sitting outside the main entrance, forlornly looking through the glass doors, as animals weren't allowed inside the hospital.

The psychiatric hospital was more of a private convalescence center than a medical institution. The cluster of secluded log cabins surrounded by the evergreen forest on a hill that overlooked the ocean made it feel more like a retreat.

The reception area had comfortable couches, a fireplace, bookshelves, and First Nations paintings of totem poles and eagles hanging on the wall. The pleasant smell of pine hung in the air.

The balding man at the reception desk put his glasses on and leaned over to look at the photo. Something about his slow and deliberate movements made Tanya watch him closely.

His face was straight and his hand gestures were controlled, but his eyes were shifty.

He's hiding something.

She looked him over. A tattoo of a gnarly cobweb spread from his jaws down to his neck and disappeared underneath his dress shirt.

He's been in prison?

Monochrome cobweb tattoos were popular among the incarcerated. It symbolized the prisoner as prey trapped inside a spider's web. The ink stood out, dark, bold, and fresh against his pale skin. This was done recently.

Tanya frowned.

Why would a psychiatric hospital hire an ex-convict? She stopped herself. *He could have been pardoned. He has the right to find a job in civilian life.*

"Never seen her before," said the man, squinting hard.

Too hard.

You're lying.

"Please look again."

The man leaned back and shook his head, averting his eyes like he didn't want to see a corpse.

"Have any of your patients gone missing?" said Tanya, putting the picture away.

"I believe my colleague already answered your questions last night. Everyone's accounted for. Besides, we don't admit anyone under eighteen anymore."

"I've been here before," said Tanya. "I recall seeing a child patient."

"A new owner bought the place a year ago. New management. New staff. New rules."

"What happened to the children?"

"Sent to a kids long-term care facility, maybe? Fostered into families? How am I supposed to know? I just work here."

"Did the new management replace the computers as well?"

He shrugged and sat back down with a harrumph, like he was done talking to her. Tanya looked at the silver nameplate on his lapel.

Paul Hammerston. Day Manager.

She leaned over the desk.

"Paul, this is a murder investigation. We're dealing with a young girl's death. I'd really appreciate you checking a name for me—"

He snapped his head up.

"Do you have a warrant?"

She wished she could reach over the desk and shake him till his teeth rattled. Tanya pushed that urge to the back of her mind, knowing that wouldn't help her solve the case.

"A girl was murdered and buried nearby. I'm asking for your help."

Paul glowered. "You think I'll hand over privileged patient information to any yahoo who comes waltzing in through the front door?"

Tanya pinched her lips.

"Turn it up," called out a voice from behind her.

She craned her neck to see a woman pointing at the large television screen in the common living room.

News had already got out. The story was about the girl on the hill. Troubled murmurs rippled through the small group huddled around the TV.

Tanya surveyed the crowd, searching for the man with the scar. There were only two males, hunched lethargically in their armchairs. Neither had a scar, but both had glazed looks in their eyes.

Drugged to the hilt.

She turned back to the manager who was staring at his computer, head bent, decidedly ignoring her.

"I thought you said you didn't see this girl before," said Tanya. "She was on the news all morning."

"Not talking to you any more, Detective," said Paul, without looking up. "You want information, you know what to do."

With a resigned sigh, Tanya stepped away from the desk and moved closer to the crowd gathered around the television. Their eyes were glued to the screen, but the news anchor wasn't sharing any details. She had none to give as far as Tanya knew, but the excitement on the journalist's face was palpable.

A dead body. Reported to be that of a young girl. No information has been released yet....

Tanya grimaced.

The anchor was clearly reveling in the news. An unidentified corpse buried in the woods meant the local channel's ratings would skyrocket, if only for a short time.

The camera panned to a group of reporters huddled behind the yellow line at the crime scene. The two junior officers were holding the fort, looking as serious as if they were guarding an Egyptian king's tomb.

Good job, thought Tanya, making a mental note to buy them coffee and donuts next time she went up.

"Hey, you can't talk to our patients either," came an angry shout from behind her. "That's harassment."

It was Paul from the front desk.

Tanya stepped away from the group and put her hands up. "Just wanted to hear the news."

Ignoring Paul's angry glower, she walked toward the exit. On the other side of the glass doors, Max wagged his tail. But just as she reached for the door, he got on his hind legs and barked loudly, as if to warn her.

"Hang on, Max—"

That was when someone tugged on her arm.

Chapter Twenty-six

A white-haired, hunched man stepped out of the shadows by the doorway.

Tanya's mind had been so busy, trying to make sense of everything she had learned so far, she hadn't even noticed him.

Max barked through the door, his hackles up. Something about this elderly man seemed to bother him. Tanya turned to the newcomer.

"Can I help you?"

"Are you the detective they said was coming?" he said in a gravelly voice. A wonky smile broke across his lined face. "You're a pretty thing to be an investigator."

Tanya didn't even answer. She spun around to leave when he clutched her arm again.

"You're searching for that cute little girl's killer, am I right?"

Cute little girl?

She turned to him with a frown.

He had to be in his mid-eighties or older, probably from a generation where female investigators were far from common, a time when no one batted an eyelid over calling women "things."

He was tall but frail, and slightly bent like his spine could no longer hold him upright. His short sleeves displayed arms covered in tattoos inked decades ago, but one stood out.

Tanya did a double take.

It was the same tattoo the day manager had, except the cobweb was on his wrinkled elbow and faded. The layers in the web usually signified the number of years the wearer had been sentenced to in prison. She counted ten.

He's been in prison, too. For a serious crime, from the looks of it.

She glanced at his leathery face. Despite his leery expression and crude words, his eyes were cold and hard.

He offered his hand. "Pendleton, Mike Pendleton. So nice to meet you, sweetheart."

The second his fingers touched Tanya's, her skin prickled. There was something dark about him. Something evil.

"Do you have any information for me, Mr. Pendleton?"

"I sure do, honey."

He came so close she could feel his breath on her cheek. Tanya wrinkled her nose as the sharp tang of his rotten breath wafted her way.

Pendleton curled his scrawny fingers around her arm. "I'm the one who did it."

Tanya leaned away from him. "Did what?"

"I killed the cute little girl. I killed Esmeralda."

Seeing her face, he cackled.

"If you do your job right, sweetheart, you'll find it all leads to me."

"Are you confessing—"

"Hey! Didn't I tell you to stop bothering my patients?"

Tanya turned to see a furious Paul march her way.

"Your patient," she said in a dry voice, "just confessed to being a murderer."

Paul grabbed the older man by the arm, more roughly than she would have expected him to.

"What are you doing on your feet, Mike?" he scolded. "Where's your throne?"

His ward craned his neck and pointed. That was when Tanya noticed the wheelchair in the corner.

She watched as Paul dragged the older man toward his chair and pushed him into it. Pendleton plopped into his seat and blinked like he was disoriented.

Outside the main doors, Max was howling, wanting to be part of the action. Paul spun on his heels and stomped up to Tanya.

"Do you like bullying the elderly, Detective?"

Seems like you're the bully here.

"For the record," she said, "he approached me."

"Mike's got dementia," snarled Paul. "He has more imagination than all of Hollywood combined. He's been saying crazy sorts of things ever since he arrived here."

He glowered at her.

"Arrest him and you'll get slapped with a human rights violation so fast, you won't know what hit you. I'm not scared of you."

"Tell me something," said Tanya, watching the day manager closely. "Who's Esmeralda?"

Paul's eyes flickered for one moment, but he composed himself quickly.

"How would I know?" he spat out.

She pointed at Pendleton who was staring into empty space, his brow furrowed like he had forgotten why he was here.

"He mentioned the name."

"Do you expect me to read his muddled mind?" Paul waved his hand, but wasn't looking at her anymore. "Please leave. You're making my patients uncomfortable."

"I'd like to remind you that withholding information from a murder investigation is an obstruction of justice."

"So, sue me."

He spun around and stepped up to the older man. Before Tanya could say anything, he wheeled Pendleton and his wheelchair back to the living room, like she wasn't even there.

Trying not to grit her teeth, Tanya stepped through the front doors.

Old Mike Pendleton didn't have the energy or the strength to kill a fly, let alone a teenage girl. But she couldn't help think there was something to his story.

Outside, Max leaped up to greet her. She petted his head to calm him down.

"Let's go, bud. We have some digging to do."

She walked over to her Jeep with Max at her heels, her mind a whirl of possibilities. The deeper she dug into this case, the more unanswered questions seem to pop up.

And she still hadn't visited the Silver Serenity residence yet.

Susan Cross or her messenger, Ray Jackson, would be calling soon, demanding a status report, and right now, that report would be completely blank.

Tanya pulled her phone out, just as it rang.

"Hey, Tanya," came Katy's breathless voice. "You won't believe this."

Chapter Twenty-seven

Tanya came to a sudden stop, her heart beating fast.

"Everything okay? Where's Lopez?"

"Don't worry," came Katy's voice. "I drove her home."

"How is she?"

"She didn't even want to take a shower. Just wanted to crawl into bed and crash. Maybe that's a good thing. That girl needs to—"

"Did she say anything? Any hints to what's been distressing her?"

"No, but she sure is hiding something from us."

Tanya sighed. If the dead girl was Lopez's daughter, she was hiding a lot more than just *something*.

"She practically kicked me out of her home," Katy was saying. "I wasn't going to leave her at her doorstep, was I? I didn't want her to crash down the stairs and hurt herself."

"You meant well, hun."

"As soon as she got inside, she told me to go away, so I left. She didn't even say thank you." Katy sighed. "She's really not herself.

But I'm happy she's home and not here, drunk crying in a corner of her office."

"Did you see anything unusual in her house?"

"She didn't let me in." Katy paused. "Was I supposed to see something? Like what?"

Tanya bit her lip.

"Katy, can you look up one thing for me?"

"Anything's better than doing the paperwork on Jack's desk."

"See if you can dig up the background of a Mike Pendleton. Caucasian male, approximately in his mid-eighties, currently a patient at the Black Rock psychiatric hospital. I'd expect a prison record, maybe decades back."

Tanya cast a sidelong glance at the hospital. It was hard to see inside from here, but she suspected everyone was watching the news now.

Other than her Jeep and a couple of staff vehicles, the front parking lot was empty. At the far end of the lot, Max was yapping at a squirrel.

On the other end, Katy was clicking away on the keyboard.

"Can you give me more info?" she said.

"That's all I have." Tanya let out a breath. "And that he confessed to killing the girl on the hill."

The typing stopped abruptly.

"*What?*"

"I don't believe him," said Tanya. "If he was fifteen years younger, I'd haul him to the station, but he's in a wheelchair, hunched over, and can't stand without getting the shakes."

"He could have got someone else to strangle the girl and dig the grave."

"An accomplice or a partner," said Tanya, nodding. "Check up on Paul Hammerston for me too, please."

"Another patient?"

"The day manager. He's stonewalling me with warrant requests, which is fair, but I think he knows more than he's sharing."

The clickety clack on the other end started again, sounding like Katy's fingers were moving at lightning speed.

"I'd say he's in his late thirties or early forties," said Tanya. "I suspect he also spent time in prison. Maybe that's where these two met. That might give us some clues to how the girl died."

"On it."

Tanya furrowed her brow.

"Why did you call me?"

Katy stopped typing.

"Oh, I followed up on your request."

Tanya scrunched her forehead, trying to recall which of the many tasks she was referring to. Katy had taken on a lot more work than was normal for the office manager of a small-town precinct without complaining.

"Tell me," said Tanya.

When Katy's voice came again, it was smug.

"I figured out who the helicopter man is."

Chapter Twenty-eight

"I called the number on the helicopter pilot's business card," said Katy.

"What did he say?" said Tanya.

"That line goes straight to the charter firm's customer service desk."

"He must have an extension."

"I wasn't looking for him," said Katy. "I wanted to talk to someone who'd give me intel."

Tanya frowned. "Who would that be?"

"The receptionist ladies who're always happy to gossip if you give them a good enough reason."

That's a stereotype, but clever....

"I told the receptionist my boss left his phone in the backseat of one of their choppers," continued Katy. "She checked the lost and found and didn't find anything, of course."

"Didn't she ask you for proof of identity?"

"All she needed was the date, approximate time and the pilot's name, and bingo, I got intel."

Tanya could feel her friend's excitement through the airwaves.

"The pilot picked up our man from the helipad at the top of the summit hotel and returned him in precisely one hour and twenty-three minutes."

"A half an hour to and from Black Rock and twenty minutes for a chat with Lopez," said Tanya. "Didn't give him much time to do anything else."

"Exactly," said Katy. "I told the receptionist I was terrified I'd get fired for losing his phone. I started crying, saying I'm going to have to find another job and a cheaper apartment, yadda, yadda. That's when I learned our man had a reputation for mistreating his employees."

"I'm not surprised," said Tanya.

"Supposedly he treats his personal assistant, you know, the woman in the pencil skirt, the worst. That's when her name slipped out. All I had to do was look her up, and guess what?"

"Please tell me."

"Second bingo. I found a parking ticket violation."

"Wow. Jack needs to pay you more," said Tanya.

"The car was registered to a business, and that told me the company she was employed at. Third bingo." Katy paused, pride in her voice. "Took a few tears and a few clicks of my mouse, but it worked."

"You're nothing but extraordinary, Katy." Tanya blew a raspberry. "So, who is our man?"

"Santiago Fernando."

Tanya screwed her eyes.

"Don't think I've heard that name before."

"He owns one of the largest privately held pharmaceutical companies in the country. That explains the charter helicopter, the beach house, and staff at his beck and call."

Tanya nodded, though Katy couldn't see her.

"Found a photo of his beach property, the one he invited me to," Katy was saying. "It's a really nice house. Guess where it's located?"

"Just tell me, hun."

"San Diego."

"So Lopez was most probably visiting him," said Tanya, speaking slowly, as she tried to fit the disparate pieces of this puzzle together. "Did you find any connection between those two?"

"Nope, but I found out his company's HQ is in Seattle. He has a home there too, but he seems to travel a lot. He's also one of the biggest sponsors of charity events in the state."

"I never trust anyone who donates large sums of money," said Tanya, "I get the feeling they're trying to make up for bad karma."

"Santiago's family has bad karma all right," said Katy, her tone turning serious. "The mother died one year after childbirth. She had the Stone Man Syndrome. It's when your skeleton hardens until it's fossilized. A horrible way to die."

"I've heard of it," said Tanya. "It's extremely rare."

"Health issues aside, they had mega legal problems." Katy's voice turned sharp. "The father was fighting three hundred plus lawsuits."

Tanya straightened up. *Three hundred?*

"What were they for?"

The sound of rapid mouse clicks came from the other end.

"Falsifying laboratory test results, misleading advertising tactics, not providing complete information on drugs and their side effects, and for trying to get too cozy with the FDA, meaning bribes, but here's the kicker...."

Tanya heard more clicking, like Katy was looking for the tab with the right information.

"Found it," came Katy's voice again. "The father was hit with a sexual harassment lawsuit from a group of unnamed plaintiffs.

He was also accused of sexual interference of a minor at one point, which is essentially the rape of a child."

"Sounds like a delightful family," said Tanya, frowning. "Not the kind Lopez would have anything to do with normally."

"There was an article about the family's charity work in a Seattle gossip magazine which went belly up decades ago. The story is short, but it has a photo of the family when the kids were toddlers. The thing is, there's no mention of them afterward. No photos. No articles. No social media posts. It's like the entire family dropped into a black hole."

"No company headshots?"

"Their website is a black box. It's a privately held firm so they don't have to disclose as much as a company with shareholders. They don't even name the board of directors, if there's one. I only found out who owns it after I dug into old news articles."

"The wealthier a family gets, the more private they become, so their media blackout is understandable." Tanya bit her lower lip, trying to think. "But what if there was something more to that?"

"Given the father's track record," said Katy, speaking slowly like something was brewing in her head, "there's a probability he abused his own kids too. Maybe that's why they went dark, so their family's dirty laundry didn't air in public."

"How many kids are there?"

"Two. They're adults now." Katy paused. "Santiago and his twin sister."

Goosebumps sprang up on Tanya's arms.

A twin sister?

Chapter Twenty-nine

"What's the sister's name?" said Tanya.

"Angelica," said Katy. "Angelica Fernando."

Tanya leaned into her phone. "Are you thinking what I'm thinking?"

"His mask was loose, so I saw his face when he came close. He looks nothing like Lopez. They can't be related."

"Did the father get sentenced for the sexual interference of a minor?"

"None of the charges stuck." Katy sighed. "News articles are sparse, but the few I found say the seven harassment charges were dropped and the sexual interference issue was resolved amicably between the parties."

"Amicably?" Tanya grimaced. "That means he paid for the victims' silence. I'm surprised any prosecutor or judge would have let that happen."

"This happened four decades ago. Things were different back then."

"Where's the sleazy old man now?"

"Six feet underground. He died of a heart attack three years ago. So, our golden boy, Santiago Fernando, took over. The sexual abuse claims have disappeared, but he's fighting the malpractice lawsuits against the company. Seems like he doesn't care much for corporate responsibility."

"The question is," said Tanya, pinching her lips, "what's Lopez doing with a bad apple like him?"

"Whatever their relationship is, she's not going to open up to us anytime soon. Right now, she's sad, mad, and in the middle of a major nervous breakdown."

Tanya racked her brain for the right words, knowing she couldn't break her promise to Dr. Chen.

"Katy, I learned something today, but we have to keep it confidential."

"My lips are sealed."

"The dead girl might be related to Lopez."

Katy gasped.

Before Tanya could explain, Max started to bark. She surveyed the parking lot but couldn't see him anymore. She scanned the woods surrounding the hospital buildings.

Where did he go off to now?

"Max?" she called out, pulling the phone away from her ear. "Where are you, bud?"

She spotted his furry tail by the tree line. He was at the edge of the lot, focused on something deep inside the forest.

Tanya brought the phone close to her ear again.

"I'd better get him in the car before the day manager starts to complain."

Max barked again.

"What's bothered him?" said Katy.

"He's probably found a family of chipmunks."

Tanya hung up and hurried over to her dog. Max was standing in his spot. Tanya's gut tightened. He would never stand still if his target had been a small animal.

He's uncovered something.

Or someone.

She gazed into the dark thicket. The massive fir trees huddled close together, concealing whatever it was that had caught his attention.

A movement came from ten yards in front of them.

Max let out a volley of barks.

Tanya pulled out her Glock and aimed it forward. Suddenly, a man popped out in between the trees, carrying something heavy in his hands. With one fleeting glance at her, he spun around and vanished into the woods.

Max sprinted after him through the underbrush, barking.

Tanya dashed after them, her heart racing.

She had only spotted the figure for a split second, but she would never forget the face that peeked through her window that morning.

It was the man with the scar.

Chapter Thirty

A pine branch snapped against Tanya's face, stinging her eyes.

"Police!" she hollered. "Stop right there!"

The man with the scar was surprisingly fast and seemed familiar with these woodlands.

Max was galloping ahead, jumping over puddles and skidding across leaves, but never losing his footing.

Tanya knew if there was anything she could rely on, it was her dog's sense of smell. She moved swiftly but quietly, staying a few yards behind him, trying not to trip over the logs scattered across the forest floor.

Suddenly, the crashing ceased, and the woods fell silent.

So did Max.

Tanya stopped in her tracks and swiveled her head, panting, but her gun at the ready.

Where did they go to?

The scarred man had been carrying something, but he had bolted so quickly, it had been difficult to make it out. If that had been a rifle, her dog was in greater danger than she thought.

She stepped through the trees, her heart thumping hard. She could hear Max panting farther down, but she couldn't see him.

"Max?"

She circled a cedar bush when she spotted him in a small clearing. She sighed in relief.

Max wagged his tail as Tanya approached him. Then, with a pointed look, he put his nose down, sniffed the ground, and trotted forward. After a few yards, he changed direction like the trail had changed.

Tanya caught up to him and folded her fingers around his collar.

"Stop, bud," she whispered, as she surveyed their surroundings. "He might be armed."

Rays of pale afternoon sunlight shimmered through the forest canopy. But the trees towering around her had grown so closely together, their thick branches shut out most of the light.

The shrill song of a red robin rang from a nearby tree, startling her and Max. As soon as Tanya looked up, the singing stopped.

She scanned the forest, her heart thudding so loudly she was sure the man with the scar could hear her.

The noise of a twig cracking came from nearby.

Max wiggled his head, fighting to get out of her grasp. Tanya gripped his collar tighter.

"Stay, bud," she whispered hoarsely.

Max stopped struggling. She released his collar and turned around slowly, surveying the surrounding thicket, scanning for shadows that didn't belong.

Max's ears were pricked and his hackles were up. Tanya noticed that his eyes were now focused on a massive oak tree several yards in front of them.

There's something behind that tree.

"Let's move," she whispered, as she stepped forward with her Glock aimed in front.

She stepped an inch at a time, her back tense and her shoulders tight. Max matched her steps, ready for her next command.

Tanya stopped when she was within six feet from the oak tree.

Rivulets of sweat ran down her back. The chase through the forest hadn't been long, but the multiple-obstacle course of low branches, massive logs, slippery puddles, and thorn bushes along the way had given her a good workout.

Where is he?

She took a slow breath in to settle her nerves and slipped behind the oak tree. That was when she heard his raspy breathing.

The man with the scar was on the other side of the tree.

Chapter Thirty-one

Tanya froze in place.

If I can hear him, he can hear me.

By her heels, Max remained stiff, but as silent as a clam.

Tanya relaxed her shoulders but kept her grip on her gun. Then, she took a slow, deep breath in. It was the best way to control her heart rate and lessen the impact of the adrenaline spiking through her veins.

The man wheezed loudly, cleared his throat, and spat.

He doesn't know we're right here.

He hacked a rough cough and took a garbled breath in, sounding like he was choking on his own spit.

Tanya craned her neck and peered around the trunk.

She caught a glimpse of his silhouette. The man with the scar was leaning against the next tree over. He was drenched in sweat and clutching his chest like he was having a hard time breathing.

Tanya's eyes traveled down to his other hand.

An ax.

She gave a silent prayer of thanks it wasn't the rifle she had been imagining.

He brushed the sweat off his face and swiveled his head, like he had heard something. Tanya didn't move, but her brain whirred with her next move.

Her Glock would win against his ax in any battle, but she recognized the unpredictability of an unnerved man who was cornered. He could run away, but he could also go berserk with that weapon.

It was time to ask what he was doing at her window, but she needed to do so without angering or panicking him any more than he was. Tanya was about to whistle to him, when the sound of people talking came from within the wilderness.

She stiffened.

We have company.

She listened to the voices as they got closer. The group was moving slowly but deliberately, like they were strolling along a trail through the woods. Whoever they were, they were in no hurry and were speaking in somber and hushed tones.

Suddenly a male voice called out. "We're ready now, ma'am."

"Good," came a woman's voice, sharp and assertive.

The voices passed by a few yards from where Tanya was. The snail-like speed at which they moved told her they weren't attempting to avoid detection.

Unauthorized hikers?

College kids playing truant on the hill?

Patients from the hospital being taken out for a walk?

No. The voices sounded older, much older. Tanya's head cleared as she realized who they were. Retirees from the Silver Serenity residence out on a walk.

Ignoring the painful cramp creeping up her leg, she waited patiently for the voices to dissipate. On the other side, the man with the scar had quietened down as well, like he didn't want to be found out by them either.

It took forever for the procession to move out of earshot. When Tanya was sure they were gone, she stretched her cramped legs.

Something rustled above her.

The red robin had flown closer. It settled on a branch and cocked its head at Max, giving him a curious look. Tanya was glad he knew when to remain silent, and also thankful it wasn't a squirrel. Max was trained, but he was still a dog's dog.

She turned back around to confront her target, when the robin let out a shrill whistle.

The man cried out in surprise.

Tanya jumped from behind the tree.

With an ungodly cry, the man whirled around and crashed into the thicket.

"Come back!" shouted Tanya. "I want to talk to you!"

Max leaped out, barking loudly. He burst into the forest after the man, and the chase was on, again.

"Police! Stop!" hollered Tanya.

She raced after him, dodging the trees, using Max's barks as her guide. To her surprise, he was heading straight out of the woods.

She halted by the edge of the forest, panting hard, and stared at what looked like a manicured park. Congregated in a circle near the middle were a dozen people, focused on something happening on the ground.

The man with the scar cut across the park, waving his ax dangerously in the air, with Max only a few feet behind him.

Hearing the commotion, the group whirled around, their eyes wide.

Without a warning, Max leaped on the scarred man and locked his powerful jaws on his arm. The man screeched in pain.

The group scattered in confusion, screaming in panic. That was when Tanya noticed the dugout hole where they had been standing.

"Max!" shouted Tanya, propelling her legs forward. "Stop!"

To her horror, the scarred man tripped on a shovel by the pit. "No!"

Max flew in the air like a spinner and tumbled into the gaping hole with the man.

Chapter Thirty-two

The crowd stared at the pit, horror etched on their faces.

"Max!" screamed Tanya, dashing over.

She teetered at the edge of the dugout. Her eyes widened.

A grave.

A wooden coffin was already lowered into the open pit.

What she had thought was a park was actually a cemetery. Tanya had been here before at night, but hadn't recognized it in the light of day, her focus being on her dog and the man they were chasing.

A painful moan came from the grave. The man with the scar lay in a fetal position on the coffin, holding on to his foot. Max had his jaws clamped onto his arm. He knew not to bite, but his growls were enough for the man to remain completely still, petrified in fear.

Tanya holstered her Glock, got to her knees, and scooted closer to her dog.

"Hey, bud. Let go."

As soon as Max relaxed his jaws, she reached in and grabbed his collar. Using both her hands, she hauled him out. A quick check told her he was fine, and in much higher spirits than the man was. Max skipped around her, tail wagging, tongue lolling, doing his usual victory dance he did whenever he caught his target.

Tanya turned back around and peered into the open grave. The injured man was rocking back and forth on the coffin now, clutching his ankle. She reached down and plucked the ax before he could hurt himself more.

She offered him her hand. "Here, let's get you out."

With a startled cry, he pushed away from her, shuffling awkwardly along the coffin to the other end.

"I'm here to help you," said Tanya, thrusting her hand toward him again. He crouched low, hugging his knees, his eyes filled in terror.

"What in all things holy do you think you're doing?"

It was the sharp voice of an angry woman, the same voice Tanya had heard on the trail earlier.

She spun around.

A middle-aged woman with striking blue hair cut pixie style was marching toward the grave. She was wearing a black skirt suit and a pearl necklace, paired with sneakers, like she had hastily changed for this funeral in the backwoods.

She stopped by the grave and stood with her hands on her hips, glowering at Tanya.

"Do you realize what you have done?"

Behind her was a small crowd of elderly folk and a female nurse, gawking at Tanya like she was an alien who had landed in their midst.

Tanya got to her feet with a sinking feeling. This wasn't how she had wanted to introduce herself to the Silver Serenity residence.

"I'm terribly sorry—"

"You interrupted a *funeral*," spat the woman in the suit. "This is reprehensible."

"My sincere apologies. I didn't—"

"You people are always giving us trouble," bellowed the woman, shaking a finger at her. "Sneaking around at all hours. Haven't I told you to stay away? They should lock you all up in straightjackets and never let you out."

She thinks I'm from the asylum.

"I'm officially lodging a complaint with the hospital, and I'm going to start a petition. Once I'm done with you, they'll never let you out!"

Maybe the girl's death has nothing to do with what's happening at Silver Serenity. Maybe we have two completely separate cases here.

The woman jerked her arms as she spoke. Her jacket flapped open for a split second and fell back in place, but not before Tanya noticed the sidearm attached to her waist belt.

A concealed weapon.

"You're mistaken," said Tanya. "I'm not a patient at the hospital."

"That's what they all say." With a furious scoff, the woman whipped out her phone and stepped away from the grave. "I'm calling the police to arrest you. Maybe you people will learn a lesson then, once and for all."

"Ma'am," called out Tanya. "I *am* the police."

Chapter Thirty-three

The woman in the suit whirled around.

Her disapproving eyes flew to Tanya's sweaty shirt, then traveled down to her army cargo pants and dusty boots. She turned her dour eyes on Max who was standing by Tanya's feet, gazing at her curiously.

In turn, Tanya appraised her back.

Carolyn Pennett-Staresinic. This has to be the Silver Serenity residence's notorious director. I finally meet the person Dr. Chen and her team warned me about.

"I'm with the Black Rock police precinct," said Tanya, spreading her hands out to show she wasn't a threat. "I was after a suspect with my K9."

"Who gave you authorization to step onto my property?" snarled the director.

A painful moan came from the pit. Tanya pointed at the man cowering inside the grave.

"Let's get him out first, shall we? He needs medical attention."

The director glared at her, then spun around to the assembly huddled behind her. The group seemed to shrink at her glance.

"Ana? Nurse Ana? Where are you? Come here right now."

A petite, blonde woman in nursing scrubs stepped out from behind the crowd. The key ring attached to her waist jingled as she walked.

"R... right here, ma'am."

"What are you waiting around for?" snapped the director. "Pull this nutcase out of here immediately."

The nurse scurried over. She stopped and gazed down at the man who was holding on to his ankle.

"I'll need to first attend to—"

"Get him out *now.*"

Tanya stepped up to the nurse. "Let me help."

Ignoring the director's glowers, Tanya assisted the nurse into the open grave. Ana stepped gingerly onto the wooden casket and kneeled by the man's foot.

"Your behavior is inexcusable. Absolutely inexcusable!"

Tanya turned around to see the director scowling at her, her hands on her hips.

"You'd better have a darned good reason for barging in on us like a crazed bull in a china shop."

Max let out a low growl from his belly.

Tanya got to her feet. "The suspect was running with an ax—"

"Hello? Someone?" called a female voice. "I need help."

Tanya glanced down to see the nurse was struggling to lift the man out of the pit.

Ignoring the director's wrath, Tanya pushed herself carefully onto the coffin, trying not to think of what she was doing. To have someone fall into your grave was a fiasco, but for strangers to walk all over your coffin was another level of awful.

A frisson went through her as her feet touched the wooden casket. Susan Cross's call had been lurking in the back of her mind all morning.

Is this the dead woman she talked about?

Are they burying a murder victim?

Tanya muttered an apology to the deceased under her breath.

Nurse Ana seemed to have calmed the scarred man down. Tanya stepped over to him and wrapped her arms around his chest.

"You take his feet," she said.

Working together, they hauled him onto the top, while the crowd watched, wide-eyed.

The director had stepped away from the scene now, and was pacing up and down with her phone to her ear. Probably calling the precinct to complain, thought Tanya as she settled the scarred man gently on the soil.

"He twisted his ankle," said the nurse, examining his foot.

Max came over and sniffed the man's foot, as if to ask if he was okay. The man jerked his head back.

"Don't worry. He won't bite you." Tanya kneeled next to him. "I'm sorry about what happened, but I thought you were a fugitive when you ran off like that."

His eyes welled in tears but he didn't speak.

"Why *did* you run off?"

He shuddered and looked away.

Tanya wondered how she could have mistaken this man as being dangerous. The left side of his face was stiff, like he'd had a stroke. His scar and his fearful demeanor told her he'd had a hard past.

She softened her voice. "I saw you peeking into my window in the cottage. Did you come to tell me something?"

He stared at her for a moment before giving her an imperceptible nod.

"Gently now," said the nurse, tapping his leg. "Lay back and don't say another word."

The man turned around and grabbed Tanya's arm.

"P... p....po...lice?"

Tanya nodded.

"Es... Es..."

"Hey," said the nurse, her voice a notch sterner. "I need you to relax. Calm down."

Tanya leaned toward him and whispered.

"What is it?"

"Es... Esmeralda," he whispered before letting her arm go.

Chapter Thirty-four

Tanya pulled back in surprise.

Did he say Esmeralda?

The creepy voice of Mike Pendleton at the psychiatric hospital swam into her mind. Tanya furrowed her brow to recall what he'd said before the day manager propelled him away.

I killed Esmeralda.

That's what he had told her.

Is Esmeralda Lopez's daughter?

She leaned over to the scarred man to ask him when a large hand clamped down on her shoulder.

She spun around.

Two nurses in scrubs had appeared at the scene, carrying a stretcher. On the trail behind them was a beige golf cart. The director must have called for them. Tanya hadn't heard them arrive, too engrossed in getting the ax man to talk.

The male nurse pushed her aside. "Move out of the way."

Tanya stared into his glazed eyes.

Is he drugged too?

"Didn't you hear? Move. Let us do our job."

Tanya craned her neck to see his female companion, a much older and more grizzled version of Nurse Ana, glaring at her.

"I'd like a minute with him once you've patched him up," she said.

Nurse Ana gave her a sympathetic look. "I'm sorry, but you have to check with Carolyn for that."

As Tanya watched, the older female nurse took a large syringe from her pocket and pushed the needle into the scarred man's forearm.

Tanya frowned. "What are you giving him?"

"It'll help him calm down," said the older nurse.

"You're sedating him for a strained ankle?"

She put an arm out to block Tanya.

"If you got no medical training, you got nothing to say." Her voice was gravelly and her eyes were bloodshot like she had spent all night drinking. "Besides, Carolyn said you pushed him in."

"I did *not* push him—"

Tanya stopped as the trio of nurses closed in on the scarred man, elbowing her out of the way. Nurse Ana turned her head and mouthed *sorry*.

Tanya jumped to her feet and stepped away from them, her mind spinning.

Esmeralda.

That hadn't been the runaway imagination of an old man riddled with dementia. Pendleton may not have killed the girl himself, but he knew who did the deed. Perhaps the ax man did too.

Tanya stopped and stared at the closed coffin in the grave, now soiled by loose dirt and footmarks. She had come up the hill to get information for Susan Cross, but that was before she had got waylaid by the ax man.

Who is inside the coffin?

How did they die?

She needed answers, but was short on time. Carolyn, the director, was still occupied on her phone, but she would be done soon and Tanya could think of no excuse to remain on their private property.

Calling Max to follow her, she walked over to the funeral guests huddled by an old tombstone. They had gathered in a circle and were speaking in hushed tones.

They stopped and stared as she approached them.

Tanya could feel the hostility in the air.

Chapter Thirty-five

Tanya offered a subdued wave to the small group, but none of them reciprocated.

She took stock.

They must have all been septuagenarians or older. One was using a walker, and another was leaning on a cane, which explained their slow stroll through the woods earlier.

"So sorry for your loss," said Tanya, trying on an awkward smile to soften her face.

A few shook their heads, while others glared at her with annoyed expressions on their faces.

"I truly apologize. I didn't intend to disrupt your funeral."

One man scoffed. Another tsked loudly.

But two women with long and wavy white hair stood out from the crowd. They were smiling at her, like they were amused.

These two weren't dressed for a funeral. They wore colorful bohemian clothes with sleeves that flapped in the breeze. One had stuck a strange flower over her ear. A rose so dark, it was almost black.

Tanya cleared her throat, wondering how to get them to open up, when Max trotted by her.

With his tail wagging, he stopped to sniff the man with the cane and licked his hands. Then, he turned to the flamboyantly dressed women, his tail swishing against their flowing clothes.

A rush of anxiety rolled through Tanya, unsure how they would react to a massive German Shepherd getting this close.

"Max, come back."

"Oooh." One of the women stooped down and petted Max's head. "Aren't you a handsome pupper?"

Max pushed his snout toward her and licked her hand.

"You look exactly like my Ranger," said the second woman, smiling. She bent down and scratched Max's chin. "I had him when I was a little girl. He was the bravest and smartest doggy I knew."

The man with the cane nodded. "This one looks pretty smart to me. Did you see how he leaped in the air? Like a cheetah from the Serengeti."

"He only chases bad guys," said Tanya, but no one was paying attention to her any more.

Max stood calmly in the center of the circle, while the group ruffled his ears and stroked his back. Tanya watched from the outside, thankful her K9 partner made up for the social skills she seemed to direly lack.

The residence director was still pacing the cemetery grounds, gesticulating while she yelled at someone on the line.

Tanya cleared her throat and leaned toward the two women with long white hair.

"Was the deceased someone you knew well?"

One shook her head.

"Never met her. She was one of Carolyn's charity cases."

"Charity cases?"

The other woman nodded sadly.

"It's heartbreaking when they have no family, so Carolyn always invites a few of us."

"It's the right thing to do," said her friend. "They say you're born alone and you die alone, but a few strangers at a funeral is better than no one."

"That's good of you," said Tanya. She pointed casually in the direction of the grave. "Was the deceased at Silver Serenity for long?"

"She wasn't one of us."

"Oh?"

"She was one of those they take to the third wing."

"The third wing?" Tanya raised a brow. "What happens in this wing?"

Chapter Thirty-six

"Didn't I tell you to leave?"

Tanya closed her eyes and exhaled as the director's sharp voice came from behind her.

"Take that mangy dog and get out of here now."

Carolyn's flushed face appeared in front of her.

"I called your office," she snarled.

Oh? And what did Katy say?

"Seems like your chief's out of town. But you can bet your pension, he's going to hear about you when he comes back. I know Chief Jack Bold personally."

Tanya remained calm, trying to think of how she could convince the director to let her inside the residence. That prospect looked bleak, if not impossible, now.

The director stepped closer and wagged her finger inches from Tanya's nose.

"Jack should fire you! Running around like this is some ghetto neighborhood. I'm livid. *Livid*, I tell you."

Tanya put her hands up and stepped away from her.

"I'm leaving," she said, keeping her voice on an even keel. "But you need to know I'm obligated to ask questions and pursue any suspects. I'm investigating the death of that young girl on the hill."

The crowd shook their heads and murmured in sympathy.

"Ah, that poor girl," said the man with the walker.

"What a terrible thing to happen," said one of the women.

The director spun around and glowered so hard at them, Tanya could almost see steam rising from her ears.

"Juvenile criminals," huffed Carolyn, her face scrunching in disgust. "These vagabonds come to the West Coast, dirty our streets, get hooked on drugs, and prostitute themselves. I have no tolerance for homeless vagrants."

She turned and glared at Tanya as if she was one of the homeless vagabonds.

Tanya motioned for Max to come with her. He stepped away from his newfound friends and trotted over. With him at her heels, Tanya slipped back into the woods.

Susan Cross's steely voice had become louder in her head. She had less than three days to investigate who they were burying and how the deceased had died.

Cross was rumored to have fired more agents than any other director at the bureau. That wasn't an easy record to hold, given that letting go of government employees was a long and bureaucratic process, mired in migraine-inducing red tape.

But that never seemed to stop Cross and her hard-nosed management style.

Tanya's heart chilled. She needed this job. She couldn't afford to lose it now.

There has to be another way inside the residence.

The sound of a small engine starting made her turn around. She glimpsed the golf cart through the tree branches.

The nurses had moved the scarred man onto the stretcher and strapped him in. He was lying horizontally across Nurse Ana and the male nurse in the backseat.

The older female nurse put the cart in gear and pulled away. Tanya watched her inch slowly away from the grave, while her colleagues in the back held precariously onto the stretcher.

The scarred man remained so still, Tanya wondered if he was still alive. A ball of bile tightened in her stomach. If she hadn't treated him like a fugitive, he would not be hurt or medicated.

Why sedate him?

If Dr. Chen had been here, she would have bandaged his foot, given him a painkiller, and discharged him without a second thought.

Tanya waited for the cart to hop onto the trail at the edge of the forest. She stepped parallel to the path and followed in the direction the cart was traveling.

There was more to Silver Serenity than met the eyes.

It was time to find out what was really going on here.

Chapter Thirty-seven

Tanya remained hidden behind the trees, glad the cart couldn't travel fast with the stretcher on the back.

She kept one eye on the vehicle and another in front of her to make sure she didn't trip and give herself away. Max trotted alongside her quietly, like he knew they were on a stealth mission.

The nurses drove along the forest trail and into the grand grounds of the Silver Serenity residence. They headed toward the back of the sprawling white mansion.

The stately structure was only one story high, but consisted of three palatial wings that connected to a central hub in the middle. Large bay windows looked out to the grounds and a small spire rose from the center. On the other end of the structure was a perfectly manicured golf course, its small golf flags fluttering in the breeze.

Tanya scanned the building.

Which one of these three is the "third wing?"

She watched quietly from behind the trees as the nurses parked their cart and carried the scarred man inside.

The back door slammed shut.

How do I get in without being seen?

The large windows meant she couldn't approach the residence without anyone noticing.

She stepped toward the front of the building and peeked through the trees. She gazed at the green lawn, the blue gazebo, and the fountain on the grounds. Three women were lounging inside the gazebo, reading books, but no one else was in sight.

Other than the birds singing in the forest, it was quiet and pleasant. Just what you would expect a place called Silver Serenity to be like.

There were no signs of ground workers or security personnel in the vicinity, and no cameras dotted the alcoves, rooftop, or facade, either.

Strange, thought Tanya. Then again, these people paid big bucks for privacy.

Time to move.

She squatted on the ground and whispered to Max to follow her lead. The trick was to stay away from the view of anyone looking out the windows.

Tanya hunkered down and shuffled toward the back door with Max by her side, his body low to the ground, his feet moving fast to keep up with her.

They slid up to the back door.

So far, so good.

The aroma of cooked herbs, onion, and garlic wafted to her nose. The sound of something sizzling came from inside.

Tanya raised her head and peeked through the nearest window. The back door opened to an industrial-sized kitchen. Bustling inside were a man in a white chef's hat and a small team of sous chefs in aprons.

The staff were engrossed in their activities, but there was no way of entering through this door without being noticed.

Tanya's mind buzzed.

Do I tell them I'm lost? Maybe that I'm hurt, and I need help?

She shook her head.

Nope, the nurses will recognize me and call Carolyn.

She was about to search for a more isolated entry point, when a low whistle came from somewhere behind her.

The hair on the back of her neck stood up. Max's ears pricked up.

The whistle came again, as brief as before, but shriller. Max let out a muffled warning bark that said *I heard you.*

"Shh...bud."

She swiveled her head when she noticed the white curtain fluttering from a patio halfway down the back wall. The curtain shimmered and waved like a flag.

The low whistle came again.

Tanya's heart raced a tad faster.

Someone had spotted her.

Chapter Thirty-eight

The curtains billowed like a sail in the wind.

Max trotted forward.

"Stay, bud," said Tanya.

He stopped, but his ears flipped back and forth.

The patio was located halfway down the wall of this annex and faced the backyard of the residence. If she and Max could sneak under the kitchen windows, they could remain concealed until they reached the curtain.

Tanya pulled her Glock out, crouched low, and patted Max lightly on the back once.

"Down, bud."

He hunkered his belly on the floor, his snout pointed at the patio doors.

"Let's go," whispered Tanya as she combat crawled toward their target, keeping close to the wall and her head below the kitchen windows. Max followed her movements, his eyes on the curtains.

When she got to two feet of their destination, Tanya stopped and listened. The curtains had stopped flapping, but the strange whistle came again.

A thump on her thighs made her turn. She looked down at Max. He had relaxed his muscles and was wagging his tail, swatting her legs as he did. He looked up at her and cocked his head, as if to say, *Aren't we going in, Mom?*

Tanya's eyes widened.

He knows the whistler.

She got to her feet and flattened herself against the wall, making sure no one could see her from the inside. She pursed her lips and whistled the same trill tone.

Whoever was behind those patio doors whistled back immediately.

Goosebumps sprang up on her arms.

"Stay, Max," she whispered.

She stepped closer to the open doors. It was dark inside, and the curtains made it hard to see.

With her heart pounding, she swung through the curtains, her Glock aimed forward.

"Hands up!"

"You wouldn't shoot an old man now, would you, Agent?" said a deep male voice from the back of the room.

Chapter thirty-nine

Tanya gawked at the plush bedroom.

Her eyes went from the luxury Persian rug to the king-sized poster bed, and to the dark mahogany bookshelves that lined the wall in the back.

But it was the tall man in the shadows that grabbed her attention.

He was dressed in silk pajamas and a matching men's bathrobe. His salt and pepper hair was brushed neatly, and his beard trimmed and groomed as always. The smell of Old Spice cologne hung in the air.

Ray Jackson.

Susan Cross's inside man.

Tanya had always thought Ray Jackson was Morgan Freeman's perfect doppelgänger. And now, in these affluent surroundings, he looked even more like the famous actor.

"What are you doing here, Ray?"

"I'm a resident of Silver Serenity."

Tanya glared at him. "And I live in Buckingham Palace."

"I'm a retired man. This is as good a place as any to spend my golden years."

Tanya scoffed. "You're what? Sixty? Sixty-one? Some of the residents here could be your parents."

Ray shook his head sadly. "I'm getting senile, I'm afraid. I wish I could still run around and catch bad guys like you."

"You don't fool me," said Tanya, holstering her weapon. "You're on a self-directed undercover mission, and Cross sent me to check up on you."

"I have no idea what you're talking about."

"You're trying to prove you've still got game, Ray."

"I don't need to prove myself to anybody." Ray glowered. "If you're going to stand here insulting me, I suggest you leave."

Tanya sighed, feeling like she was having a conversation with the cocky Cheshire Cat of *Alice in Wonderland*.

She turned toward the open French windows and clicked her tongue. Max skipped across the threshold and dashed toward Ray, his tail a blur of brown fur.

"Max!" With a sudden smile, Ray dropped to his knees to nuzzle the dog.

"How come you never visit me any more? Is your mom working you too hard? She's a meanie, isn't she? I should rescue you one of these days."

"Over my dead body." Tanya glared. "Do you want to tell me what the heck's going on?"

"I thought I told you to go away."

"I've been trying to get a hold of you, Ray. Why didn't you pick up?"

"The front desk has my phone. We're only allowed them for emergencies."

Tanya raised her brows. "You must be joking."

"It's a wonderful policy. That way, meddling people can't reach me." Ray shot her a side glance. "Besides, screens are bad for you. Why do you think there's a spike in depression among young people? Your generation will go insane and blind before you reach my age."

Tanya frowned.

Maybe Susan Cross's suspicions had some merit after all. Taking away the residents' only private communication channel was a good way to isolate them.

"I like it here," said Ray. "I even have two girlfriends."

"Two?" Tanya shook her head. "Senile, my foot."

"Selectively senile," said Ray with a glint in his eyes. "When I want to be."

"What I'd like to know is how does a retired agent even afford to—" Tanya stopped. "Did the bureau pay the one hundred grand to snag you a spot here?"

Ray Jackson got to his feet. A smirk came on his face.

"Close but no cigar, Agent Stone."

Chapter Forty

"I admit to twisting an arm or two at the bureau."

Ray pursed his lips.

"Everyone was convinced this case was dead on arrival. The director, on the other hand, wired me the money."

Tanya crossed her arms, unsure how much to believe him.

"How did you get admitted at your age?"

"My application was convincing. I said I was a lifelong smoker and heavy drinker on a fast-food only diet. Divorced three times, and the lucky recipient of a triple bypass." He grabbed his chest and groaned. "Worked like a charm."

"Didn't they review your medical records?" said Tanya. "Or did you falsify them as well?"

"A health checkup for this place?" Ray chuckled. "They only care for the money. But I'm not complaining. I've had worse undercover digs before."

He pointed his chin at an entertainment unit that encased the largest television set Tanya had seen.

"Fifty-inch Sony. All the channels. Not bad, eh?"

"*Susan Cross* paid for this?" said Tanya.

"It was a private loan, and this is a personal quest." He shot another irritated glance her way. "That's why you don't need to be here."

"I'm not going anywhere."

With a heavy sigh, Ray shuffled toward the liquor cabinet.

He poured a ruby-colored liquid from a decanter into a tumbler, and soon the luxurious smell of oak distilled rum filled the room. He turned and offered the half-filled glass to Tanya.

She put her hands up. "I'm on the job."

"Suit yourself."

He opened a beer fridge and plucked out a can of Coke. He filled his glass up with the fizzing liquid, before opening a cabinet and plucking out a bag of potato chips.

"Jalapeno chips with rum and Coke?"

"I usually stick to chips and Coke on weekdays, but seeing you makes me want something stronger."

Tanya stared at the plastic bags of processed snacks rammed into the top shelves of the cabinet.

"That's not very healthy."

"Don't judge. Everyone has their favorite poison."

Tanya stepped up to the liquor table.

"Do you have any water here? We were running through the backwoods and I was sweating like a pig by the end."

She picked up a jug that had a looping double "S" logo engraved on it.

"Silver Serenity? Fancy," she said, sniffing the clear liquid in it.

"That's supposed to be healthy water, whatever that means," said Ray, pointing to the jug. "Personally, I don't drink that stuff."

Tanya plucked an empty ice bucket, filled it up, and placed it on the floor. Max trotted over, sniffed it, and turned away, his nose in the air.

"I thought you'd be dying of thirst, bud," said Tanya, pouring herself a glass. She downed a few gulps before setting the glass back on the table with a grimace.

"Tastes funny."

"They put all sorts of minerals and vitamins in it," said Ray. "I don't touch that stuff."

Tanya barely heard him because she noticed the rectangular card tucked under the liquor tray. She pried it out, her heart ticking a beat faster.

"What's this? This week's menu?"

Ray gave her a side glance. "Are you hungry now? They do room service."

"Look at what they served two nights ago," said Tanya, tapping the menu item just beneath the looping double "S" logo of Silver Serenity.

"Rare Châteaubriand with truffle butter mushroom sauce, accompanied by a warm goat cheese salad encrusted with roasted walnuts and cashews."

"I didn't know you were a gourmand," said Ray. "I always took you to be a vodka and potatoes kind of gal."

Tanya turned to him.

"We found a homicide victim buried on the hill."

He nodded somberly. "Heard the news. The culprit's probably a lunatic from the asylum."

"The dead girl's stomach contents consisted of rare steak with walnuts and cashew nuts," said Tanya, staring at him. "A coincidence? I think not."

Chapter Forty-one

"Wasn't me," said Ray, with a shrug. "I never fed the girl. I never even saw her."

Tanya dropped the menu on the table.

"Someone did. There's a high probability that girl had a meal here the night she died."

"The probability is zero."

"Why?"

"Kids aren't allowed at Silver Serenity. Residents need to make special requests when families with children visit, and that only happens once in a blue moon."

Tanya narrowed her eyes. "My gut says her death is connected to this residence."

"You're hallucinating."

She stared at him. "Are you protecting someone in here?"

"Are you kidding me?" His voice rose in pitch.

He stepped over to an armchair and settled down with a groan. Max, who had been sniffing all the corners of the bedroom and the ensuite bathroom, trotted over and settled down by his feet.

Traitor.

Tanya walked over to the chair across from Ray and sat down. "Why did Cross send me here?"

He shot her a dark look. "I wish she hadn't."

"I don't have time for games," said Tanya. "I'm investigating the death of a young girl."

"Go do your detective work at the hospital next door, then."

Tanya let out an exasperated sigh.

"Tell me about the deaths at the residence."

"I know much less than you think."

"What's the director like?"

"Brash, narcissistic, bad-tempered, an addict, a gambler....everything but a human trafficker." Ray's eyes gleamed. "The rumors are vicious."

"Do you know she carries concealed?"

"Spotted the gun the second I walked in."

"Why would anyone carry a weapon in a residence for the elderly?" said Tanya. "This isn't a high-security prison."

"I'm sure she has a good reason."

"Is she behind the deaths?"

Ray shot her a stern look. "Haven't you learned anything by now?"

"Carolyn rules the roost, carries a gun, and was burying a dead body when I met her. Plus, she wasn't too happy to see a cop on her property." Tanya held his glare. "She's at the top of my list until I find evidence that shows otherwise."

"It's not her."

"How can you be so certain?"

"The most likely suspect at first glance is the least likely," said Ray. "We need to look deeper."

"You're the one who taught me the principle of Occam's razor," said Tanya. "The explanation that requires the fewest assumptions is the correct one."

Ray leaned back in his armchair with a sigh.

"In theory perhaps, but in real life, that's not always accurate."

Tanya threw her hands in the air.

"How did you find out about the deaths at Silver Serenity?"

"An anonymous tip. Got a letter two months ago."

"What did it say?"

"Someone is bringing women in here and killing them off, one by one."

Chapter Forty-two

Tanya frowned.

"How did the letter writer know your address in Black Rock?"

"It was sent to HQ in Seattle," said Ray.

"Where's the letter now?"

"Probably sealed in a box in an evidence room at HQ."

"Who sent it?"

"There was no signature."

"Didn't forensics check the handwriting, the paper, the ink?"

Ray raised his eyes. "Forensics' resources are limited and their projects are prioritized. This case is at the bottom of the pile."

"Why? Do they think the letter is a hoax?"

"They aren't even thinking about the letter. They have much bigger fish to catch. But since Silver Serenity is just around the corner from me, I told Cross I would make a few inquiries."

"Meaning you get yourself admitted into a senior home?"

Ray didn't answer, and instead took a sip of his rum and Coke. Tanya watched him as he sat silently, eyes downcast.

He isn't sharing everything.

"Cross told me an actress died here two nights ago," she said. "How did you find that out?"

Ray shrugged. "I have a tendency to wander around and forget where I am. It's a terrible affliction."

"And convenient."

"I was passing the main office after supper one evening and overheard a phone call."

"I told you the director is involved."

Ray gave her a dismissive wave.

"Carolyn was telling whoever was on the other line that she lost Isabella Rose. She was worried the tabloids would get wind of it. A nurse caught me in the corridor and shooed me off, so I missed the rest, but I remembered the name."

Tanya nodded, surprised he was sharing all this with her, especially since he didn't want her here.

"Not to speak ill of the dead," Ray was saying, "but I tried watching Isabella Rose's movies. They're unbearable. I didn't even know she was staying here."

"Do you think she was coerced into coming here?"

Ray cradled the glass in his hands. "Your guess is as good as mine."

"How did those women die?"

"Their death certificates point to various terminal illnesses, but they were all moderately healthy when admitted."

"None of them were typical retirement residents?"

"We're talking women in their forties and fifties."

"Have you seen them?"

Ray stared gloomily into his glass. "If I had, I wouldn't be sitting here, chatting with you."

"You seem to know an awful lot about the victims."

Ray sighed.

"Because it's all in the death ledger."

Tanya's eyebrows shot up.

"Death ledger?"

Chapter Forty-three

Tanya leaned toward Ray.

"What's in the death ledger?"

"A list of names."

"Where did you find it?"

"In the director's office during one of my impulsive forays. I scanned it quickly, I don't recall them all, except for Isabella Rose."

"Was there anything in the ledger that pointed to foul play?"

"Didn't get that far."

"What about the women's families?" said Tanya. "Hasn't anyone inquired about their deaths?"

Ray's eyes flickered.

"The emergency contact column in the ledger was empty," he said. "So, I presume none of them had any family or connections to speak of."

Tanya watched him closely. "Who signed the death certificates?"

He looked up, the lines around his eyes more visible.

"I'm on your side, Ray," said Tanya, a ball of frustration bubbling in her belly. "I came here to figure this out with you. If you want, you can take all the glory when we're done."

Ray sighed and waved dismissively at her.

"There's a doctor who flies down from Seattle. Used to come once a month, or so the others tell me, but he's here weekly now. He doesn't give a hoot about the residents, I can tell you that. He spent five minutes checking me and took off like he had more important people to meet."

Ray shrugged. "Good thing too, because I have perfect blood pressure for my age."

"Does he spend most of his time in the third wing, where they keep the women?"

"No one knows, but everyone complains of his rushed bedside manner. Once he's done here, he collects a big paycheck from Carolyn and flies off in his helicopter."

"Helicopter?"

"You could afford one too if you're at the beck and call of celebrities, politicians, and wealthy retirees."

"Seven women were admitted over the past year," said Tanya, looking thoughtfully at the ceiling, trying to recall the little information Susan Cross had shared with her. "Three have died. One woman is being buried today. That leaves three alive."

She turned to Ray. "Where is this third wing?"

Ray rubbed his eyes, like he was getting tired.

"No idea. I had two minutes to scan a few pages before Carolyn poked her gun in my face. She said she'd shoot me next time she caught me in places where I shouldn't be in."

Tanya's eyebrows shot up.

"After all that, you still don't suspect her?"

"I found the book in the lost and found basket by the door," said Ray, "which means it wasn't hers. If she was trying to hide it, she wouldn't have left it there."

"She held a gun to your head because you were rooting around her lost and found basket?"

"She accused me of stealing the drugs she keeps in her office. I didn't argue. I told her I was confused and shuffled out of her office like a drug-addled old man would."

"You didn't accost her?"

"And have her kick me out?" Ray glared at her. "You've got it wrong, Stone. Her impulsive and explosive personality doesn't jibe with a methodical serial murderer."

"She's burying the fourth body today," said Tanya. "Why aren't you at the funeral?"

"I was hoping to snoop around while she's occupied."

Tanya shook her head. "It's all fun and games until they target you too, Ray."

Chapter Forty-four

Tanya scurried along the main corridor toward the director's office.

She was thankful there were no security cameras inside or outside Silver Serenity. *Privacy is paramount*, Cross had explained. It was one of the biggest attractions for the well-to-do who came here seeking peace and quiet.

Tanya passed the biggest grandfather clock she'd seen when she spotted the open doorway farther along the hallway. She crept toward the room and peeked inside.

Nurse Ana was standing next to a trolley filled with syringes, thermometers, and blood pressure monitors, her back to the door. The quick movements of her hands told Tanya she was on her phone.

She wondered what had happened to the man with the scar. *Please be okay,* she thought as she stepped away.

Tanya hurried along. She had been fortunate not to bump into anyone so far, but she couldn't rely on luck. The funeral would be over and Carolyn would be back soon. She didn't have time.

It was a relief to see the double wooden doors with the bronze-embossed plate that read *Manager, Silver Serenity Residence.*

Tanya stepped up to the office. The door was ajar. She spotted movement through the narrow opening.

Carolyn's back already?

She swiveled her head, but the corridor remained quiet. From the far corner, she caught sight of a satin bathrobe disappearing from view.

Ray.

He was following her.

If he had been incensed to see her at the residence, he was now outraged she had decided to seek the death ledger on her own. Tanya wasn't sure she could rely on him.

She wished Max was with her, but she'd locked him up in Ray's room with a bowl of water and the curtains drawn, so no one would know they were inside the building.

Tanya took another step closer to the manager's office. The sound of something falling on the floor came from inside.

She sighed, realizing it was too late to get the ledger now. She was about to step away when a loud bang came from inside, followed by a curse.

Her eyebrows shot up.

It was a male voice.

She peeked in through the narrow opening. A man in a light blue top was fumbling with an object on the floor.

Blue scrubs.

A nurse.

The nurse picked up what looked like a heavy plaque and placed it on the desk. Then, he wandered around the office, coming into view for a few seconds before disappearing, like he was searching for something.

It was the male nurse who had arrived at the cemetery with his colleague to pick up the scarred man.

Is he after the ledger too?

While she watched through the opening, the nurse checked the drawers, the bookshelf, and behind the furniture. He kept rattling the cabinet on the wall by Carolyn's desk that was labeled *Restricted*.

Sweat poured down his face. Whatever he was seeking, he was desperate about it.

With a frustrated hiss, he searched the desk again, opening all the drawers until he got to the bottom-most one. With a stifled cry, he pounced on something and held it up to the light. Relief crossed his face.

Tanya peered in to get a better look.

A key.

The nurse snapped around and stepped up to the cabinet. With trembling hands, he pushed the key into the lock and yanked the doors open.

Tanya stared at the rows of medication bottles on the glass shelves.

He's not after the ledger.

The nurse seemed to know exactly where to find what he had been looking for.

He plucked a brown bottle from the shelf, unscrewed it, and spilled a handful of pills onto his open palm. After picking one and putting it under his tongue, he slipped the remaining tablets into his pocket.

Drug addict, thought Tanya, remembering his glazed eyes at the cemetery. *He's done this before.*

The nurse spun around like he knew someone was watching him.

Tanya pulled back.

She heard him close the cabinet doors and lock them. The sound of drawers opening and shutting came soon after, like he was straightening the room to hide evidence of his presence.

Tanya stayed behind the door, ready for him to emerge, her heart thudding.

The nurse pushed the door open and hurried out, tripping over the rug.

"Hello there," said Tanya.

He jumped a foot high.

"Who... who...what are you doing here?"

Tanya scanned the name tag on his lapel.

"Matt Benson? I'm investigating a complaint about drug theft."

Chapter Forty-five

The color drained from the nurse's face.

He blinked rapidly, but Tanya kept her gaze steady. "What were you doing in the director's office?"

"I, er, was looking for my...er, leave application. I n... needed to change d... dates...." He stepped away, stammering. "Gotta go. Nurse Ana needs me."

He spun around and scrambled down the corridor, like he couldn't get away from her fast enough.

After a check in all directions to make sure no one had noticed her presence, Tanya slipped inside the office and locked the door.

If anything, Carolyn was neat. Given her explosive personality, Tanya had expected her office to be a mess.

She pulled out a pair of gloves from her utility belt and put them on before kneeling next to the lost-and-found basket. She rummaged through the hats, mugs, socks, slippers, umbrellas, and other miscellaneous items. It didn't take her long to learn there were no books in it.

She flipped through the files on the desk. They were new applications for the residence. She placed the files back in place and scanned the room.

Where's the death ledger?

She worked quickly, trying the drawers, the bookshelf, and even the medicine cabinet now she knew where the key was hidden. She searched under the desk, behind the furniture, and yanked the rug back to see if Carolyn had shoved it underneath the carpet.

Nothing.

Where would I hide a small journal if I didn't want anyone to find it?

She surveyed the room.

Did Nurse Matt Benson steal it during one of his drug raids?

She shook her head. Addicts are rarely that focused or determined to do anything other than get their next hit.

A ping came from the computer. Tanya circled the desk and stared at the screensaver of Silver Serenity's looping double "S" logo. Using a gloved finger, she tapped the keyboard. A blank box popped up.

Password-protected.

She let out a frustrated hiss, when she spotted a bright yellow paper sticking out from under the keyboard. She pushed it aside.

A sticky note.

Scribbled on it was a muddle of numbers and letters that made no sense whatsoever.

Bingo.

Tanya typed the characters into the password bar and hit enter. The desktop flickered into view.

That was easy.

Every year, local FBI task forces tried to educate citizens on computer security, but it was always a spectacular failure. Tech companies charged a fortune to install firewalls, set up private networks, and conduct penetration tests. What they didn't tell you was, while the threat of online hacking was serious, the weakest link was usually the people authorized to be on the systems themselves.

Like Carolyn was now.

Tanya clicked through a series of folders on her desktop, but they contained generic administrative details on ground maintenance, bill payments, and staff salary. After a few minutes of poking around, she sat back in exasperation.

She glanced at the clock on her phone. Carolyn would be here any minute. What she needed was Asha, her private investigator friend from New York, who had the necessary gadgets and skills to download information in bulk to be checked later on.

Another ping made Tanya sit up.

A yellow envelope icon flashed on the screen.

New email.

She clicked on the email program and scrolled through the unread messages, taking care not to touch them. There were an unusual number of replies from online poker gaming sites.

Carolyn's a gambler.

Tanya's fingers itched to open them, but she knew anyone with a modicum of knowledge in cyber security could easily find out she had been snooping.

She scrolled down to the emails that had already been read from a few days ago.

A handful of messages sent over the past week had no subject line. The sender's email address was from a generic service provider that millions of people around the world used.

Tanya pulled the mouse down and clicked on the latest read message from that sender. Her eyes widened as she scanned the unsigned note.

We know where you came from and we know what you're up to.

Tanya took a photo of the email and moved to the next note from the same sender.

Your life will be over if the owner finds out. You'll be ruined.

The third opened email from the sender was even more ominous.

Pay up now or you're a dead woman.

Tanya glanced at her phone again. She had spent more time than she had planned in the office. She closed the email app and stepped away from the desk, her mind whirling.

Carolyn Pennett-Staresinic was being blackmailed. Perhaps she had a good reason for carrying that sidearm.

Who was blackmailing the director?

And why?

Chapter Forty-six

The sound of metal scraping against wood came from the door. Someone was inserting a key into the lock.

Carolyn.

Tanya sprang toward the medicine cabinet.

Carolyn stormed inside the office and halted abruptly. She glared at Tanya, a crimson flush rising up her neck.

"What the heck are you doing in my office?"

"Oh, hello," said Tanya, keeping her voice casual. "Glad you came so quickly."

"I told you to get out, didn't I?" bellowed Carolyn. "How did you get in here?"

Tanya tapped the medicine cabinet.

"You have a serious theft problem. Expensive drugs. I thought I'd take a look."

"I reported the missing medicine months ago!" screeched Carolyn, making Tanya's ears ring.

It worked.

"I'm afraid we've had a slew of murder investigations on our hands," said Tanya. "We're short-staffed—"

"That's your problem! First, you ignore my reports, then you have the temerity to stroll through my estate and into my office without permission. How dare you?"

Carolyn stomped over to her desk, picked up the wooden plaque, and threw it in Tanya's direction. Tanya ducked just in time. The heavy object hit the wall and crashed to the floor.

"Get out!"

Carolyn let out an angry wail.

"I will file a complaint. You useless, stupid, incompetent cops.... Get out!"

The doors banged open and Ray Jackson came rushing in, clutching his chest.

"Help me," he warbled. "Please... help me."

Ray was hyperventilating and holding on to the door frame like he was about to fall any moment. Carolyn gaped at him like she had never seen him like this before.

"Help me," he cried, his eyes closed tightly like he couldn't bear the pain. "It hurts...."

Ray staggered toward Carolyn, one arm reaching out, but the director scooted away in fright.

With one swift gesture, Ray swept the stack of files off the desk, scattering them on the floor. Just as Carolyn fell to her knees to scoop up her papers, Ray winked at Tanya, buckled his knees, and crashed to the floor.

Tanya stared.

Did he just wink at me?

Nurse Ana ran in.

"What's going on?"

"Heart attack, I think," said Tanya, pointing at Ray, who was now writhing on the floor. "Do something."

"It hurts so bad," gargled Ray.

Nurse Ana jumped into action while Carolyn watched, speechless for a change.

Tanya stepped out of the office, her heart thumping hard. She was thankful Ray had backed her up, and hoped he wouldn't overact.

She knew Nurse Ana and Carolyn could try to sedate him, but he was a trained agent who had got out of messier situations before.

She hurried along the corridor toward Ray Jackson's room, before the director could call for reinforcement. She opened the door and slipped inside, sighing in relief to see Max again.

He was sitting by the closed French doors, his ears up, his back stiff, and his eyes on something in the backyard. He didn't even turn to look at her, but wagged his tail to acknowledge her arrival.

"Hey, bud, whatcha looking at?"

He thumped his tail but stayed in his spot. Tanya stepped up to him.

"What is it, Max?"

She moved the curtains aside and peeked out as the eerie whistle came to her ears. It was the same tune Ray had made when he'd wanted to get her attention.

Max barked.

"Hush, bud," whispered Tanya.

She surveyed the yard and scanned the beginning of the trail that wound through the wilderness toward the cemetery in the woods. There was not a soul in sight.

The low whistle came again.

A chill went down her spine.

Is someone trying to get Ray Jackson's attention?

Tanya glanced back at the closed door. She could no longer hear Ray's fake yells for help.

It's time to get out of here.

Feeling bad for leaving Ray behind, Tanya unlocked the French doors.

The kitchen windows at the far end were now ajar. The faint sound of pots and pans banging, and the chef's hollering instructions came to her ear.

She glanced down at Max again. He was ignoring the kitchen noises and staring into the woods.

The eerie whistle came again, more urgently this time.

Holding her Glock, Tanya stepped out through the patio doors.

Chapter Forty-seven

Tanya and Max dashed toward the forest.

They stopped at the tree line, and Tanya scanned her surroundings. Max stood by her, squinting into the darkness. For one bizarre moment, it seemed like the entire wilderness was holding its collective breath, waiting to see what would happen next.

Tanya surveyed the forest floor for footprints, trampled grass, broken branches, but there were no clues to the whistler. Or signs of any life, for that matter.

She trod deeper into the woods, gripping her gun, swiveling her head, her eyes and ears on alert, but whoever had whistled seemed to have vanished into thin air.

She was about to investigate a clump of birch trees, when her mobile buzzed. She pulled her phone out and glanced at the screen.

Katy.

Tanya frowned, hoping Lopez's condition hadn't worsened. She didn't believe her colleague was guilty of anything other than being severely distraught by her daughter's death.

Maybe she's finally talking.

She clicked on the call, her hopes rising.

Katy started speaking before she could even say hello.

"He's a serial killer."

Tanya jerked her head back.

"Who is?"

"That man you told me to look up. He killed three of his wives. Alleged to have killed. The allegations were never proven, but the newspapers dubbed him a modern-day King Henry."

Tanya's brain spun into high gear. So much had happened in such a short period, it seemed like anyone could be the guilty party now.

"Who is this serial killer?"

"Mike Pendleton," came Katy's annoyed voice. "He has a long rap sheet."

"For what?"

"Domestic violence. He was also arrested for murdering his third wife. That initiated questions about his second and first wives' deaths, but the charges were dropped due to insufficient evidence."

Tanya frowned. "He was a bigamist?"

"Nope, but I think he was a murderer. All his wives died in accidental circumstances at home while Pendleton was present."

"When did this happen?"

"Decades ago. He was in his early thirties."

More mouse clicking came on the other end.

"Seems like the police didn't take the women's calls for help seriously," continued Katy, "and when they eventually died, they botched the investigations. They failed to secure the evidence, lost important files, and the cases fell apart."

Tanya shook her head. "Not good."

"Typical for that era," hissed Katy. "If the victims had been men, they would have done a proper job."

Mike Pendleton's cobweb tattoo sprang to Tanya's mind.

"He was incarcerated, wasn't he?"

"Ten years, but he got out with a pardon," said Katy. "That's a small price to pay for taking the lives of three women, in my opinion."

Tanya's mind whirred as she tried to make connections between the past and the present, and between the psychiatric hospital and the retirement residence.

Katy sighed. "Does any of this help you at all?"

"It tells me Mike Pendleton has a criminal mind," said Tanya, speaking slowly. "He may no longer have the capacity to commit a serious felony, but he's sharp, despite what the day manager said. The question is, who does he have influence over?"

Tanya grimaced.

"At first glance, everyone I've met on the hill could be a suspect. The residence's director, the nurses, the manager at the hospital. They're all hiding something."

Even Ray Jackson.

"But I'm skating on thin ice. I have no motive and no evidence if the women's deaths are even true homicides. All we know is a girl was killed and buried on the hill."

"I found three Esmeralda Lopezes." Katy's voice was glum. "A thirty-something teacher in Barcelona, an eighty-year-old university professor from Mexico City, and finally, an aging porn star in LA."

"Keep digging."

"I'll be checking Paul Hammerston's records next."

"Is Lopez talking at all?" said Tanya.

"I've been phoning her every hour on the hour, but the last time I called, she told me to stop bothering her." Katy sighed. "Oh, and she signed the consent form."

Tanya's eyebrows shot up.

"For the official DNA test?"

"Dr. Chen's been harassing me about it all morning, so I sent Lopez an electronic form."

"Did she ask why you wanted it?"

"Given the state she was in, I don't think she read it. Probably thought it was admin paperwork, scrolled down, and initialed it on the screen." Katy paused. "I kind of feel bad. I didn't mean to trick her...."

"If she has nothing to hide, she has nothing to worry about," said Tanya, speaking slowly. "If she was guilty of a crime, she wouldn't be this distracted."

"Dr. Chen's waiting for the official lab results, but there's a backlog—"

Max, who had been sitting quietly at Tanya's feet, got up. He whirled around and stared at a nearby thicket.

"Gotta go," whispered Tanya. "Thanks, Katy."

A rustle came from the woods like someone had been listening in to her phone conversation.

Max barked.

Before Tanya had a chance to do anything, he leaped over a log and disappeared into the bushes.

Chapter Forty-eight

A *cabin in the middle of nowhere?*

Tanya stumbled onto the shores of a small green lake and halted, panting.

She had chased Max's tail through the deep woods, hoping he would lead her to the whistler. She surveyed the small lake, but it was the crooked log structure beyond the pond that held her interest.

Is this a hunter's lodge?

The cabin's front door was wide open, but there was no one in the vicinity.

Firewood had been stacked into neat pyramids in the front yard, and an ax was stuck on a tree stump. The warped roof jutted over the front entrance. Hanging from the rafters was a row of dead animals. Tanya gaped at the rabbits, raccoons, and squirrels swaying to the wind in a macabre dance of the dead.

A prepper?

Whoever lived here was self-sufficient.

Arranged in neat rows next to the house was a vegetable patch. Early saplings were already sprouting from the ground and curling up the iron trellises. Multicolored rose bushes bordered the garden, still budding, but creating a striking contrast to the lush greenery around them.

Tanya stared at the dark rosebush in the corner. She recalled the peculiar flower in the woman's hair at the cemetery. She walked over to the garden and bent down.

The black rose.

She felt the velvet petals with her fingers.

Are these even real?

Max trotted over and cocked his head at her, as if to ask if they could keep moving.

"Let's go, bud," she whispered, getting to her feet.

It was at that moment she heard the peel of laughter. She spun around toward the cabin. It wasn't coming from inside the house. She scanned the dirt yard, but couldn't see anyone.

Tanya had been prepared for anything but the sound of women laughing happily. She gestured for Max to retreat and slid back into the woods.

"This way," she whispered, as she stepped through the trees.

They were going to take the circuitous route that meandered around the cabin. Making sure to not step on dried twigs, she made her way slowly and deliberately toward the back of the structure.

The laughter came in waves, interspersed with the low rumblings of talking. She strained to listen, but she couldn't make any words out. The voices were female. Older women. Not many. Three at most.

They sounded familiar, but the only person Tanya could imagine staying in this isolated house was sedated and under watch at the residence. The scarred man with the ax.

The smell of burning wood came from nearby, but there was no smoke. A bird chirped in a tree, and one of the women broke into giggles.

Tanya circled the cabin and stopped. She now knew why they sounded familiar.

Two good-looking septuagenarians were seated on a swing bench in front of a fire pit. Next to them was a broken plastic chair with a half-empty bottle of red wine on it.

The women were swinging gently back and forth, sharing a glass of wine between them. Each wore a black rose in their long white hair. Tanya stared at them, wondering if she was imagining this surreal scene.

They were the same women she'd met at the cemetery. They were still in their flamboyant bohemian clothes that flapped in the wind.

Did they whistle at me?

Max was watching them intently, but his hackles were down and his body was relaxed. Tanya holstered her weapon.

She stomped her feet to make noise, then stepped on a dry twig for extra measure. The laughter stopped. Tanya peeked through the trees to see them staring in her direction.

She cleared her throat.

"Hey, Max? Let's go say hello, shall we?" she said out loud, before stepping out of the woods.

The women gasped as she and Max appeared into view.

"Hi there," Tanya waved. "Nice to see you ladies, again."

"Ooh, the police officer," said one of the woman.

Her friend leaned forward. "Are you here for the body?" she whispered.

Tanya raised a brow. "Didn't you bury her this morning?"

"That we did." The second woman nodded, her face turning somber. "But we're expecting another funeral tomorrow."

Chapter Forty-nine

"You had another death?" said Tanya.

"Seems like we did," said one of the women. "We'll know for sure when Carolyn asks us to come to the funeral."

Tanya frowned. A headache was coming on and her temples were throbbing.

Something didn't add up.

Why would the director invite the residents to the funerals of the people she murdered?

Most killers go to great lengths to hide the bodies, not make a display of it. Maybe Ray's anonymous letter was a hoax. Maybe the women weren't being murdered. Maybe Susan Cross is right, and this case is unfounded.

The fruity, earthy aroma of red wine hung heavily in the air, mixed in with the smoke from the fire pit. Tanya put a hand on her stomach, wondering why she felt sick all of a sudden.

"You look like you could do with a drink, sweetie," said one woman, extending her hand with the wineglass. Her pretty smile wrinkled the edges of her blue eyes that reminded Tanya of the wide-open skies of Ukraine.

Tanya took one look at the drink and felt nauseous.

"I'd love to, but I'm on the job."

"That's too bad," said the woman before throwing her head back and gulping down the last drop.

Tanya pulled up the broken chair and sat down. Her legs felt strangely wobbly. Max trotted up to the women on the swing, his tongue lolling. With happy cries, they leaned over to pet him.

"What a beautiful pup," said the first woman, stroking his back. "What's this gorgeous boy's name?"

"Max," said Tanya.

"Hey, Max, I'm Sahara," said the second woman with the long snowy white hair that glistened in the afternoon sunlight.

"And I'm Ocean," piped up the first woman.

Ocean and Sahara? These can't be their real names.

"Hi, I'm Tanya." She waved at them, but they were too busy cooing over her dog.

"So, ladies," said Tanya, trying to get their attention, "is this your cottage?"

Ocean pushed back a strand of hair and gave her a coy smile. "We come up here when we want to have some fun."

"Carolyn's so strict," said Sahara, looking up from petting Max. "No smoking, no drinking, no sex. Those are the rules."

"Harsh."

"Not complaining though, because we do have superior accommodations, a gourmet chef, excellent service, and privacy," said Ocean. "Carolyn does her job, but she's been so stressed lately."

Tanya sat up.

"Stressed? Why?"

"That woman's so bossy and works everyone to the grind," said Sahara. "She needs a vacation, if you ask me. She should sit on a beach with a book or something."

"Or join us for a quiet smoke and drink." Ocean chortled. "She would have a heart attack if we invited her up here, though."

A spasm rolled across Tanya's abdomen, but within seconds, it passed. She swallowed the pain and turned to the women. They were too distracted by Max to notice her sudden change in demeanor.

She pointed at the cabin. "Who lives here?"

"The poor man you were chasing, sweetie," said Sahara, tsking.

"Is he a resident?"

"He's our handyman and gardener," said Ocean. "He does odd jobs. Sometimes he takes things from our rooms, but I really don't think he deserved to be chased down like that."

So, we have a nurse who pilfers from the drug cabinet and a handyman who steals from the residents?

"Any idea how he got that scar?" said Tanya.

"Something happened to him when he was a young boy," said Sahara. "No one knows, but I'd say he had a hard life."

She peered at Tanya.

"Did he steal the butcher knives again?"

Tanya blinked. "Butcher knives?"

"How do you think he skins the rabbits?"

"He can be a bit odd," said Ocean, "but he wouldn't hurt a fly."

"It's so boring up on the hill," said Sahara, shooting Tanya a guilty smile. "You and your puppy chasing him across the cemetery was the most exciting thing that has happened all year."

"Carolyn nearly lost it, didn't she?" grinned Ocean. "I was sure she'd have a heart attack, and we'd have to bury her too."

Sahara laughed. "One can only hope."

Tanya felt another involuntary convulsion in her stomach. She dug her fingers into her thighs to suppress the pain.

What's happening to me?

Chapter Fifty

Tanya leaned toward the women.

"Do you know why Carolyn carries a sidearm?"

Ocean shrugged. "To keep us safe, I guess."

"We have a guard, but he's a one-man security team," said Sahara.

"A nice-looking man, too," said Ocean, "but sadly, too young for us."

"I'm so glad we found someone close to our age," said Sahara with a bright smile. "A debonair gentleman with wonderful manners. Looks a lot like that famous actor. Now, what's his name?"

"Morgan Freeman!" cried Ocean, clapping her hands.

Tanya gaped.

"Such a hunky silver fox, isn't he?" said Sahara to her friend. "I love it when he walks around shirtless."

"Lots of cuddles with no attachments," giggled Ocean. "Just the way we like it."

Tanya grimaced. The thought of Ray having intimate encounters with these two ladies was as icky as imagining her parents having sex.

The nausea came over her again. This time, she wasn't sure if it was whatever was ailing her or if it was what these women were oversharing.

"Sweetie, we stopped caring what people think a long time ago," said Sahara, seeing Tanya's face.

Tanya leaned back in her chair, one hand on her stomach, wondering how to get the intel she had come for.

"I've heard there's been unusual activity here recently."

Ocean frowned. "Has someone complained about us sneaking into Ray's room at night again?"

"Not that kind. What about strangers hanging around the grounds?"

"Tall, dark, handsome strangers?" giggled Sahara. "We'd be the first to know."

"Carolyn's serious about her rules," said Ocean. "Family visits are restricted to afternoons in the conference room, but we hardly get visitors. My own folk would rather go to the Maldives for a vacation than visit me."

"Family's overrated." Sahara slipped her hand into the folds of her harem pants and pulled out a cigar. "As soon as you get a few gray hairs, they expect you to take up knitting and sit quietly in the corner, waiting to shrivel up and die."

Ocean took the cigar from her friend. Sahara took out a lighter, and soon the smoky aroma of expensive tobacco filled the air.

They swung back and forth, taking puffs of their cigars, satisfied looks on their beautifully lined faces. Max had settled himself at their feet, and didn't seem to mind the smell at all.

Tanya shifted in her seat, trying to ignore the cramps in her stomach, wondering what had made her so sick. She hadn't drunk the wine or tried their cigars. She hadn't eaten much all day either.

"Our husbands are dead and our children are all grown up," said Ocean, blowing a perfectly round smoke ring. "We spent our entire lives meeting their needs and now, it's our time."

"I got past the sell-buy date and my family thought it was time to stick me in a cheap pension home," said Sahara. "That's the day I sold the house and came here to get pampered. I will die with every last dollar of their inheritance spent."

"Life really begins at seventy." Ocean smiled and took another puff. "This is freedom."

Tanya balled her hands into fists and swallowed the agony roiling in her belly, wishing the women would stick to the topic.

Sahara leaned forward.

"You feeling okay, hun? You look a little peaked."

"I'm good. D... did you... did you see the girl they found on the hill?"

"This is a child free-zone—" Ocean stopped and turned to her friend. "Wait, didn't you tell me you saw a kid hanging by the woods two nights ago?"

Tanya's heart skipped a beat.

Sahara's brow furrowed. "I was going to Ray's room when I saw a shadow, but it was dark and my eyes were playing tricks on me."

"What did the shadow look like?" said Tanya. "Tall? Short? Thin?"

"I'd had a couple of glasses of wine with dinner, so...."

"A couple?" Ocean slapped her friend's thigh. "You had a whole bottle by yourself, sweet woman, you could barely walk."

Sahara flapped Ocean's hand away.

"It was a girl, I think. She was in pink pajamas, which I thought was weird to be out and about in. That's when I realized maybe I had too much wine that night."

Tanya's heart beat faster.

"Pink pajamas? Are you sure?"

Ocean pursed her lips and turned to Tanya.

"She was completely wasted. I wouldn't trust her to remember her own name after a half a bottle of wine."

Chapter Fifty-one

Tanya's stomach churned, like it was fighting to digest a heavy meal.

"How did that woman die? The one you buried this morning."

"Heart attack," said Sahara.

"How do you know?"

"That's what the doctor said." Ocean shook her head sadly. "Carolyn was really upset."

"Is that right?"

Another sting cut through Tanya's stomach, followed by something bitter that came up to her throat.

"She started an addiction rehabilitation program last year," said Sahara. "It's for women who need to get away from families and recover in peace. But they keep dying. It's really sad."

Tanya tried to sit up and concentrate. They were sharing valuable information. But another wave of nausea hit her. Stronger, this time.

"Carolyn really needs to stop taking on extra projects. Everyone's overworked," Sahara was saying. "Personally, I think she needs to stop the program."

Ocean tsked. "I swear that woman will snap one of these days if she doesn't stop to breathe."

Tanya's stomach turned again. She hadn't eaten more than a toasted bagel and coffee from Lulu's café that morning.

"Are you feeling all right, sweetie?" said Sahara, turning concerned eyes on her.

Tanya nodded. "You said there will be a funeral tomorrow. How do you know?"

"It's one of the charity cases, but Carolyn doesn't like talking about these things because it dampens the mood."

Tanya put a hand to her stomach, willing it to stay still. As if sensing her discomfort, Max got up and stepped up to her. He licked her hand and put his snout on her thigh.

She directed her focus on the women.

"If Carolyn didn't talk about it, how do you know someone has died?"

Ocean plucked the black rose from her hair and waved it gently in the air.

"Every time we find a rose in the towel room," she said, tucking the flower back behind her ear, "we know a burial is coming up."

Tanya pointed her chin at the cabin. "I thought you took that from the garden up front."

"We'd never do that," said Sahara. "Stu would be heart broken."

"Who's Stu?" said Tanya. "The guy who lives in the cabin? The man with the scar?"

"We only take cut flowers," said Ocean. "They're going to die anyway, so why not enjoy them?"

Tanya wished they'd answer her questions directly. "Who leaves these roses in the towel room?"

Sahara turned to Ocean. "Didn't Carolyn hire a new undertaker? We used to have wreathes at the funerals. I never saw single flowers before, so they must have switched things up."

"Black baccara roses, I think they're called," said Ocean, pointing at her flower. "Fitting for a funeral but beautiful to wear any day. I don't think the nurses know what they're for and leave them behind. What a pity."

A painful rumble came from Tanya's belly, but her mind was racing with questions.

"How many roses have you found in the towel room so far?"

Sahara took another puff of her cigar. "Three? Four, I think?"

"A baccara rose is much more tasteful than an ugly wreath." Ocean turned to her friend. "Would you put one on my coffin when you bury me, hun?"

"You got it, sweetie," said Sahara. "Do the same for my funeral, will you?"

"What is it with these depressing funerals?" scoffed Ocean. "Make mine a celebration of life."

"Me too. Make mine a party."

A wave of pain rode through Tanya's belly to the small of her back, making her gasp out loud. Max whined and pawed at her leg.

Sahara and Ocean stared at Tanya in alarm.

"Honey, you've gone pale."

"You need to lie down, sweetie."

Tanya doubled over and vomited into the fire pit.

Chapter Fifty-two

Tanya staggered down the hill.

Max circled her, whining. He knew something was wrong.

Tanya had wanted nothing more than to dig into Silver Serenity's background, but the pain in her stomach grew with every minute she sat on that broken chair by the fire pit.

Her legs shook and her head felt heavy, like a ton of rocks were tumbling through her brain.

Ocean and Sahara had urged her to come to the residence to let Nurse Ana look her over, but that was the last thing Tanya wanted. Something told her that her illness had originated at the residence.

She was always careful about what she and Max put in their bodies. Staying fit, healthy, and strong was a job requirement. With Lopez out of commission and both Deputy Fox and the chief out of town, she couldn't afford to get ill too.

She tripped over a log and grabbed onto a fir branch to steady herself. She leaned against the tree trunk and forced herself to breathe slowly.

She wasn't too far from her cottage.

Just a few more steps.

Max kept circling her and whining, as if he was asking how he could help her.

Tanya squeezed her eyes and took another breath in. The loud buzzing of her phone in her pocket cut through her aching head like an ear-splitting drill.

She opened her eyes and blinked.

The world was distorted. Small black dots flickered in her sight, and the woods seemed a blur of gray, green, and brown.

Am I going blind?

A jolt of fear struck through her heart.

The water jug in Ray Jackson's room.

It was poisoned.

Her phone buzzed again.

She fumbled in her pocket and pulled her cell out with trembling hands. The screen floated in front of her eyes, but she made out a fuzzy red button.

A new message.

Holding the phone close to her eyes, she clicked on the text and squinted. The words on the screen swam in a disjointed pattern. Ignoring the searing pain in her stomach, she asked the phone's voice assistant to read it out aloud.

The robotic voice complied.

Your brother's alive. Don't you want to see him? ANON.

With an angry hiss, Tanya slipped her mobile back in her pocket.

I don't have time for these stupid pranks—

Something bitter surged into her throat. She blinked and looked around her.

Where's Max?

She scrunched her eyes and peered into the thicket. She could hear him bark in the murky distance.

"Max?" she called out.

Her throat was hoarse, like she had been shouting all night.

"Max, come back," she hollered, but her voice sounded more like the unrecognizable warble of a drunk woman.

Tanya pulled out her mobile and tried to focus on the list of the most recent callers.

Katy.

Where's Katy?

She clicked on her friend's name and held the cell to her ear, breathing raspy breaths.

Please, pick up.

"Hey," came Katy's friendly voice from the other end.

"P...p... poisoned. H...help."

"Tanya? Is that you? I can't hear you, hun."

Tanya took her hand off the trunk to position the phone closer to her ear, when her legs gave way.

"Tanya?" came Katy's voice through the speakerphone. "What's going on?"

Tanya stared at the forest floor. It was rushing toward her. She put her hands out but she couldn't stop it. She crashed to the ground.

She tumbled down the hill, out of control, gathering speed.

She clutched at roots, logs, anything to slow her rapid decent. But she traveled faster and faster, throwing loose rocks in the air, scraping on dry branches, feeling like her skin was being ripped off.

"Katy! Max!"

Tanya screamed but she couldn't hear her own voice.

Then the world went black.

Day Three

Chapter Fifty-three

S he was hurting everywhere.

Tanya pried her eyes open but all she could see was a gray background. She blinked, but the blurry image remained. A pang of fear struck through her.

Is this what death looks like?

She thrust her hands around her. She was lying on something soft.

Her throat was parched, her muscles were stiff, and her entire body was too weak to move.

She placed a hand on her thighs, and another on her neck. She moved one hand over to her opposing shoulder and squeezed it gently.

I'm alive.

A strange image flashed across her mind, like she was reliving a bad dream.

She was sitting by a dying fire pit in the middle of the woods. Perched on a wooden swing were two older women in white robes, looking like angels. She scrunched her forehead as she tried to recall the distant memory.

Think, girl, think.

The fuzziness cleared slightly. There were shapes now, inanimate shapes, in front of her.

A loud bang came from somewhere. She turned her head. She couldn't see much, but she could make out a few more objects, none of which looked human. Or dog.

Her heart leaped to her throat.

Where's Max?

Memories of his fading barks rushed to her mind. She was in the woods again, stumbling down, trying to get to her cottage before she passed out. A swirl of panic spiraled up her spine.

Max!

Where did you run off to?

Her heart pounded inside her rib cage. She couldn't breathe.

Why didn't you stay with me?

She scrunched her eyes and tried to focus on something else. She was in flight-or-fight mode, thinking only of the worst-case scenarios. A wiser voice inside her told her this wouldn't help.

She drew in a deep breath to calm her nerves.

Eerie memories mashed together in her befuddled consciousness. All of a sudden, she was no longer incapacitated, but back in Ray Jackson's plush bedroom at Silver Serenity.

Like watching a movie, she saw herself pour a glass of bubbly water from a jug. She took a gulp and placed it back on the tray with a grimace. Then, to her horror, she poured the water from the same jug into an ice bucket and set it on the floor for Max.

No!

I gave him poisoned water.

Something caught in her throat.

Did he drink it?
Tanya's brain whirled in a tornado.
No. He knew—
Someone touched her arm.
Tanya jumped, startled. A dark figure was standing by her.
She curled her hands into fists, ready to fight.

Chapter Fifty-four

"Tanya?"

Tanya blinked and stared.

"It's me, hun," came the voice again. "How are you feeling?"

Relief flooded through her body.

Katy.

"We found you in the woods, a few yards from your house."

Tanya opened her mouth to speak but nothing came out. She reached out and clutched air. Katy clasped her hand in hers and squeezed.

"You're going to be okay, hun."

Where's Max?

She tried to get the words out, but her throat was constricted. She closed her eyes and opened them again, and realized her vision was slowly returning.

A second silhouette was stepping toward her bed. She snapped her head around and blinked. She tried to focus on the figure.

Who's this?

"Stone?" It was a familiar female voice, stern and firm.

Dr. Chen.

Something cold and hard pressed against her chest. Her eyes flickered. The doctor was pressing a stethoscope on her.

"Don't move. You must rest."

Tanya cleared her throat. She had so many questions, but her throat was sore.

"I flushed it out," Dr. Chen was saying. "You vomited all over yourself, so I knew you had ingested a toxin."

Tanya struggled to sit up.

"My team's running a rapid toxicology test as we speak," said the doctor, tapping her shoulder. "Say ahh."

Tanya opened her mouth.

"Someone tried to poison you, Detective."

Tanya blinked and tried to focus.

"M...Max... is he okay? she croaked.

Katy leaned over and patted her arm. Tanya turned to her, her eyes tearing up.

Wh... where is... he?" she whispered hoarsely.

Katy stared at her for a second before glancing up at the doctor. Then, she whirled around and disappeared through the door.

"Your back, please."

Dr. Chen was pushing Tanya forward, holding her shoulders tightly. She felt the cold of the stethoscope between her shoulder blades and shivered, but kept her eyes on the doorway.

All of a sudden, a long snout with a black nose pushed the door fully open. It was followed by a large brown head with pointy ears.

A jolt of joy struck through Tanya.

"Max!"

He scampered over to the bed, his tongue lolling, and his tail wagging so fast it was a blur of brown.

Tanya heard Dr. Chen say something sharp about dogs in her examination room, but she didn't care. Max jumped up and slapped his paws on the bed, whining happily. With tears of joy, she enveloped him in a hug.

"I will *not* make this exception again," said Dr. Chen, but Tanya was too happy to be mad at her.

"He saved you, hun."

Tanya looked up to see Katy had returned.

"He went to get help," said Katy, stroking Max's back. "He's a very good boy."

Tanya hugged Max tightly. There was so much she wanted to say, but all the words seemed to dry up in her throat.

"Your phone was on," said Katy. "I heard him barking. Then, I heard him come back with the two cops who were at the scene on the hill."

Tanya's heart felt like it was about to burst, this time out of love, not fear. She hugged her dog even tighter while he licked her face all over.

"If those officers hadn't found you in time," came Dr. Chen's voice from behind her, "you wouldn't be sitting up so quickly, I can tell you that, Stone."

Tanya turned to her.

"W...water... It was in the water."

She looked up in horror.

"Ray," she whispered. "R...Ray Jackson."

"Who's that?" The doctor frowned. "Is he the man who killed our girl?"

Tanya slid off the bed and searched for her clothes.

"I was collateral damage. They were trying to poison him, not me."

Chapter Fifty-five

"Fifteen hours?"

Tanya turned to Katy in shock.

"Dr. Chen sedated you," said Katy, her hands on the wheel and her eyes on the road.

Tanya fumed. "I lost a whole day while a killer's roaming on the hill?"

They were winding up that same hill in her Jeep. It was early morning, and the sun was shining, twinkling through the trees. The forest no longer looked forbidding, but Tanya knew life on the hill wasn't as peaceful as it seemed.

She was riding shotgun in her Jeep while Katy drove. Max was lying in the backseat, his eyes moving from Katy to Tanya and back again, his ears pricked as the conversation turned heated.

"For heaven's sake, we all know if she hadn't, you would have gone running off again."

Katy changed the gear. Tanya cringed as the Jeep's engine screamed in protest.

"Either learn to work the manual shift, or let me drive my own darn car."

"You're not fit to drive, let alone leave your bed." Katy put on the voice she reserved for her daughter, Chantal, when she had been naughty. "You should thank me for convincing Dr. Chen. She was ready to strap you down."

Tanya massaged her temples, a feeble attempt at fighting the migraine threatening to overcome her. She was still woozy and her body ached, but she hadn't admitted any of that to the doctor or Katy.

"I wouldn't let her."

"I wouldn't test that woman."

Tanya didn't answer, knowing Katy was right. The diminutive physician had more fight in her than anyone twice her size.

After a lot of grumbling, Dr. Chen had released her, and an intern had lent Tanya her spare scrubs. Then, Katy had driven her to the cottage for a shower and a change of clothes, and to give Max his meal of the day.

Before they left the clinic, Tanya had called the Silver Serenity residence, demanding to speak to Ray Jackson.

The older female nurse had picked up the phone. Tanya had recognized her gravelly voice. The nurse had objected, saying she wasn't allowed to disturb him. She had relented only when Tanya had threatened to bring a team of officers with a warrant to search the premises for stolen drugs.

But the nurse had been right. Ray Jackson hadn't been pleased at all.

"I already told you," he'd said. "I can take care of myself. You shouldn't have been here in the first place."

Tanya had gritted her teeth. "Someone doesn't want you at the residence. They will try again, Ray, and next time you might not be fortunate."

"Let them try."

With that, Ray had hung up, leaving Tanya gnashing her teeth.

Katy took a curve on the road that wound up the hill.

"Doesn't he realize I'm trying to save his skin?" said Tanya.

"How do you know he's not involved?" said Katy. "Dr. Chen is right. If anyone can get away with killing a bunch of women and that girl, it would be a man who's been trained for this sort of thing."

Tanya turned to her friend. "What's his motive?"

"We haven't figured it out yet." Katy turned to her briefly. "How do you know he wasn't trying to poison *you*?"

"You're seriously entertaining that theory?"

"It's a working theory. Just watch your back around him."

Katy pressed on the accelerator as the incline turned steeper.

Tanya sighed.

"According to the two women at the cabin, there was another death at the residence yesterday." She glanced at her phone to check the time and date. "If their story is true, Carolyn would have buried the victim already."

"Can we exhume the bodies?" said Katy. "Maybe they were all poisoned, like they tried to do to you."

"Jack will have to ask for a slew of authorizations. That's going to take time." Tanya hissed. "I can't believe I drank that water. I should have been investigating two homicides, not sleeping on the job."

Katy moved her foot to the clutch and changed gears.

"Trust me, you weren't sleeping, hun. Every time I checked on you, you were moaning like you were having nightmares."

Tanya blinked but said nothing. Normally she remembered her bad dreams, but this time, she recalled nothing after her fall down the hill.

"There it is."

They had just entered the grounds. Katy pointed to the Silver Serenity residence which loomed at the end of the long driveway.

Tanya stared at the stately white mansion. From the outside, the institution seemed to live up to its name, but she knew strange things were brewing inside, things she couldn't yet explain.

"Slow down," she said.

Katy pressed on the brakes. "What's the plan? Barge in, show your badge, and ask to see the death ledger?"

Tanya put a hand up. "Stop the car now."

"Here?"

Chapter Fifty-six

"We're going to walk the rest of the way."

Tanya pointed at a little clearing in the woods. "Put the Jeep in off-road mode. We'll park in there."

Katy scanned the vehicle's dashboard, her brow furrowed. "What's the button for off-road mode?"

With a sigh, Tanya put her left hand on the gear shift. "Just do as I say."

"Fine." Katy pressed the brakes and turned the wheel, grumbling. "Who buys a manual these days, anyway?"

In the backseat, Max got to his feet and thumped his tail, like he knew they were about to get back in action.

Following Tanya's instructions, Katy maneuvered the Jeep over the ditch and into the clearing. The vehicle swayed as it rolled over the uneven terrain. Katy drove the car behind a large bush so anyone coming up the road wouldn't spot it.

Katy got out and peered into the woods. "It's going to be a long walk."

"Stay sharp," said Tanya. "We might bump into the handyman. He carries an ax."

Katy turned to her, eyes wide.

"Ray's room faces the woods in the back," said Tanya, gesturing for Katy to follow her and Max. "Stay behind me."

Locking the Jeep, they slipped in between the evergreens and headed in the direction of the residence. Max trotted ahead, stopping every few seconds to make sure his team was keeping up. Tanya slipped behind him, one hand on her Glock, ready if anyone accosted them.

But her instincts told her the killer wasn't someone who'd jump from behind a tree and stick a gun in your face. The killer of that girl and potentially these women was someone more subtle, someone who played their murderous games quietly.

Tanya was running on pure adrenaline now, driven only by the deep desire to find the girl's killer and figure out what was happening to those women. She knew her body would pay dearly for jumping out of Dr. Chen's clinic so soon.

But tomorrow was another day. Today, she had a job to finish.

Tanya stopped when they reached the edge of the woods that looked over the backyard. Ray Jackson's room was visible from here. The patio doors were open, but the curtains were drawn. They fluttered in the breeze as they watched.

Tanya scanned the fogged-up windows of the kitchen only a few yards from Ray's room. They were cooking up a storm in there.

"No one's around," she whispered, scanning the empty grounds.

"Do we make a run for it?" said Katy.

Tanya nodded. "Let's go."

She scurried over to Ray's patio, with Max and Katy right behind her. Squeals of laughter came through the window as they approached the wall.

Katy raised a brow. "Does he have visitors?"

The laughter turned to playful giggles.

"Sounds like they're having an orgy in there," whispered Katy.

Tanya reached over and rapped on the glass. The giggling stopped abruptly, followed by a loud thud, like someone or something fell.

A hand emerged between the curtains and ripped them back.

A furious Ray Jackson appeared at the threshold in nothing but yellow banana shorts.

Chapter Fifty-seven

R ay glowered at Tanya.

"What are you doing here?"

"Making sure you're not dead."

"Ooh, we have visitors," came a gleeful voice from inside the room. Soon, Ocean, wearing a man's flannel shirt, appeared next to Ray Jackson. Sahara popped her head under his shoulder.

She smiled. "Oh, hi, sweetie. So nice to see you again."

"Did you catch the man who killed that poor girl, hun?" said Ocean, turning her blue eyes on Tanya.

"You looked quite awful yesterday," said Sahara, "but you took off before we could give you a cup of tea or something."

Ocean leaned toward Tanya, a concerned expression on her face. "You look a little pale, honey. Are you sure you should be up and about?"

"Feeling much better, thanks," said Tanya, with a weak smile. "Sorry to throw up in your fire pit."

Sahara reached over and squeezed her arm.

Tanya turned to Ray. "I need to talk to you alone. It's business."

Ocean turned to him, her eyes widening. "Oh, dear. Did you do something terrible? Is she going to arrest you?"

An angry twitch had come on Ray's face. "I told you not to interfere."

"Visiting hours are so restrictive, Uncle Ray," said Tanya, trying on an amiable smile.

"Ooh, I didn't know you two were related," said Sahara, glancing from Ray to Tanya and back. "But I can see the resemblance...I think...."

Ray's jaws clenched. Sahara and Ocean clung to him, giggling like teenage girls with their crush.

"Can we speak alone, Uncle?"

"You can't gallivant up here and expect me to jump whenever you call," spat Ray.

"Uncle Ray," said Tanya, keeping her voice even. "This is urgent."

With an angry hiss, he turned away from her and put his arms around Sahara and Ocean.

"Why don't you beautiful ladies come back later tonight?"

They kissed his cheeks before leaving.

Ray walked over to the poster bed and threw on a bathrobe with the looping double "S" Silver Serenity logo stitched to the lapel.

Tanya stepped inside the room.

"I thought you were on the job, Ray, and here you are, partying it up."

"I was gathering intel." He glowered at her. "If anyone knows anything, it's those two."

"You're *using* those ladies for intel?" Katy turned to him with an incredulous stare. "That's awful."

"For the record, they approached me first. They call me their boy toy."

Katy opened her mouth and shut it, then shook her head like she had no words.

Tanya put a hand up. "I don't even want to know."

She stepped over to the liquor tray on the cabinet, slipped on her gloves, and examined the water jug. It was exactly as she had left it. Her half-filled glass sat next to the ice bucket with the liquid still in it.

Katy came over, putting on her own gloves. She sniffed the water.

"No odor."

"It tasted metallic," said Tanya, picking a stainless steel lid from the tray and tightening it on top of the bucket. "Dr. Chen's team can test it for us."

"I brought my own supplies for a reason," said Ray.

Katy turned to him with a glare. "Did you know what's in this? You nearly killed Tanya!"

Ray raised his hands. "I told her not to touch it."

Katy looked him up and down. "Tanya could have got badly sick if she had drunk the entire glass. Max, too. How could you?"

"I didn't know," said Ray. "Do you really think—"

"Okay, Casanova," said Tanya. "Pack your bags. We're leaving. You're too close to the heat."

Ray put his hands on his hips and turned his glare on her.

"If it wasn't for me, Stone, you wouldn't even have known to come here."

"Susan Cross ordered me to. So, I'm going to find the death ledger."

Ray shook his head. "You did such a good job of that last time, didn't you? I saved your skin, if you recall. And all I get is accusations of trying to murder you. Not one thanks!"

Tanya pointed at Katy. "That's why she's here. She's going to help us find the book."

Ray stared at Katy.

"So, she's looking for a nice room for her grandmother, okay?" said Tanya. "She'll go through the front doors to talk to Carolyn, ask for a tour, see all the rooms, and stall, stall, stall. That should give me ample time to find that journal."

"I don't have all day," said Katy, turning to her, a worried look on her face. "Peace is making supper tonight. I promised him I'd be home early and help Chantal with her homework."

"I need two hours tops. I'll work as fast as I can."

Ray turned from Katy to Tanya. "Is that why you returned? For the ledger?"

"And to make sure I won't have to take you home in a body bag," said Tanya.

With a loud sigh, he turned around and ambled to the nightstand. He waved a leather-bound book in the air.

"No need for any of your shenanigans."

Katy took a sharp breath in. "Is that the death ledger?"

"I searched for it everywhere in the office," said Tanya.

"Someone removed it." Ray tossed it toward her. "It was in the towel room, under a stack of bath sheets."

Chapter Fifty-eight

"Seven," said Tanya, as they negotiated their way through the woods back to the Jeep. "And now, we're down to three."

"Two, if we believe Ray Jackson's cougar girlfriends," said Katy, clutching the ledger in her hands.

"They concluded that based on a flower arrangement. We can't rely on their words. Besides, Carolyn hasn't held another funeral yet." Tanya paused. "The question is where *are* these women kept?"

"Didn't those folks at the cemetery say there's a special wing dedicated for rehabilitation?"

"Rehabilitation," muttered Tanya, "or, homicide by any other name?"

She furrowed her brow.

"Carolyn's rough around the edges, but seems to have a soft spot for people dying alone. Ray just might be right about her. She may not even suspect something nefarious is going on."

"Remember, she's the big boss," said Katy, as she hurried to keep up with Tanya's long strides.

"Lots of things can happen behind a boss's back."

"So, Carolyn's a wild card?" said Katy.

"This whole case is a wild card. We don't even know if we're looking at homicides or deaths due to natural causes. An anonymous letter and a gut feel won't get us a warrant or justify an arrest."

"Speaking of wild cards," said Katy. "Santiago Fernando has a criminal record."

Tanya turned to her. "Why doesn't that surprise me?"

"He was incarcerated for three years."

"His crime?"

"Assaulting a journalist. Witnesses say she accosted him on the street about his father being a child rapist, and he turned on her. Hit the reporter so hard she ended up in a coma."

"Three years for putting a woman in a coma?"

"He had a powerful father with lots of connections." Katy grimaced. "The judge gave a media suppression order on the trial, so there's very little information to go on."

Tanya frowned. Something about this story bothered her. She felt like she had overlooked an important clue.

What am I missing?

"There's something odd about all this."

Katy gave her a side-eye. "Ray Jackson gave up this ledger way too quickly, don't you think?"

Tanya sighed.

"I don't trust your confidant," said Katy with a huff.

Tanya couldn't help but agree. She was still fuming.

Ray Jackson had outright refused to leave with them. She'd had no choice, as the alternative would have been to kick up a fuss, which would have given their presence away to the residence's staff. Katy had the right to doubt his intentions. His bull-headed behavior didn't engender trust.

"What if this ledger is not a real ledger at all?" said Katy, waving the book in the air. "What if it's a red herring to drive us away from what's really happening on this hill?"

Chapter Fifty-nine

Max barked from within the woods, as if he was calling them.

He had trotted ahead of them in the direction of the Jeep several minutes ago.

Tanya surveyed the thicket around them.

"I don't like us hanging out here. Someone could see us snooping, and the culprit, or culprits, could go underground."

"You're worried about the killer disappearing?" Katy shivered. "I just hope they don't come after us."

"Not on my watch," said Tanya. "Let's see if we can find out what's going on here before you go home for supper."

"Now that would be a miracle." Katy made a face but followed Tanya, as she hurried through the woods.

Max was waiting for them by the car. He thumped his tail as they emerged from the bushes.

Katy stepped up to the vehicle and placed the book on the bonnet.

"This isn't much of a ledger." She bent over and scrolled her finger down the list, her brow knitted. "Just a few names and their respective health conditions. My goodness. They were really sick."

"Ray's anonymous letter supposedly said the women were in moderate health," said Tanya.

"But according to this," said Katy, flipping through the book, "they were diagnosed as terminally ill, and those who died, died of justified causes."

She stopped.

"These names are familiar."

Tanya straightened up. "You recognize them?"

"Isabella Rose. Why is that so...." Katy snapped her fingers. "Isabella Rose starred in a soap opera. I've seen her on TV."

Tanya nodded. "She was an actor."

"She was the star of *The Sexy Sisters*, I think it was called," said Katy. "I remember because it was awful. They had finished filming when Isabella got caught for drinking and driving. She spent two weeks in a minimum-security prison and had to do community service. It was splashed all over the tabloids."

Tanya opened the Jeep's back door for Max to hop inside.

"Were all these women from Hollywood—"

Katy gasped.

"Hang on. A page is missing."

Tanya stepped up to her. Katy held the book up and shook it, to see if loose leaves were tucked among the pages.

"Someone ripped out a page, right here." She squinted as she tried to make out the remaining words scribbled on the leftover piece. "I can read a few letters, but..."

"The state forensics lab might be able to help," said Tanya, peering over her shoulder. "I get the feeling that page may be exactly what we need."

Katy looked up at her, her face clearing. "I remember where I saw these names before."

She slammed the ledger shut.

"While you were knocked out at the clinic, I dug into the background of Santiago Fernando, the man who flew over to have a fight with Lopez."

"And?"

"I went through police records, newspaper articles, blogs, social media, anything that mentioned him or his pharma company. That's when I came across these names."

"Wait. There's a link between the women at Silver Serenity and our mysterious helicopter man?"

Katy nodded.

"An undeniable one."

Chapter Sixty

T anya jumped into the driver's seat.

Katy scrambled over to the passenger side, clutching the ledger to her chest. She pulled out her phone and swiped through her research findings.

"All seven women," she said, scanning an article, "were part of a class-action lawsuit against the pharmaceutical company three decades ago."

"What was the suit about?" said Tanya, putting the Jeep into gear and reversing out of its hiding spot.

"Sexual abuse."

"How old were the women at that time?"

"Late teens," said Katy. "All of them."

The Jeep swung up and down as Tanya crossed the small ditch that separated the woods from the road.

"Only one defendant was named in the records," continued Katy. "Hugo Fernando. Santiago's father."

Tanya checked both sides for incoming vehicles, before rolling the Jeep onto the road.

"Is he still running the company?"

"He died from a cardiac arrest three years back. The son, Santiago, took over the firm soon after."

"Curiouser and curiouser," murmured Tanya.

"Even more mysterious is how the whole story vanished off the face of the earth," said Katy. "There's nothing more about the lawsuit, the claimants, or any indication of how it was resolved, if it ever was."

"I bet they settled," said Tanya, tapping the wheel with her finger. "He could afford to pay them off."

"But how did these women end up at Silver Serenity, decades later?" Katy frowned. "And why?"

"Maybe they refused to remain quiet." Tanya kept her eyes peeled for vehicles coming from either direction. "We need to dig deeper into our helicopter man. He's our connecting link."

Katy sighed. "I hate leaving those last two women alone. They could die by the time we get the warrants."

"Carolyn has justification to throw us out if we barge in now. Then, we may never see them alive."

"What if they're being murdered right now?" said Katy.

Tanya took a deep breath in to steady her nerves. "I'll bear that burden. We need to tackle this by the book or it's going to backfire, and the killer could get away."

"I still hate it," said Katy, more to herself than Tanya.

"Eliminating two more women so soon after one died will raise suspicions," said Tanya. "I think our killer is smarter than that."

Katy flopped back on her seat. "I sure hope Jack gets those warrants fast."

"He's called the nearby counties for reinforcement. The state is sending a crime scene response team, ready to search the hospital, the residence, the cemetery, the woods, inch by inch, and do it legally. That way, no one can throw this case—"

Tanya's phone buzzed.

Keeping her eyes on the road, she pulled her mobile out of her pocket and placed it on the dashboard.

"Stone?" came a clipped voice.

Katy turned to Tanya. "It's Dr. Chen."

"You need to get down here ASAP," came the physician's voice.

"What's going on?" said Tanya, as she barreled down the steep incline.

"The DNA connection troubled me so I checked Lopez's office. I found something interesting in her desk drawer."

"How interesting?"

"That woman's been lying through her teeth."

Chapter Sixty-one

D r. Chen was pacing up and down the bull pen at the precinct.

"You rarely come to our offices," said Katy as she opened the secure inner door.

"I have justifiable cause." Dr. Chen raised a plastic card in the air. "And the entry key you gave me as this town's unofficial coroner."

Tanya raised a brow. "Have you got the verified DNA results already?"

"Still waiting. State bureaucrats are slower than molasses. Give me the funding and I'd have a world-class forensics lab set up in no time."

"So you've been sleuthing on your own?"

Dr. Chen sighed. "I want to find out who killed that girl just as much as you do. It's not like you have sufficient resources anyway, do you?"

"What did you find?" said Tanya.

"Left on the printer." The doctor picked up a paper from the desk and flapped it back and forth. "Three e-tickets to Buenos Aires, scheduled for three days from now."

Katy's eyes widened.

"One ticket is in Lopez's full name," said the doctor.

"Hold on," said Katy. "Why is Lopez going to Argentina?"

"What I'd like to know is," said Tanya, taking the paper from the doctor's hands, "who are her flying companions?"

"The name on the second e-ticket reads Esmeralda Lopez," said Dr. Chen.

A frisson of horror ran down Tanya's back.

"The dead girl." She paused. "At least, according to two men on the hill."

"The third ticket," said Dr. Chen, "is for an Austin Lopez."

"He could be her husband or an ex," said Katy. "Maybe a brother or a cousin."

"Whoever he is," said the doctor, "they're planning to get out of the country next week."

"This trip was organized before Esmeralda died." Katy dropped her shoulders and shook her head. "I have no idea what's going on anymore. Not with Lopez. Not with the helicopter man. And not with whatever's going on on the hill."

"Sounds to me like our Deputy Lopez," said the doctor, giving Tanya a pointed look, "needs to be arrested for withholding information to a homicide investigation."

Chapter Sixty-two

Tanya raced the Jeep down the road that led to Lopez's home.

She entered the cul de sac and slowed down. This was a quiet, tree-lined neighborhood, not where you would expect to see a police presence, but two junior officers were sitting inside their squad car at the entrance to the rotunda.

They saluted Tanya as she drove up. She stopped the Jeep and rolled down her window.

"Anything to report?"

"No activity, ma'am."

"Who's watching the back door?"

The men jerked back and exchanged a horrified glance. One scrambled out of the car. "Right away," he mumbled as he scurried off to the back of Lopez's house.

Tanya rolled into the driveway of the single-story brick home.

"Maybe there's a connection between Esmeralda's death and the women at Silver Serenity, after all," said Katy. "I swear this case is growing legs that keep tangling up."

Tanya put the Jeep in park and turned to the backseat. Max was already on his feet, wagging his tail, waiting to be let out.

"I'm sorry, bud, but you have to stay in the car," said Tanya. "Be a good boy, now."

He whined in reply and shook his head, as if to say *Please can I come?*

"Shouldn't we take him inside?" said Katy. "Maybe Lopez will open up?"

"She's hiding from something or someone," said Tanya, getting out. "If they come looking, Max will warn us."

"What about the cops?"

"I'd trust him over them, any day."

Leaving a whining Max in the vehicle, they marched up the driveway. Tanya jumped up the front steps and rapped on the door.

They waited.

"She must be sleeping off her hangover," said Katy.

Tanya glanced around the front yard of the modest home. "I don't see her car."

"It's at the precinct," said Katy. "I drove her home because she was in no state."

Tanya banged on the door.

"Lopez! Open up!"

They waited, but the house had fallen silent.

"Carmen?" called out Katy. "We need to talk, hun. It's really important."

No answer.

"I don't like this," said Tanya. "Maybe the killer—"

The sound of the bolt turning came from the front door.

Tanya and Katy waited with bated breath.

The door swung open, and an angry Lopez stood on the threshold.

Chapter Sixty-three

Lopez's face was pink and blotchy. The lines under her puffy eyes had deepened.

"What are you two doing here?" she snapped.

Tanya hunched slightly to not tower over her. "You need to tell us what's going on."

"It's none of your business," said Lopez, her voice hardening. "I had a bad holiday. I just need to get it out of my system."

"Honey, you were crying drunk in your office." Katy put a hand on Lopez's arm, but Lopez jerked back like she had been stung. "And you're jumpy as heck."

Lopez stared at her but didn't speak.

"You're the last person I would have expected to find like that," said Katy. "What happened in San Diego?"

Lopez looked away, her face scrunching like she was trying hard not to cry.

Tanya stared at her colleague who seemed to have undergone a one-hundred-and-eighty-degree transformation.

"If someone has threatened you or has hurt someone close to you, we can help."

Lopez blinked. "You can't do anything now."

"Can we come in, hun?" said Katy, taking a step forward. "For a cup of tea and a chat?"

"Why can't you do the decent thing and leave me alone?" Lopez stepped inside and swung the door.

"We know what happened to Esmeralda," said Tanya. "We can't help her anymore, but we can help you."

Lopez stopped. Her eyes widened. She opened her mouth as if to speak, then closed it. She shivered like it had turned cold all of a sudden.

"Oh, honey," whispered Katy, stepping toward her. "I'm so sorry."

Lopez buckled at the knees and clutched at Katy's arm.

She didn't protest as Katy led her inside the house.

Tanya glanced around. Papers were strewn all over the living-room floor, mostly printouts of maps of the local area. In the midst of the mess was a laptop, a tablet, and her phone, like she had been in the middle of a research project.

Tanya pushed a stack of papers off the couch for her to sit down, while Katy plucked a wool blanket from an armchair.

Katy placed the blanket around Lopez's knees and stepped toward the kitchen.

"Shall I make some tea, hun?"

Lopez hung her head. She took a raspy breath in and tears rolled down her face.

"I just want my baby back," she whispered hoarsely.

A pang of sorrow crossed Tanya's heart. If there was one thing she couldn't do, it was to bring a girl back from the dead.

Tanya sat on the couch next to her.

"How did Esmeralda come to be in Black Rock?" she asked in a soft voice.

"I brought her over...." Lopez warbled through her tears. "From San Diego..."

Katy came over and crouched by her feet.

"How old was Esmeralda, honey?"

"Fourteen."

Lopez's chest heaved.

"She was a kind soul. She... she used to get mad at me if I vacuumed a spider web in the house. She caught them and let them out in the garden. She wanted to be a veterinarian when she grew up."

Her sobs grew louder. There was nothing they could do at that moment except let her cry it all out.

When her crying receded, Tanya bent down.

"Do you have any idea how this happened, hun?"

Lopez took a shaky breath in and looked at her through watery eyes.

"Do you think I'd be sitting at home if I knew who did this?"

Her tone, voice, and body language signaled the truth.

Tanya shook her head. "We'll figure it out for you. I promise you that."

Lopez wiped her face and glanced up at her. Her face darkened.

"Whoever it is, I'll twist the sick animal's neck and make him pay."

Tanya sat up.

"Do you believe the perpetrator to be a man?"

Lopez slammed her fists on her thighs.

"I don't know. I don't care. Whoever it is, when I find out, I'll kill them. "

Tanya leaned toward her.

"Can you tell us who Austin Lopez is?"

Lopez jerked her head back, like she hadn't expected the question. She buried her face in her hands.

Tanya exchanged a curious glance with Katy over their friend. Something about that name had distressed her, but this time, Lopez was hiding her face, not crying.

Tanya scanned the living room, trying to understand how Lopez could have come to such a low point. She was about to gather the maps to see what she had been looking at, when she saw it.

She sprang to her feet and stepped over to the mantelpiece above the fireplace. She picked up the gold-framed photograph and held it out up Katy could see.

Katy squinted at the happy couple on the patio of a luxury beach house, the woman in a bridal gown and the man in a tuxedo.

Tanya walked back to the sofa with the photo and tapped Lopez's shoulder.

"Hun?" said Tanya in a quiet voice. "Is Santiago Fernando your husband?"

Chapter Sixty-four

"We're...s...separated," stammered Lopez, not looking at the photo. "I want to leave him."

Tanya and Katy stared at her tear-stained face.

"Why can't you?" said Katy, leaning forward. "If you want to divorce him, he can't stop you."

"Because he...." Lopez's shoulders drooped. "Do you know who he is?"

"Does it matter?" A ball of fire lit inside of Tanya. "For heaven's sake, this isn't Saudi Arabia or Brunei."

Katy touched Lopez's arm. "Is he threatening you, hun?"

"There's just too much at stake."

"What kind of stakes?" Tanya frowned. "Was he holding your daughter hostage?"

Lopez looked away, but not before Tanya noticed a pink flush creep up her neck.

"He's a powerful man...." Her lips quivered. Her eyes flicked back and forth as if she feared Santiago Fernando would appear in front of her at any moment. "He'll punish me...."

"Why did you go to San Diego?" said Tanya.

"Because.... because I learned something." The pink flush on her neck turned scarlet. Lopez hung her head. "It was something my mother told me two weeks ago...."

Katy furrowed her brow and turned to Tanya. Tanya shrugged to say, *I didn't know her mother was alive either.*

"What did your mom say, hun?" said Katy.

Lopez didn't reply, but a large teardrop fell on the rug.

The image of Esmeralda's corpse swirled in Tanya's mind. She would never forget the scars on the dead girl's back.

"Was he the one who hit Esmeralda?" said Tanya. "Is that what your mother told you?"

"It's not him."

Tanya cocked her head. "Then, who hurt your daughter?"

"Her grandfather....that was a long time ago."

Katy's eyes widened.

"Hugo Fernando?" She gulped. "Oh, honey, how did that happen?"

"I didn't know! He hated her. He thought she didn't...she shouldn't be part of the family...."

Lopez covered her face.

Tanya was struggling to repress the frustration gnawing inside of her. Something from Lopez's past had come to haunt her. Forcing her to explain would go nowhere, but this wasn't helping her find the girl's killer.

Tanya got on her haunches and looked into Lopez's eyes.

"I need you to tell me what happened to your daughter after you brought her to Black Rock. How did she end up on the hill? Did she run away? Did Santiago hire someone to kidnap her? Was it him?"

Lopez shook her head. "He didn't know she died. He was devastated when I told him."

Tanya and Katy exchanged a surprised glance.

"He was so angry, he didn't believe me. He told me I was playing a disgusting game to get more from the divorce."

"That's what you were arguing about in your office," said Katy.

Lopez nodded. More tears rolled down her cheeks.

Tanya frowned. "How can you be so sure he didn't hurt Esmeralda? He sounds highly capable to me."

"He loves her," said Lopez, wiping her tears. "If he was going to kill anyone, it would be me. But he would never touch his own daughter. He adored Esmeralda since she was a baby."

Tanya shook her head in astonishment.

Lopez was parroting the exact words she had heard from victims of domestic violence over and over again. Victims always defended their abuser, and couldn't seem to fathom them harming their children, despite the glaring, and most times horrific evidence.

Does she have Stockholm syndrome?

Tanya leaned toward her. "Who is Austin?"

Lopez sat up with a gasp and put her hands over her chest.

"You should have never come." Her voice had hardened. "You're only making things worse."

She got to her feet shakily and pointed at the half-open door with a trembling finger.

"Get out."

Tanya and Katy gaped at her.

"Get out of my home, now!"

Lopez spun around to Tanya, fury in her eyes.

"You told me you wanted to help me. Why are you wasting your time?"

"I'm trying to—"

Without any warning, Lopez flew at her with her fists. Tanya staggered back, protecting her chest with her arms as Lopez rained blows on her.

"Carmen," cried Katy. "Stop it!"

"Find out who killed my baby girl!" screeched Lopez, spittle flying from her mouth. "Do your job!"

That was when Max started to bark outside.

He had spotted something.

Tanya stumbled away from Lopez and leaped toward the open door. She jumped down the front steps, her ears ringing from Lopez's cries and her arms smarting from her blows.

She couldn't believe what had just happened.

Max was whirling around the backseat, howling, like he had spotted an intruder. Tanya scanned the yard, her heart thumping hard, but it was quiet and empty, other than the squad car at the start of the cul de sac.

The driver's side door of the police car opened and out stumbled the junior officer. He adjusted his shirt and walked over casually.

"What's going on?" he called out as he strolled over to the Jeep and peered inside. Max's barks grew louder.

Tanya surveyed the neighborhood.

Someone had come by the house, but not via the street.

"No!"

She whirled around to see Lopez was pushing Katy out of the front door.

"Wait," cried Katy, "you're hurting me."

Lopez pushed her down.

With a startled cry, Katy stumbled down the steps, clutching air.

Chapter Sixty-five

"How are we doing for the warrants?" said Tanya, speaking into her phone.

"The judge is at the summit," said Jack. "She's pushing back, saying we don't have any justifiable reasons. I'm going to try her again before dinner—"

He stopped as someone called out his name. Tanya could hear people chatting in the background. Jack hollered that he was on his way.

His tired voice came through the airwaves.

"I'm in the middle of a meeting with the mayor."

"I have a dead teenage girl on my hands, and we just got confirmation of a familial DNA match. The victim is Lopez's daughter."

Jack fell silent. He was quiet for so long Tanya wasn't sure if the call had dropped.

"Are you still there?"

The chief's voice was more somber when he spoke again.

"Seems like there's a lot to Lopez I didn't know."

"Me neither," said Tanya. "She's not telling us the whole story, which makes me wonder if she's protecting someone."

"How did the girl die?"

"She was strangled and buried in a shallow grave. Not too far from the psychiatric hospital."

"They don't admit children in there, not anymore."

"She wasn't a patient, at least according to the hospital administration. My hypothesis is Esmeralda was visiting someone at the asylum or at the retirement residence when she was killed."

"Sounds like you've got your hands more than full. I wish I could be there."

"Hang in tight and fight the good fight for us, Jack. Katy and Dr. Chen are helping me...."

Tanya glanced behind her at Dr. Chen's closed office door.

"Katy got a few bruises, but the doctor's patching her up at the moment."

"How did that happen?"

"Lopez pushed her down her front steps and slammed the door on her. I don't think she meant to hurt Katy, but she didn't want us around, that's for sure. She's completely freaked out."

"You can't put civilians in danger, Stone." Jack's voice was firm. "Sheriff Reginald is sending his people, and so is the chief of Mountain View. Wait for them to arrive in town. Leave Katy and the doctor out of this."

"We don't have a lot of time," said Tanya. "Lopez is scared out of her mind, like she's expecting something terrible to happen."

Her mind whirled with the thought of the seven women at Silver Serenity. She didn't have time to explain how she knew about the strange goings-on at the retirement residence.

"There's an odd connection between the hospital and Silver Serenity, Jack. If we don't act fast, we may have more than just one dead girl on our hands."

Chapter Sixty-six

Footsteps came from the other end and Jack went quiet.

The chatter receded, and his voice came back on.

"Go after the husband and pin him down," he said in a low voice. "The probability he killed his daughter to spite his wife who's asking for a divorce is high. How many times have we seen that happen?"

"Lopez denies it, but I can't trust her judgment right now," said Tanya, biting her lip. "Funny thing is I never knew who she was married to."

"What do you mean?"

"Her husband is Santiago Fernando. He owns the largest privately held pharmaceutical company—"

"Hang on." Jack's voice was sharp. "Did you say *Santiago Fernando*?"

"Do you know him?"

"His company is sponsoring the summit." His pitch had jumped up a notch. "He's giving the keynote speech at dinner tonight."

Tanya's eyebrows shot up.

"Did he leave in the middle of the summit around midday yesterday?"

"He's been with us the whole time."

"I don't think so. He flew down in a chartered helicopter. He had a heated argument with Lopez at the precinct before flying off. The chopper was booked at the last minute, so this trip wasn't planned. I'd say he was gone for an hour or two, tops."

"I'll dig around here, discreetly. Maybe the hotel staff or the conference organizer noticed him leave."

"He was wearing a weird disguise," said Tanya.

"Like?"

"A black hat, sunglasses, a scarf around his neck, and a pandemic type blue mask. I'd say he covered up as much as he could, so no one would recognize him."

"Huh," said Jack, like he was digesting the news. "That certainly isn't the man I met here."

Tanya sat up.

"What I don't understand is how his company got to sponsor a government event."

"The state's pushing us into private-public partnerships, all in the name of efficiency." Jack sighed heavily. "If you ask me, this is just another means to grease the wheels of lobbying. It's a schmooze fest with lucrative government contracts as the payout."

"But what does a *pharmaceutical* company gain from picking up the tab for an anti-crime summit?"

Jack sighed again. "I can tell you I'll be asking more questions tonight."

Tanya's brain whirled. "Are there journalists at the hotel?"

"Cameras and recording devices are banned," said Jack. "The attendee list is controlled and not shared, not even with me. And there won't be a press release at the end, like usual. This is strictly a working summit."

"No cameras?" said Tanya. "So our man can scoot out for a few hours without leaving a trail?"

Jack went quiet on the other end.

"How much would you bet he's sponsoring your summit for personal gain?" said Tanya.

"What's his endgame?"

"Santiago Fernando," said Tanya, speaking slowly, "created the perfect alibi for himself."

Jack groaned. "The highest law enforcement officers in the state."

"Exactly."

"I'll fight for those warrants," he hissed. "As soon as I get them in my hands, I'm heading back down."

"Don't you have to—"

"Black Rock's facing a bigger menace than I thought. I've left you alone to handle it, and that's not fair."

The Silhouette by the Window

So, Tanya Stone's not backing down, is she?

The dark silhouette was framed by the large bay window. They were alone in the room, gazing out at the view. But their mind was elsewhere.

She can try to find me. But she's never going to come near me.

The lines on their forehead deepened. They were nearing the end of a project that had been a lifetime in the making. They could almost see the finish line.

I'm smarter than them all put together.

The person's face turned hard.

Why can't they understand what I'm doing is good?

I'm working to make this world a better place. I have dedicated my entire life to eradicate this evil and help humanity. And yet, they chase after me, trying to destroy me.

The silhouette let out a heavy sigh like they carried the entirety of the world's problems on their shoulders.

I'm a savior, not a criminal.

They should reward me, not hunt me down like a wild animal.

The silhouette turned around. If anyone else had been in the room, they would have noticed the strange expression on their face.

The figure stepped toward the door, their footsteps as sure and solid as the new goal in their mind.

Tanya Stone is getting close, but I'll be ready.

I'll be waiting.

Chapter Sixty-seven

Tanya finished her call with Jack and glanced around Dr. Chen's clinic.

Where did Max go off to again?

She had been standing in a corner of the reception area, keeping her voice low, and her face away from the handful of patients waiting to see the physician.

A clerk and a nurse were bustling behind the reception desk, and Katy was in the examination room, having the gash on her forehead looked at.

Tanya had caught Katy before she had crashed onto the concrete steps, but not before she had scraped the side of her head on the rusty railing. Tanya had helped her into the Jeep and pressed a gauze from the first-aid kit to her wound.

Only when she pulled out of the driveway, she had spotted Lopez staring out the living-room window.

Lopez's face had been pale and her eyes had been wide in shock. If Tanya had to guess, she had known Katy was hurt, but something significant had a tight grip on her, so much so, she feared to come out and check.

Tanya had stared back at the face that was so familiar, yet so unlike the colleague she had known all along.

Why are you so scared, Lopez?

Tanya hadn't acknowledged her, but had turned the Jeep around and driven to Dr. Chen's clinic, ignoring Katy's protests that she was fine.

Tanya stepped up to the front desk now and leaned toward the clerk, who was tapping on her keyboard.

"Have you seen my dog?"

The clerk looked up.

"Oh, it's you."

She gave her a sheepish smile and swiveled in her chair. Tanya spotted the furry brown back hunched under her desk. Max was crouched low, munching on a pile of cookies.

"Max?"

Tanya snapped her fingers.

He looked up, his ears down and a goofy grin on his face, the remnants of a biscuit dangling from the side of his jaws.

"Drop that, right now."

Max swallowed it in an instant and licked his lips.

"It's...it's organic," stammered the clerk. "It's got real ginger too. No chocolate, I promise."

Tanya shot Max a stern look. "Get out of there now."

He trotted around the desk, his head bowed, and his tail tucked in between his legs.

"You knew that was wrong, but you did it anyway."

Max bowed his head and whined.

Tanya turned to the clerk. "He's on a strict raw food diet."

Sanctioned by the bureau.

The clerk fluttered her eyelashes.

That's not going to work on me.

"He looked so hungry," pleaded the clerk. "I was about to have a cookie when he saw the packet in my hands. He looked at me with those big brown eyes. How can anyone say no to that face?"

Max came over to Tanya and stood in front of her, his head low, like he was expecting a berating.

"Oh, bud."

Tanya bent down and ruffled his head, not having the heart to scold him. He worked hard for her day in and out. An unhealthy but rare treat seemed forgivable.

"Just make sure your vet doesn't hear of this, Max."

"I won't tell," whispered the clerk. "Promise."

"Fine, but no more—"

Tanya's FBI burner phone buzzed in her pocket. With a curse under her breath, she fumbled for it.

Speaking of the bureau. That's got to be Susan Cross, asking for a report.

All Tanya had were pieces to a disturbing puzzle, pieces that didn't seem to be connected by any logic.

There was the murdered girl in the shallow grave near the asylum. Her shocking relationship to Deputy Lopez, and Lopez's wealthy husband whom no one had known existed until now.

She didn't know how much she could rely on Sahara's memories of a drunken night, but Tanya's gut told her the girl's fate had been tied to the mysterious deaths at the retirement community.

But she knew none of these disparate discoveries would satisfy the director. With a sigh, she flipped the phone over.

The words *Silver Serenity* scrolled across the screen.

Her heart jumped to her mouth.

No one in Black Rock knew about her undercover role or her employment at the bureau, except for Ray Jackson, and Katy and Asha.

Her heart pounded as she clicked on the green button and put the phone to her ear.

"Stone? I found something."

Tanya closed her eyes in relief.

Ray Jackson.

"I thought they took your phone. Where are you?"

"At the nurses' station." Ray was whispering, and his voice was uncharacteristically shaky. "There's a landline in the back."

Tanya frowned. "Everything okay?"

"Can't talk, but—"

He stopped abruptly.

Tanya gripped her cell tighter.

"Ray? What's going on?"

Chapter Sixty-eight

The sound of a door banging came through the phone.

Tanya's heart raced.

Then came a clattering noise, like something heavy was moving along a hard surface. Ray Jackson had fallen silent on the other end, but she could hear his laborious breathing.

Tanya straightened up as she realized someone was rolling a medicine or food trolley along a corridor. The sound faded as the trolley moved away.

Ray's voice came back on the phone. "I found the ripped page from the death ledger."

"What? Are you—"

"Get over here right now," he hissed.

"Ray, you need to get out—"

The phone clicked.

Tanya pulled the mobile away from her ear and stared at the screen. Ray Jackson had hung up. Worst-case scenarios swirled through her mind.

Ray didn't get rattled easily and had always proven to control the situations he'd found himself in. Then again, it had been a couple of decades since he had worked in the field.

"I'm fine," came a familiar female voice. "I've got to get back to work."

Tanya spun around to see Katy and Dr. Chen emerge from the back of the clinic. Katy had a bandage on the side of her head, and Dr. Chen was giving her a disapproving look.

The physician thrust a bottle into Katy's hands.

"When you get a headache later, you're going to thank me."

Tanya slipped her phone into her pocket and stepped over to her friend.

"You need to go home."

Katy winced. "I look worse than I feel."

"Listen, I've got to go. It's urgent."

Katy narrowed her eyes. "Where?"

"Silver Serenity. Ray Jackson needs help."

"I'm coming with you."

Tanya shook her head.

"If you're really up for it, look into Santiago Fernando. He's at the crux of this mystery. If he killed his own daughter, we need to nail the rat."

Dr. Chen wagged a finger in her face.

"You're one to talk. You think you can go running around like this? You will crash soon. You should be lying down, resting."

Tanya squared her shoulders. "I've never felt better," she lied.

"You're going to regret not taking my advice," scoffed Dr. Chen. "Seriously, I feel like you all have gone completely nuts on me."

"Is that your official diagnosis?" said Katy with a weak smile.

Ignoring her, Dr. Chen turned to her receptionist.

"Postpone my afternoon's appointments. I'm going to have a serious chat with Lopez. She needs to know about the DNA test results directly from me."

"Not a good idea," said Tanya. "She already knows it's her daughter, plus, I don't think it's safe for you to visit her right now."

Dr. Chen scowled.

"What are you doing about the dead girl in my morgue? She needs closure and a proper burial."

Tanya sighed. "I'm working on it."

She turned to Katy.

"Jack's getting warrants for Silver Serenity and the hospital. If you see anything, can you send them to me ASAP?"

Katy nodded. "I'll guard the fort, but are you sure you want to go up the hill alone?"

"Reinforcements are supposed to arrive today. As soon as they report to the precinct, can you get two more officers stationed at Lopez's house? Send the rest up the hill to the retirement residence."

Katy stared at her. "I'm just the office manager."

"Take whatever powers you need," said Tanya, ignoring Jack's warning words about civilians being involved creeping around the back of her head.

"I need all the help I can get. Besides, the officers don't know your position. Let them think you're in charge."

Without waiting for Katy to answer, Tanya spun on her heels and stepped out of the clinic.

Max raced ahead of her toward the Jeep, like he knew where they were heading.

Chapter Sixty-nine

"We're under a lockdown order."

Tanya's mouth went dry.

She stared at the woman through the glass doors. It was the older nurse who had driven to the cemetery in the golf cart to pick up the man with the scar.

Her name tag read Nurse Priya.

Her face was twisted into a dark scowl and she was glaring at Tanya through the front doors of Silver Serenity. Behind the nurse was the foyer and the main doorway into the retirement building.

Where Ray Jackson was.

"Why the lockdown?" said Tanya, her heart beating faster. "Is everything okay inside?"

"It's the interfering media," said the nurse, unsmilingly. "The paparazzi came up here this morning and started bothering everyone. So, no one is allowed inside or out. Not until the director says so."

"Where's Carolyn? I'd like to speak with her."

"She's busy. She told us not to interrupt her, no matter what."

"This is an emergency."

The nurse's frown deepened.

"You can't come in."

Tanya let out a frustrated hiss. Max was whirling around her legs, as if he wanted to tell her something, but she focused on the nurse behind the glass doors.

"I'm from the Black Rock police precinct. I got a call that someone's in trouble. You need to let me in."

"Must have been a prank call. Everyone's in their room, having lunch. No one's in trouble."

"How do you know that for certain?"

"Because I just finished the rounds and checked up on each resident. You got the wrong information."

Tanya put a hand on the door handle.

"I'd like to double-check."

The nurse pursed her lips.

"Carolyn said you need a warrant to come inside."

Tanya let out a resigned sigh and muttered under her breath.

Hurry up, Jack.

The nurse spun around, stomped through the foyer, and slammed the interior doors shut.

Time to sneak in through the back, like last time.

Tanya stepped away from the main entrance. She turned around to see Max was watching her from halfway down the driveway now. He barked once, as if to call her over. She walked over to him.

He whined as she approached.

"What is it, bud?"

As soon as she got to three feet of him, he whirled around and trotted past the Jeep. He continued down the driveway like he had picked up a scent.

Tanya's heart ticked a beat faster.

Where's he going?

She followed him, swiveling her head back and forth, on high alert.

"Hey."

She jumped, startled to hear the disembodied voice.

Max stepped off the driveway and headed toward the white gazebo in the grounds. Tanya followed him, maintaining her distance a few yards behind her dog.

With another glance back to make sure she was following him, Max climbed up the steps of the hut and disappeared inside.

With her Glock in her hand, Tanya crept up to the gazebo.

Chapter Seventy

"Don't shoot!"

Tanya stared at the two women, hunkered on the floor inside the gazebo. Max was licking their faces, his tail wagging.

"You're such a good boy," whispered Ocean, nuzzling him. "You heard our whistles, didn't you?"

"So, it was you who whistled at me from the woods the other day?"

Ocean pointed at Sahara. "She thought it would be fun to play with you and lure you in."

"Lure me? Seriously—"

"Get down," hissed Sahara. She pointed at the building behind them. "Or Carolyn will know we're in here."

Tanya holstered her weapon and kneeled, her angry eyes darting between Sahara and Ocean.

"I don't have time for games, ladies."

"She's locked us all in," whispered Ocean hoarsely. "She said a bunch of journalists were heading up here to take our pictures and sell them to the tabloids. All because of the woman we buried this week."

Sahara squinted at Tanya. "She was a Hollywood actress, did you know that?"

"How did you two manage to get out in the middle of a lockdown?" said Tanya.

"We never make a fuss, so they don't watch us," said Sahara. "They have their hands full with the others who always want an extra fluffy towel, a sponge bath, more hot tea."

Ocean's blue eyes flashed. "We hate being cooped up in our rooms, so we sneak out of the windows in the back while the staff is busy with the others."

"We told your uncle Ray to do the same, but he made a big mistake last night," said Sahara, her face grave.

Tanya's heart skipped a beat.

"Is he okay?"

Ocean leaned toward her, like she was about to tell a secret.

"Nurse Ana found him wandering around the corridors in the middle of the night. He had another bout of sleepwalking, you see."

"Sleepwalking?"

"He has insomnia, sweetie," said Sahara. "Didn't you know?"

"And he's highly allergic," said Ocean. "He brings his own food and is very careful what he puts into his body. He didn't even eat the chocolate I got him."

"Don't take it the wrong way if your uncle doesn't share these things, sweetie," said Sahara, patting her arm. "He didn't want to bother you, that's all."

"I knew," said Tanya quickly. "I thought he'd got therapy for his....conditions."

"Carolyn was hopping mad last night," said Sahara. "We all heard her. She screamed at Nurse Ana for letting him run about, like it was all her fault. Ray shouted at Carolyn for shouting at Ana. Oh, boy. Big mistake."

Tanya's heart raced. "Where's he now?"

"Stuck in a gilded cage," said Ocean. "Pacing up and down in his room, like a caged tiger, most probably."

"She put a guard by his door." Sahara shook her head. "We tried to tell Ray it's best to fly under the radar, but he's stubborn as a.... Anyway, he asked us to keep an eye out for you."

Tanya raised her head and glanced over the gazebo wall, but the grounds were quiet. She got to her knees and tapped Max on the back.

"Let's go, bud. Time to talk to Uncle Ray."

"Oh! He told us to give you this," said Sahara, reaching into the folds of her oversized blouse. "Where is it, now? I was so sure I put it in the third pocket in my left...." she muttered as she fumbled through her clothing.

Tanya crouched low, wondering if they were pulling her leg again.

"How did you talk to him, if he was locked up and under guard?"

"Benson's a sweetheart," said Ocean.

The male nurse. The one I saw pilfering drugs from Carolyn's office.

"Such a nice young man," said Sahara, still poking around her clothes. "He does anything we ask."

The image of them smoking cigars and drinking wine by the cabin swam to Tanya's mind.

"Nurse Matt Benson's your dealer, isn't he?"

"Dealer?" Ocean pursed her lips. "That's a terrible word. It's not like we've asked him for street drugs or anything."

With an irritated hiss, Sahara got to her knees and fluffed her clothes like a bird shaking its feathers. A cream-colored piece of paper dropped to the floor.

Tanya pounced on it.

She unfolded the note and stared at the neatly written letters. She recognized the handwriting. It was the same she had seen in the ledger that was now held in the evidence cabinet at the precinct.

This was the torn page she and Katy had been searching for.

"Do you know where he got this?" said Tanya.

"I think he came across it during his sleepwalking episode last night," said Sahara. "No idea exactly where."

Tanya read the torn page again.

She scanned the seven names she had seen previously in the ledger. In front of each name was a date and a time, but it was the fourth line that grabbed her attention.

It was the day before the funeral she had crashed into.

Her eyes scrolled down. The next date had been crossed out and a newer date scribbled over it.

Last night.

The last two names had future dates next to them. Tanya's heart raced as she realized what she was holding in her hand.

This wasn't a routine record of patients' names, ages, their illnesses, or even their deaths.

This was a *murder* ledger.

Chapter Seventy-one

Tanya squinted at Sahara and Ocean.

"What happened to the black rose in your hair?" she said, trying to recall which one of them had it pinned behind her ear.

"I put it in a little vase in my bathroom," said Sahara. "Really brightens up the space."

"Did you see a new rose in the towel room after that?" said Tanya, as she glanced down at the dates on the torn page.

"After the lockdown," said Ocean, "we didn't dare to roam inside the building."

"Not because we're scared of Carolyn, mind you," said Sahara, giving Tanya a pointed look. "We have a reputation to uphold."

Tanya glanced behind her, at the residence. The building looked serene, in contrast to the anxiety rising inside of her.

The dates were clear. One victim had died the night before. Another was due to die that evening.

"Ray called an hour ago," said Tanya, swallowing something bitter. "He sounded agitated. I get the feeling something will be coming down soon, and it won't be safe for you to be here."

Ocean sat up, her eyes flashing. "You mean it's going to get dangerous?"

"Why don't you get away for a few days? Find a nice bed-and-breakfast by the ocean in Black Rock."

"But we're having the time of our lives," said Sahara. "So many things have been going on. Exciting things, especially after Ray came to stay with us."

Tanya wasn't sure, but she thought she caught a gleam in their eyes. It was a smug look that said these two ladies knew more than they were sharing.

Ocean nudged her friend's arm. "I'm ready for a smoke break at the cabin. What do you say?"

Tanya shook her head. "You shouldn't be out in the woods alone."

"We're too old to worry about dying, sweetie," said Sahara, brushing past her.

She shuffled on her haunches toward the gazebo entrance. Ocean blew a goodbye kiss at Max and followed her friend out.

A ball of frustration curled in Tanya's stomach as she watched them creep along the grounds and disappear into the forest. She didn't have time to keep an eye on them.

Her priority was Ray.

She was about to call Max, when her public phone buzzed.

"Are you okay?" said Katy on the phone. A hum of low voices came from somewhere behind her.

"Haven't seen Ray yet," said Tanya.

"Dr. Chen called. Her team just finished the toxicology test. It was ricin."

Ricin?

Tanya took a deep breath in. That explained her nasty experience after drinking the water.

"So, somebody was trying to poison Ray."

"Reinforcements are here," said Katy. "I got two more officers to watch Lopez's home. She called me upset, accusing me of spying on her."

"Make sure they keep an eye on the entire perimeter. I have a funny feeling the husband will try to contact her, or send someone to."

"Good thing there's nowhere nearby to land a helicopter," said Katy.

"What about the rest of the team?"

"I divided them into two camps. One for the psychiatric hospital and the other for Silver Serenity, but we're still waiting for one last thing."

Tanya's heart sank.

"The warrants."

"Jack's going to have another chat with the judge. He called it a delicate diplomatic situation, which I gather to mean another hour or two. Should I send the teams, anyway?"

"Hang tight," said Tanya. "I don't want these guys blazing up the hill, alerting Carolyn or whoever."

"Roger that."

"All we have is circumstantial evidence," said Tanya. "We need to work towards a tight case that will hold up in court."

Katy cleared her throat.

"On that note, I dug up some dirt on Lopez's in-laws."

Chapter Seventy-two

"A group of women sued Santiago's father thirty years ago," said Katy on the other end. "Or tried to sue him, anyway."

Tanya frowned. "What was the lawsuit about?"

"A small-time ambulance-chasing attorney represented them. He was asking for a million dollars in damages. The family retaliated with a counter-suit, saying they were being blackmailed."

"Do we have the names of the women?"

"Only the lawyer's," said Katy. "There's nothing after that. It's like the case fizzled out. As usual."

"Did they say how many plaintiffs there were?"

"Seven."

"That can't be a coincidence. These women had to have been extorting money from the Fernandos, and now they're paying for it with their lives."

"Women?" said Katy. "They were teenagers back then. Fifteen, sixteen-year-old girls."

Tanya fingered the torn page of the ledger in her hands.

A teenager thirty years ago would be in her mid to late forties now. She sat back silently, her mind buzzing.

Katy's voice came again. "This time, they were accusing Hugo Fernando of taking their children."

Tanya's jaw dropped. "I thought this was about the sexual abuse claims."

"That was the first civil suit. Those charges were dropped."

Tanya leaned back, trying to gather her entangled thoughts.

"In exchange for giving up their toddlers," Katy was saying, "the teen moms got taken off the streets. According to the article, they got a new home, a car, jewelry, and luxury cruise tickets."

"They sold their children?"

"Imagine a desperate and homeless teen mom trying hard to make ends meet. They probably thought their babies were going to have better lives. We're talking about children who had children. My heart breaks for them."

Tanya could hear Katy click her mouse furiously on the other end.

"The girls got first-class tickets to Mexico with their babies, but returned sans kids and a whole lot richer." The clicking stopped. "If you ask me, Fernando senior was running a child trafficking ring."

"Child traffickers usually bring babies into the US, not take them out." Tanya furrowed her brow. "There's more to this story, Katy."

"I'd bet the lawyer was as crooked as Father Fernando," said Katy. "He saw an opportunity to get a big paycheck by suing the owner of a profitable company. Grosses me out there are people like this in the world."

"Wasn't he attempting to reunite the children with their mothers?"

"Brace yourself," said Katy.

"Can it get any worse?"

"The lawsuit was merely asking for more money for having given up the kids. They didn't want the kids back. Or, at least, that's what the lawyer was demanding."

Tanya recoiled in disgust.

"Where was child protection services? Why didn't law enforcement do their job once this story broke? This should have been a criminal case."

"This article was in the back of *Stars and Scandals.* The feature news that day was on an alien abduction, so you can imagine the reception this got."

Katy's voice broke.

"I can't stop thinking of those poor babies. What happened to them? Where are they now? It's really sad."

Tanya's mind whirred as she forced the puzzle pieces to come together in her head.

"Carolyn could be working for the Fernando family. Maybe she was paid to get rid of these women and silence them for good. Esmeralda just happened to be a bystander and got caught. If I can get Carolyn to open up, we can nail Santiago and his entire corrupt family."

"I don't know what's going on up on the hill, hun," said Katy, her voice high pitched. "But I'm really worried for you. Please wait for reinforcement to join you, okay?"

Tanya glanced back at the building looming in the middle of the grounds.

Not when Ray and the last woman alive might be at risk of death tonight.

Chapter Seventy-three

Tanya hung up and slipped the phone into her pocket.

She gestured to Max.

"Let's get Ray out of here before he becomes victim number eight."

He thumped his tail.

Tanya shuffled toward the edge of the gazebo and crouched low. If anyone was gazing out of the windows, they would be in clear line of sight, but she had no choice.

"Down," she said, getting on her stomach. Max followed her movements, flat on his tummy, his body stuck to hers like glue. Together, they army-crawled across the grounds towards the woods.

Once she was behind the tree line and out of sight, she got to her feet. Tanya was halfway toward Ray's room, when she realized her dog was no longer by her feet.

She whirled around. He was staring in the opposite direction, his ears pointy and his body stiff.

Tanya drew her Glock.

"What is it, bud?" she whispered.

Max wagged his tail to acknowledge her question, but he didn't take his eyes off his target, whatever it was.

Tanya stood quietly next to him, her ears on alert for sounds, her eyes scanning the woods for movement.

It seemed like everything in the world was delaying her main objective. She surveyed the trees, seeking for shadows, but not a leaf stirred. The woods were silent, but she felt the presence of the stranger in her bones.

Whoever they were, they were watching and waiting.

Suddenly, a low whistle came from the woods.

Max's ears pricked up, and he growled a low growl.

Tanya clenched her jaws.

Is that Sahara and Ocean? Are they playing with me again?

She glanced down at her dog. His eyes were beady and his hackles were up. Only moments ago, he had been licking the faces of the two women, his tail wagging happily.

It's someone else.

She signaled to Max and scurried behind a large tree trunk. Max rushed over, but kept his snout doggedly pointed at a thicket several yards ahead.

Tanya aimed her weapon in the direction he was staring at.

Suddenly, a rustle came from behind the bush.

Max growled.

Tanya aimed her Glock at the thicket. Max stood still, his face squinched.

Come out. Come out. Whoever you are.

The bushes rustled some more.

Max leaned forward, ready to pounce.

Tanya put her finger on the trigger.

"Show your face or I shoot!"

A figure stepped out from behind the thicket. The man with the scar.

Chapter Seventy-four

The scarred man was unarmed.

"Stay, bud," said Tanya in a hushed tone, her eyes on the man.

Max sat on his haunches, but ready to attack on command.

The last time Tanya had met the man with the scar, Carolyn had screamed at her and the nurses had elbowed her out. This time, it was just them.

Tanya took a good look at the stranger in their midst. He was tall and thin, and his hair was scraggly and unwashed. His work pants were muddied, and his T-shirt was ripped, like he had been running through the thorny underbrush.

His glazed eyes stared at the barrel of her Glock, like he was hypnotized by it.

"Who are you?" said Tanya.

He turned to her, terror etched in his eyes. He opened his mouth, but only a strange moan rolled through his lips.

Did I frighten him to silence?

Between her, Max, and the Glock, he was completely outnumbered. She withdrew her weapon and holstered it.

"You can put your arms down."

The man moved his hands in a jerky, hesitant fashion, like he wasn't sure if she would draw her gun again and shoot him at any moment.

"What's your name?" said Tanya.

He pushed his chest out and tried to speak again, but the words were even more warbled than before.

Tanya pointed at herself. "Tanya."

Then, she pointed at him. "And you?"

He cleared his throat and swallowed hard.

"S...S...Stu..."

Tanya nodded. "Stu?"

He pointed at the scarred side of his face. "S... S... st...stroke."

"You had a stroke?"

"I... I c... can't...t...t..."

"Talk?" said Tanya. "You can't talk because of a stroke?"

Stu nodded and sighed in relief like he was thankful she understood. Sweat poured down his face like saying those few words had drained all the energy out of him.

Max got to his feet. Stu glanced down at the dog and threw his hands up again.

"I...er...I..."

"This is Max," said Tanya, pointing to her dog. "He doesn't like anyone sneaking up on us. That's why he ran after you."

Stu's eyes traveled from Max to Tanya and back, the lines on his forehead deepening.

"He won't hurt you," said Tanya. "If you relax, he'll relax too."

Stu tilted his head to the side and furrowed his brow.

Tanya put a hand on her chest.

"Breathe. Do like me. Take a deep breath in."

Still frowning in confusion, he inhaled, his entire upper body moving with his breath.

"Good. Now take another deep breath and let it out."

By her feet, Tanya could feel Max softening his posture as well. Her tone had helped more than her words. Max knew instantly when she was under attack, and when she was assisting a victim. This unusual man wasn't a threat anymore.

"What are you doing in the woods?" asked Tanya.

He opened his mouth and shut it, then stared helplessly at her.

Tanya racked her brain on how to communicate with him.

"Stu, I need to know what you were doing outside my window the other day."

Stu pointed into the woods with a shaking finger. Warbled sounds rolled out of his lips, like he had something important to say, but his words were tripping over one another.

"You want to show me something?" said Tanya.

Stu nodded.

"Is that why you whistled at me right now?"

Stu lifted his chin up and let out a whistle, making Max bark.

"It's okay, bud."

Tanya turned to Stu.

"Stu, I'm really sorry I chased you through the woods and got you hurt. I truly am. Is your ankle better?"

Stu blinked.

"Yesterday, when the nurses were strapping you to the stretcher, you mentioned a name. Do you recall what you said?"

He nodded, this time with more vigor than before.

Tanya stepped closer.

"You said *Esmeralda*."

Hearing the name, Stu whipped around and pointed in the direction he had before.

"Chi... chi... Es... Es... Esmeralda."

Chi? What's he talking about?

Esmeralda was lying lifeless in Dr. Chen's morgue at that very moment.

But Stu was insistent. "Es... Esmeralda."

Tanya stared at him. "You know what happened to her, don't you?"

Stu blinked rapidly.

"Show me," whispered Tanya. "Show me what you saw."

Without answering, Stu whirled around and disappeared into the trees.

Chapter Seventy-five

Max dashed after Stu, barking.

Tanya leaped in between the trees before she lost them both.

Stu was scrambling through the woods, meandering around clumps of bushes, giving wide berth to a line of tall spruce trees that seemed to make up the perimeter of the forest.

Tanya followed him and Max deeper into the thicket, maintaining her distance.

Stu seemed to know the path and was sure of his footing, while she had to focus to not trip over rotten logs or slip into potholes hiding under fallen leaves.

"Stu," she called out. "Where are we heading?"

He craned his neck and gestured for her to hurry, but didn't reply.

"Are we going to your cabin?"

He gave her another wave that could have meant anything.

Tanya plodded after him, her eyes alert for intruders.

Soon, the line of trees thinned out and short stumps appeared in their place. They had been moving in parallel to the trail that snaked through the woods.

Through the foliage, Tanya glimpsed a human-made structure. They were walking toward a compound of log cabins arranged in a clearing. The timber walls and high-pitched roofs appeared and disappeared from view as she followed Stu.

She now knew exactly where they were heading.

The psychiatric hospital.

Stu turned around and put a finger to his lips. Whatever he was planning to show her, it wasn't something he wanted to advertise to the world.

He circled the log cabins and stopped at the edge of the compound. Tanya stepped closer to see what he was peering at. He was checking out a nondescript square building situated in the back of the campus. The only window next to the closed back door had been boarded up.

A storage facility? wondered Tanya.

A rotten odor wafted to her nose.

Garbage.

She glanced around to see two massive steel bins at the corner of the building. One had the word *Recycle* on it and the second said *Waste.*

Stu poked his head out from the treeline and swiveled it from side to side. Then, without a word, he scuttled toward the back door.

Tanya scanned their surroundings. There was no one in sight. Her heart skipped a beat.

Maybe I don't need a warrant to get in.

"Let's go, bud." Tanya bent low and scurried over to where Stu was, with Max following in tandem.

She wrinkled her nose. The smell was getting worse.

Stu was fiddling with something near the garbage chute. He was trying to open a small wooden hatch on the side of the wall.

He was pulling on a steel latch, but his fingers kept slipping. Tanya wanted to help, but waited quietly in the background, knowing she couldn't afford to startle or scare him. Not when he was showing her a way to enter the hospital. He was her immunity for trespassing on private property.

With a grunt, Stu finally yanked the latch off and got the hatch open. Tanya cringed at the creaking sound, wondering if anyone could hear from inside the buildings.

Stu stepped through the opening and vanished into a tunnel.

Tanya's hand automatically went to her Glock.

She pulled her weapon out, ducked her head, and followed him inside.

Chapter Seventy-six

Max trotted after Tanya, while Stu scurried in front of them.

They had entered a narrow concrete passageway that inclined downward, like it was heading to the basement of the building.

The foul odor of garbage hung heavy in the air. The only light illuminating the damp corridor was a yellow incandescent bulb that hung from the ceiling in the far end.

Stu was hurrying like he was pressed for time, or he was worried they would be discovered.

Keeping her head bent, Tanya hastened her steps, knowing how bad it would look if anyone found out a member of the Black Rock police precinct had entered the premises without permission.

A loud bang from somewhere in the building made her jump. From behind her, Max growled. Tanya gripped her gun.

"What was that?" she whispered.

Stu turned around and gasped out loud as he saw her Glock. He threw his hands in the air. Even in the darkness, Tanya recognized the horror in his eyes. That explained why he ran off when she had accosted him in the woods.

She leaned toward him.

"Did someone hurt you at one point...with a gun?"

He shuddered visibly and nodded.

"I'm not going to harm you, Stu," she whispered, pushing the gun behind her. "This will protect us. I'm only carrying it in case someone's waiting for us down there."

His eyes widened at those last words, and the color drained from his face. She could smell his terror.

"Whoever you're scared of, they're not going to get you. I'm a police officer. It's my job to keep you safe."

He didn't move.

Tanya narrowed her eyes. Whatever he wanted to show her might be the last pieces to the puzzle she was struggling to build.

She tried again. "Do you want me to go first?"

Stu nodded.

Tanya reached for the flashlight in her pocket and stepped around him. There was a steel door about five yards ahead of them, where the lonely bulb hung from the ceiling.

She turned her light up to see what was above their heads. It was a plain concrete slab. That was where the bang had come from.

"Are we under the kitchen?" she whispered.

Stu shook his head. "Ware...ware...house."

Tanya walked over to the steel door at the end.

"Is anyone in there?" she whispered. Stu cowered like he didn't want to even imagine the thought.

Aiming her Glock forward, Tanya pushed down on the handle. To her surprise, it opened easily and quietly.

She stepped into the small space. Behind her, Stu shuffled in and touched something on the wall by the door. A pale light flickered to life.

It was a stockroom with not much ventilation. The air reeked of an unwashed musty smell.

The shelving against the walls were stacked with cans of food, packages of dried staples, water barrels, and firewood. Along the far wall was a row of flower pots, garden utensils, and a lawn mower that looked like it had reached the end of its life.

Whoever came down here kept things neat and tidy. But it was the center of the room that had Tanya's full attention.

Two naked mattresses lay side by side on the ground, with a pile of blankets, sheets, and pillows neatly folded on top.

She turned to Stu who was hovering by the door, eyes averted like he was trying hard to not notice her gun.

It was time for some answers.

"Was Esmeralda here?"

Chapter Seventy-seven

Stu stood in his spot, his eyes darting nervously back and forth.

"Y...y...yes...."

Tanya pointed at the second mattress.

"Who was she with?"

Stu blinked but didn't answer.

"Was it you?"

He jerked back, horror etched on his face. He flailed his arms.

"No! N... No! No!"

"It's okay. I believe you," said Tanya. "Was it another man?"

He moved his head from side to side.

"Was it a woman?"

Another shake of his head.

"A second girl?"

He sighed and looked away.

"Or, was it a boy?" said Tanya, leaning in.

Stu clamped his mouth shut.

"What are you hiding from me?"

"I.... can't... she... she... told me... I can't... I mustn't...."

"Who is this *she*?"

Stu covered his face.

"Who are you afraid of, Stu? Is it Carolyn? The director of Silver Serenity? Or someone else?"

Stu kept his hands on his face, hiding his expression.

Tanya stared at the mattresses, wondering what motive Carolyn would have had to keep Esmeralda in this musty little stockroom.

Was Esmeralda brought here to be abused? Was she kept captive for ransom? Or was it an abduction for reasons she couldn't even fathom yet?

She scanned the shelves for clues. There were no clothes, leftover food, personal items, or any evidence of a girl's presence, other than the mattresses and the neatly folded sheets. A forensics team might discover DNA evidence, but for that, she would need a warrant.

Tanya stepped to the steel door on the other end of the room and tried the handle. It was locked. She looked back at Stu, but he shrugged like he didn't know how to get in either. Or he was too afraid to open it for her.

"What's on the other side?"

"M...more s...sto...."

"Storage?" said Tanya.

"Y...yes."

In an alcove next to the steel door was a closet, or what looked like one. Tanya stepped up to it and slid the wooden door to the side.

She flipped the light switch on. It was a tiny bathroom with a sink, toilet, and a showerhead in the corner. It was impeccably clean inside.

A small shelving unit carried towels, wrapped soaps, and toothpaste. Stacked on the bottom most shelf were four ceramic plates with silver forks on them. She stared at the double "S" Silver Serenity logo engraved on the plates.

She stepped back into the stockroom where Stu was waiting, his nervous eyes on Max.

"You brought Esmeralda her meals."

Stu gave her a startled glance, then nodded.

"Did you get free dinners from the residence's kitchen in exchange for your handywork?"

He nodded again, swaying on his feet.

"That's how her...." Tanya stopped herself in time.

That's how her stomach contents contained the remnants of a Chateaubriand steak and a gourmet salad.

Was Stu trying to hide the girl from danger?

Or was he keeping her prisoner?

She turned to close the bathroom door when she saw it. The glass vase was tucked behind a pile of firewood on the floor.

It was an uncanny anachronism to find in this dingy underground room. Tanya blinked, wondering if she was seeing things.

There was no water in the vase, but the long-stemmed black rose stood gracefully on its own.

It had been freshly cut.

Chapter Seventy-eight

S tu was watching her, wringing his hands.

Tanya pointed at the vase.

"Did you bring that flower here?"

He nodded.

"It's from your garden, right?"

"Y...yes...."

"Is it a signal?"

Another nod, but the fear in his eyes deepened.

"I...want...wanted t..to...to...t...te...tell....abou...about...the...d....deaths." He let out a breath like he was exhausted just to put those words together.

Tanya's heart ticked faster.

He was trying to warn someone about the deaths.

Stu stared at her hopelessly like he wished he could explain himself better. Tanya pulled out her mobile.

"Can you type out what you're trying to tell me?"

He stumbled back and waved her away, like he didn't want to touch the device.

"What if I gave you a piece of paper and a pencil?"

"I....c...can't...." He mimed writing. "I...can't write...anymore...."

The stroke.

Tanya tapped her foot on the floor in impatience.

"Stu, we've got to find a way for us to communicate. We need to know what happened to Esmeralda."

Stu stared at her helplessly.

"Point at a picture. Say the name. I promise you, I'll make sure you'll be safe from whoever it is."

Stu's eyes filled with tears.

"Es... Es... Esme...Esmeralda is d...dead."

Tanya could see the heartbreak on his face.

She wanted to reach out and tell him it was going to be okay, but a calloused part of her also wondered what role he played in the kidnapping and murder of Lopez's daughter.

Who commissioned Esmeralda's death? Was it Santiago Fernando? Carolyn? Or both? Did they force Stu to kill the girl?

She stepped closer to him.

"Did Esmeralda ever visit Silver Serenity?"

Stu nodded.

"Often?"

Another nod.

"Do you know who she was—"

A loud thud came from the floor above, making them jump. The sound was followed by heavy footsteps, like someone was stomping right over their heads.

Stu whirled around, with a stifled cry.

Before Tanya could do anything, he scrambled around and disappeared back into the tunnel.

Chapter Seventy-nine

Max raced after Stu with Tanya right behind him.

Stu leaped out of the hatch and zoomed along the wall, moving at lightning speed.

Tanya jumped out of the tunnel, expecting to race after him into the woods, but he dashed toward the back door, pushed it open, and slammed it in Max's face.

Max stood in front of the door, his hackles up, barking.

Tanya yanked the door handle just as the bolt locked into position. The door shook but held steady.

She glared at the entrance, her heart racing. She lifted her eyes and examined the boarded-up window, cursing herself for not being fast enough. Her gut told her Lopez and Esmeralda's secrets lay inside this building.

Max stopped barking. Tanya was about to bang on the door and call out to Stu, when he whirled around and stiffened.

A crash came from somewhere in the building, followed by running footsteps.

Someone's coming this way.

The footsteps got louder.

Tanya pulled her Glock out. She scuttled to the end of the wall with Max in lockstep with her. The sound of someone cursing came from around the corner.

Tanya pressed her back against the wall, her shoulders taut, her weapon at the ready.

Suddenly, the profile of a short, plump male appeared around the corner.

Max barked.

The man jumped a foot high. He staggered back, tripped over a dead branch, and crashed to the ground. He lay on his back, gasping, staring at the dog.

The cobweb tattoo on his neck was even more exposed now. He wasn't wearing his badge, but Tanya hadn't forgotten the day manager she had met at the front desk.

Paul Hammerston.

This was the man who had steered the aging serial killer away from her, moments after she heard Esmeralda's name for the first time.

A quick glance told Tanya he wasn't armed. She lowered her weapon but didn't holster it. He struggled to his feet and brushed the leaves from his trousers.

"What are you doing here, Paul?" said Tanya, keeping her voice casual.

His face turned purple in fury.

"What the hell are you doing on *my* property?" he spluttered in rage.

"Your property? I didn't realize you owned this entire institution."

He stopped and stared at her. Tanya noticed a flicker cut through his eyes, but it disappeared quickly.

"Put that thing away!" he bellowed, pointing at her Glock. "Guns aren't allowed here. Neither are animals. Take this beast and get out. You can't intimidate us."

Max watched him, growling, like he wanted nothing more than to pounce on him.

"He's a trained K9," said Tanya, in her calmest voice. "We're not here to intimidate anyone."

"You pointed a gun at me!"

"I thought you were an intruder."

"Intruder?" Paul spluttered. He shook a fist in the air. "How dare you? *You're* the one trespassing!"

Tanya holstered her weapon and dropped her shoulders, trying to look more friendly.

"I'm here because I'm investigating the murder of that young girl."

Paul hissed. "Didn't I tell you? We don't take kids in here."

"How many times do I have to remind you, Paul? She was buried next to your compound. That fact isn't going to go away."

"I don't know how she got up the hill," yelled Paul. "I have no idea how she got buried there, and I sure as hell don't know how she died!"

Tanya pointed at the recycling and garbage bins at the back.

"Who comes back here, usually? Your kitchen staff? The cleaners?"

"Don't be stupid. The kitchen has garbage and recycling chutes. No one comes here, except for the city garbage truck once a week." He glared. "Whatever stupid story you're concocting in that dumb head of yours isn't going to fly."

Tanya inclined her head and gave him an innocent look. "If no one needs to come here, what are you doing out here?"

That dark flicker crossed his eyes again.

"I... I heard a sound in the back, so I came to check. It's my job."

Tanya glanced around the leaf-strewn backyard, then at the bins.

"If you wanted to hide a young girl without anyone seeing, this would be the perfect spot, wouldn't it?"

He stared at her, his mouth open.

"Are you accusing me of kidnapping, Detective?"

"I just want to understand what happened to the victim. Maybe one of your staff knows."

"This is a reputable institution. We have strict procedures. We don't hire any idiot off the streets."

But they sure seem to have no issues with ex-convicts, thought Tanya.

"What do you know about organizational policies, anyway," he sneered. "You're just a dumb cop."

Tanya ignored the insult. "Have you hired anyone recently?"

"Everyone's been here for years."

"How long have you worked here?"

His face turned red. He pointed a shaking finger at his chest. "Do I look like a murderer?"

Way to avoid my question.

"Criminals come in all shapes, sizes, colors, classes, and genders. We, dumb cops, try not to make the mistake of stereotyping."

Paul stepped up to her. He only came to the level of her shoulders, but his eyes blazed in fury.

"If you don't have any reasonable grounds for arresting my staff or myself for this horrific crime," he said through gritted teeth, "I suggest you leave now."

Tanya looked down at him, her gaze steady.

"If you have nothing to worry about, why don't you cooperate? I'll take a quick look around the premises and get out of your hair. I promise I won't disturb your patients."

Paul shoved a finger in her face.

"Like hell I will let you in. Not even if you stick that gun on me again. You need a warrant and you know that. Now, get out!"

Paul stepped away from her.

"If I see you on my property again, I'll complain to the mayor. I'll complain to the press. I'll let the whole world know you've been harassing us. This is nothing short of excessive use of police force, I tell you."

With a furious hiss, he twirled around and stomped back in the direction from where he came.

Tanya watched him leave. She hadn't missed the small contractions on his face and dark flickers in his eyes as she asked her questions.

Excessive force?

Thou doth protest too much, Paul Hammerston.

Chapter Eighty

"R ay?"

Tanya tapped on the French windows.

The curtains were drawn across the locked patio doors, and his bedroom was plunged in darkness.

"It's Stone. Are you in there?"

She put her ear on the glass panel, but it was quiet inside.

At her feet, Max wasn't wagging his tail or whining to be let in so he could say hello to his friend. He saw her look down and cocked his head.

"Hang on, bud," she whispered. "I'm going to find a way in."

They had been fortunate. They hadn't bumped into anyone as they had slinked through the woodlands back to the retirement residence.

Jack still hadn't secured the warrants. The teams down at the precinct were getting antsy, but Katy was keeping them under control. For now.

The men guarding the dead girl's grave were still at the crime scene. The officers stationed at Lopez's house had nothing new to report, and Lopez herself seemed to have headed to her bedroom and fallen asleep.

All quiet on the western front.

But Tanya knew it was always calm before hell broke loose.

There was still one woman alive inside this building. She was determined to save her and Ray before either were harmed.

Tanya reached into her pocket and brought out her Swiss Army knife.

She surveyed the backyard and the woods to make sure no one was watching. The afternoon sun was shining on the hill, but she was starting to see shadows everywhere.

Bending down so she was at eye level with the lock, she slid her knife in the crack between the doors, and jimmied the latch up and down. It took two long minutes to hear the click of the lock opening. With a sigh of relief, she pushed her fingers in between the glass panels and slid them apart.

She stepped inside and stared into the empty room.

The building was supposedly under lockdown, which meant Ray should have remained in his bedroom. That was, unless he had decided to pretend to sleepwalk again.

Though it was still warm, Tanya felt a chill.

Where is he?

Is he in trouble?

She called to Max. He jumped across the threshold and trotted around the room, sniffing all the corners.

She closed the curtains and turned her flashlight on. Tanya watched her dog work, waiting to see if his sensitive nose would discover clues her human eyes or mind couldn't.

Max did two rounds of the room and the ensuite bathroom. He even sniffed inside the wardrobe which Tanya opened for him.

She reached inside and plucked Ray's bathrobe, which had been hanging on the hook of the wardrobe door. He had worn this when she saw him last. It was still crumpled and had a water stain on the lapel. He hadn't washed it yet.

Perfect.

"Hey, bud," said Tanya, holding it low so Max could sniff the cloth and start his search. That was when the sound of something steel clanked on wood.

Someone was at the door.

Her heart ticked a beat faster.

Ray? Is that you?

She heard keys jingle. Then came the sound of a key being inserted into the lock. The door rattled. A second key was inserted, followed by another rattle of the door.

That meant only one thing.

This wasn't Ray.

Chapter Eighty-one

Tanya switched off her flashlight.

She placed Ray's bathrobe on the hook and closed the wardrobe.

Whispering for Max to follow her, she tiptoed over to the bathroom, and gently closed the door until it was only an inch open.

Max settled on his haunches behind her, his snout pointed at the gap in the door. His body was tense, which meant he didn't know or didn't like the person trying to enter Ray's room.

Tanya waited in the dark, listening to keys being inserted one after the other. It took six excruciating tries. Finally, the person opened the door with a loud exclamation.

The lights turned on.

Matt Benson?

Tanya stared at the male nurse whom she had caught stealing from Carolyn's office.

He pocketed his key ring and closed the door shut. He didn't look anxious. It was like he had been certain Ray wouldn't be in his room and wouldn't be returning soon. But his eyes were shifty. He knew he shouldn't be here.

Benson made a beeline to the nearest bedside table.

He opened the first drawer and rummaged through it. With a disappointed sigh, he slammed it shut and opened the next drawer. After checking the drawers, he straightened up and scanned the room, a frown on his face.

Tanya pulled back. The bathroom door had an embedded stained glass deco in the middle. She wasn't sure if he could see their shadows behind it, so she crouched low, her heart thumping.

Is Benson the killer?

Or did the killer send him to find the missing ledger?

Tanya reached into her holster and brought her Glock out, silently praying Ray wasn't in danger. Or worse.

She peeked through the opening.

Benson was going through the second bedside table now. Suddenly, his back stiffened. He straightened up and held a yellow plastic container to the light, and a wide smile broke across his face.

Pills?

Tanya's brow furrowed.

Is he stealing drugs from the residents too?

She glanced down and nodded at Max. He understood what that meant. He got to his feet, his tail swishing, as if to say he was ready.

Tanya pushed the bathroom door open and slipped inside the room. She crept toward the poster bed with Max glued to her thighs, their feet sinking into the thick carpet. Nurse Benson was so busy searching for his pills, he didn't even hear them approach.

Tanya came around the bed and stepped closer to him.

She placed the barrel of her Glock on the base of his nape.

Benson let out a bloodcurdling wail and leaped onto the bed. Tanya jerked her head back as a steel blade slashed the air in front of her face.

Benson had a small dagger in his hands.

Tanya thrust her Glock toward him.

"Put that down!"

Chapter Eighty-two

"**G** it away from me!" screeched Benson, slashing the air.

Max howled at him, ready to jump on the bed and take him down on command.

Ray had told Tanya these rooms were soundproofed, but still, Benson's screams and Max's barks could attract attention she didn't need at the moment.

"For heaven's sake," said Tanya. "Would you calm down?"

The nurse stopped waving his knife and stared at the barrel of the gun, his face white in fear.

"I'm not going to shoot you," said Tanya in a low voice. She pointed at his dagger. "Put that away and I'll holster my weapon."

His face flushed.

"I don't wanna go to jail again."

Tanya reached over and pried the blade from his fingers.

"What were you incarcerated for?" she said, as she slipped the dagger in her pocket.

Benson looked away and brushed the sweat from his forehead.

"Opioids...," he mumbled.

Why does everyone I meet on this hill have prison records?

"I already told the cops," said Benson, his voice high pitched. "My friend pushed his stash on me. He knew they were coming after him. He told me to stick it under my mattress. He was the dealer, man. Not me. I swear."

Tanya watched his face as he babbled nervously.

"I never sold no drugs." He turned pleading eyes on her. "I'm a junkie. I know I gotta get clean, man. Don't you think I know that?"

"I believe you," said Tanya.

Benson's jaw dropped. "You won't haul me to jail, then?"

"You procure alcohol and tobacco for Ocean and Sahara. Only a good man would risk his job to give those ladies some joy." She paused. "If you cooperate with me, I'd be happy to negotiate a deal for you."

Benson stared at her. "What do I gotta do?"

"Talk," said Tanya, holstering her weapon. "Where's Ray Jackson?"

"Saw him in the kitchen just now."

"What was he doing there?"

"Snooping like usual. Don't know what he's looking for, but he's always in places he shouldn't be."

"Was he okay? Did he look like he was in trouble?"

Benson furrowed his brows.

"Looked fine to me. He had his head in the fridge when I came here. I like him snooping around because I get to...." He gulped.

"Come here and steal drugs?" said Tanya, finishing his sentence. He gave her a glum look. "Didn't mean any harm, I swear."

Tanya leaned in.

"Did Carolyn know you had a prison record when she hired you?"

Benson shrugged. "We all got records here."

Tanya raised a brow.

Really?

"How did she find you?"

"She used to be a prison guard." He looked up at Tanya. "Man, everyone was so scared of her. She got death threats every day, but she was a tough one."

That could explain her concealed carry.

"She told me she'd get me out early if I took on a job. I got lucky, man. A nice bed, real good food, and—"

"Access to free drugs," said Tanya, pointing at the spilled pill bottle on the floor.

Benson's shoulders drooped. "I swear I didn't mean to. I was just... some days are real rough, you know...."

He looked as miserable as a true junkie would, being delayed of his next fix.

"If I stayed in prison, they'd have killed me, man. Carolyn saved my life." He spread his arms out. "This place is heaven. I couldn't believe it when she told me this was my new home."

"I bet you practically work for free."

Benson shrugged. "I got my freedom, man."

"What about the other staff members?" said Tanya, glad he was talkative.

"She got five of us out early for good behavior. Three from the men's prison and two from the women's."

Cheap labor.

"She seems to be well-connected."

He nodded. "She even bribed the parole officers to stop harassing us."

Carolyn sounds like a law breaker in her own right.

Tanya leaned in and locked eyes with Benson.

"Who is blackmailing Carolyn?"

"I dunno."

"I think you do," said Tanya. "Someone found out she hired ex-cons to run an affluent retirement community without the knowledge of the patrons, and now she has to pay for their silence. Am I right?"

He gaped at her.

"No, man. She's good. She took us in. We're super thankful we don't have to sleep in a cell with a dirty toilet anymore. Why would anyone blackmail her?"

"You tell me."

"She gave us a second life," said Benson. "Except for Ana, but she didn't need it."

Tanya frowned. "Where did Ana come from?"

"Walked in a year ago. Came with a real nurse's certificate too, and all that jazz. Got a job on the spot."

Chapter Eighty-three

"Tell me about Nurse Ana," said Tanya.

"She's a keener," said Benson. "Keeps to herself, but everybody loves to diss her because she works like a dog and makes the rest of us look bad. She's Carolyn's pet, you know what I mean? She's nice to me, though. I like her."

Tanya nodded.

Benson rubbed his face like he was getting tired.

"If she ever found out she's working with a bunch of ex-cons, she'd run away screaming, I swear."

Tanya furrowed her brow. Carolyn had got away with too much for a mere employee of an institution that catered to wealthy seniors. Someone higher than her must have known of her unconventional hiring practices.

And approved of them.

She checked her phone but there were no new messages from Jack or Katy. She turned her focus on Benson again.

"Who owns Silver Serenity?"

"How would I know?"

Tanya leaned toward him.

"Tell me where the third wing is."

He blinked.

"Why are you asking me?"

"You're a staff member here."

"I stick to the wings I'm allowed in. Carolyn tells us nothing. Especially me."

"Have there been any unusual deaths in the residence in the past twelve months?"

"Everybody stayed alive, even old Mrs. Bennington. She's always telling us she can't wait to die and leave her money to her cat, and let her family suffer."

He wrinkled his brow.

"Mr. Wong in room fourteen was super sick when he came in. He never gets out of bed. The doctor keeps saying he's going to die anytime, but he's been hanging on for seventeen months now. Probably gonna outlive everyone else."

"What about the charity cases?" said Tanya.

"The what?"

"The younger women who are admitted with addiction issues. Who takes care of them?"

"Oh, those." Benson shrugged. "Never seen them. Carolyn's super strict about who does what, so we don't know everything that's going on here. I think that's Nurse Priya's job."

Nurse Priya?

That was the woman with the gravelly voice and stern scowl who had refused Tanya entry, only moments ago.

Is she in with Carolyn?

"Are there any rooms that are closed off to you?"

Benson scrunched his eyes. "What do you mean?"

"Where has Carolyn forbidden you to go inside the building? Think hard."

Benson's frown deepened.

Something heavy bumped against the closed door. Then came the jingle of keys. Benson swiveled around the bed with a gasp. Tanya pulled her weapon out.

"Oh no," the nurse whispered hoarsely. "If she finds me here, she's gonna kill me."

Whoever it was, was having better luck than he had. The key slid in to the keyhole and the lock turned.

Is that Ray?

Benson leaped down and scrambled under the bed. Tanya yanked Max by the collar and scurried into the bathroom.

The door creaked open. Benson peeked at Tanya from under the bed, a terrified expression on his face.

Tanya put a finger on her lips and gently closed the bathroom door.

Chapter Eighty-four

From inside the bathroom, Tanya heard the door scrape against the rug.

Through the stained glass deco on her door, she spotted a silhouette. It was a woman.

Is that Carolyn?

The newcomer gasped and flicked the light switch off and on, like she hadn't expected the room to have been lit up. She shut the door behind her and turned the bolt. Whoever it was, she wanted privacy for whatever she was up to.

Tanya strained her ears. A drawer opened and shut like she was on the search for something, like Benson had been.

Everyone's interested in Ray Jackson's room today.

Under the poster bed, Benson had gone completely silent.

Another drawer slammed shut, startling Max who was sitting by Tanya's feet. Tanya placed a hand over his head and stroked his ears to keep him calm. She gripped her Glock, wondering how she got to the point of cowering in a toilet of a pension home.

Where are our warrants, Jack?

"Where is it?"

Tanya almost jumped in surprise. She recognized the voice that had hissed with impatience. It was Nurse Ana, the woman they had just been talking about.

She peeked out through the gap in the door.

Nurse Ana was searching the bookshelf. A book fell to the floor. The nurse dropped to her knees to pick it up, then settled on the carpet and flipped through the pages.

The death ledger, thought Tanya. *Ana's hunting the journal that was locked up in Black Rock's precinct—*

"Please don't hurt me!"

Benson.

Tanya peered out of the narrow gap.

Nurse Ana had spotted him.

"What are you doing under there?" said Ana, bending to see underneath the poster bed.

"I just came to c... clean the r.... room," stammered Benson, scrunched under the bed. "I thought you were... you were.... Carolyn...."

Nurse Ana sat back on her haunches with a sigh.

"You were looking for drugs again, weren't you?" She shook her head. "How many times do I have to tell you, Matt? You're going to get in so much trouble one of these days."

Benson crawled out from under the bed and folded his hands in front of him.

"Please don't tell Carolyn. Please. I'll do anything. I'll do laundry next week. Heck, I'll do *your* laundry, if you want me to."

Ana sighed.

"Didn't she book you in for therapy? You need to go already. It'll do you good."

"I hate doctors," said Benson, looking away. "Why can't everyone just leave me alone? I'm not hurting anyone, am I?"

"You're an addict." Ana's voice had hardened a notch. "You have underlying triggers that drive you to these pills. Get yourself checked or you'll end up on the streets."

Benson hung his head.

Tanya listened quietly, gauging their relationship.

It seemed like Ana hadn't known her colleague that well. Benson had already hit rock bottom and ended up in a far worse place than the streets, if jail could be worse for a junkie.

With a disappointed sigh, Ana got to her feet.

"I won't tell her I saw you. If you don't tell her you saw me either."

Benson looked at her, his brow furrowed.

"Wait. What are you doing here?"

"I'm looking for a book."

"You came for a *book*?"

"A small leather-bound journal," said Ana, scanning the room. "Did you see it?"

"Nope."

She whirled around to him. "Aren't you supposed to be giving Mr. Wong his bath?"

"Er...I... er..." stammered Benson. "Yeah, you're right. I gotta go now."

He didn't wait to be told twice. He scooted out and closed the door behind him.

An eerie silence fell in Ray's room.

Behind the bathroom door, Tanya stopped breathing. She could feel Ana's pulsating presence on the other side.

She wondered if the nurse could feel her too.

Chapter Eighty-five

Tanya moved her eye toward the gap in the doorway.

Ana was examining Ray's liquor cabinet.

The nurse hovered over the alcohol tray. She slipped one hand into her pocket, brought out a purple vial, and loosened the lid. Tanya watched as she slipped a few drops into Ray's rum decanter.

Is that ricin?

Ana's target had been Ray all along. Since he hadn't drunk the contaminated water, she was going for his favorite drink.

But this was good news. It meant he was alive, somewhere in the building.

Tanya scrunched her eyes to recall the criminal psychology cases she studied as a recruit at Quantico. Something about Ana's behavior didn't make sense.

The nurse had moved to the cupboards, opening and shutting them, scrutinizing Ray's personal stash of snacks and beverages.

Tanya unfurled herself to her full height and looked down at Max, who cocked his head. It was time to unearth who Nurse Ana was really working for. With a nod to her dog, Tanya put her hand on the handle.

A thud made her freeze.

Tanya's heart hammered. For one split second, she imagined Ana had spotted her silhouette through the bathroom door.

The knock came again.

Someone's rapping on the door.

Ray's room was more popular than a train stop on a weekend.

Who is it now?

Tanya peeked through the opening, wondering if Ocean and Sahara had arrived for their regular tryst with their boy toy.

Ana opened the door and popped her head out. Whoever was on the other side, didn't speak.

"Coming right away," said Ana, like she had been summoned by someone important.

Carolyn?

Nurse Ana shut the cupboard doors, and gave the room a sweeping glance as if to make sure everything was as she had found it. Then, she scurried out, like she was in a hurry.

Behind the bathroom door, Tanya relaxed her shoulders.

What's going on in this place?

Her phone buzzed in her pocket. She scrambled for it and checked the screen.

"No one wants to touch Silver Serenity." Katy sighed on the other end. "It's like sacred ground. Jack's been getting the run-around from judge to judge, but he's pressuring them hard."

Tanya frowned. "With Santiago Fernando sponsoring the gig, I wonder if there's been undue influence."

"Jack said he's beginning to feel like a ping-pong ball."

"He won't give up. He'll find a way."

"I sent the backup teams to the foot of the hill," said Katy. "They're ready and waiting for the green light."

"As soon as you see even a hint of a warrant, tell them to come up. I'll take the blame if we get flack. Send half to the asylum and half here. They have a lot of ground to cover."

"Roger that." Katy paused. "What about you?"

"I saw Nurse Ana trying to poison Ray's rum. I need to find him pronto. Hopefully, safe and in one piece."

"Don't tell me you've gone inside on your own."

"There's one more woman left, and I'd prefer to find her alive."

"Jack said you have to wait for backup."

"I'm not alone," said Tanya, glancing down at her dog, sitting faithfully by her.

"Tell Max to keep an eye on his mommy."

"I've survived the killing fields of Ukraine, I can handle rogue hospital staff and a few retirees."

"Famous last words," muttered Katy on the other end. "Are you both wearing your vests?"

"Don't worry. No one's going to shoot at us inside a pension home."

Tanya hung up and stepped out of the bathroom.

Chapter Eighty-six

The corridor outside Ray's room was eerily quiet.

Tanya wondered about the other residents. Being locked up for hours, in even the most extravagant of accommodations, would wear out anyone's sanity.

She stepped up to the door next to Ray's room and put her ear against it.

She knew Silver Serenity's most prized attribute was privacy, but she wasn't sure if her inability to hear anything meant everyone was sleeping, drugged, or if the rooms were just heavily insulated.

Making sure to remain in the shadows, Tanya crept down the labyrinth of corridors. She kept a sharp eye out for Nurse Ana and her mysterious companion. Max trotted close to her, his body glued to her thighs, and his ears pricked.

He wasn't growling or stopping to sniff any of the closed doors they passed. But Tanya kept her sidearm at the ready, stopping at every junction to scan all sides before walking into a new hallway.

She retraced her steps back to Carolyn's office.

The office door was wide open, but the director was nowhere to be seen. Tanya slipped inside and appraised the space while Max guarded the door, his snout pointed toward the corridor, ready to warn her of anyone coming their way.

Everything seemed to be in place. The drug cabinet in the back was locked. Nothing seemed amiss. Tanya approached the desk and pushed the keyboard aside. The yellow sticky note with Carolyn's password was gone.

She narrowed her eyes.

Carolyn's smartened up.

Tanya was about to leave the room when she spotted the book with the gold-embossed font on the spine. It was an oversized tome that jutted out from the top shelf. The title read *Silver Serenity, Twenty-Five Years of Service.*

She stepped up to the bookshelf and plucked it out.

How did I miss this?

She opened to the table of contents and scrolled down the list. Her eyes traveled down the history of the residence, its famous donors, noteworthy fund-raising events, and stopped on the line she was looking for.

Architecture.

She flipped to the middle of the book and stared at the image that spread across the centerfold. It was a schematic representation of the building when it was constructed.

Tanya scanned the three wings.

The two primary annexes faced the front of the residence's grounds, and were sectioned off into compartments, labeled as residents' rooms, nurses' stations, doctor's office, staff break room, business office....

Her fingers scrolled to the shorter section that jutted out from the back.

Storage & Delivery.

There seemed to be what looked like a large entrance that separated this structure from the rest of the building.

The third wing.

Is this where the women were kept?

She snapped a photo of the map from her phone and placed the book back in its spot.

Max craned his neck and thumped his tail as she came over to him by the door.

"Good job, bud," whispered Tanya. "We have a rescue mission to get to."

Chapter Eighty-seven

Tanya scurried in the direction of the third wing, using the photo to guide her.

She was glad to have a schema of the building, as once she left the main area, the hallways got more convoluted.

She turned a corner and stared at the closed double doors that greeted her eyes. She looked down on her phone to situate herself.

The third wing.

Without the map, it would have taken her longer to get to her destination.

Tanya crept stealthily along the hallway toward the entrance, when she noticed an open door only a few feet down the corridor.

Her heart beat faster.

Gesturing for Max to slow down, she snuck toward the open door. After a check to make sure the coast was clear, she pressed her back to the wall and listened.

At her feet, Max was waiting for her next move, watching her calmly. That meant only one thing. There was no one inside the room.

Tanya inched closer.

A loud gong made her jump. The hair on the back of her neck sprang up. It took her a second to realize what it was.

The grandfather clock.

Tanya stood shaking, as the clock chimed. She took a deep breath in and peeked in through the open doorway. Max was right, as usual.

It was an empty stockroom.

She stepped inside and surveyed the stainless-steel shelves stacked high with high-end monogrammed bed linen, thick and fluffy towels, and a variety of toiletries for the residents' rooms.

A recent memory stirred in the recesses of her brain. She racked her mind to recall the details, but they slipped from her. She scanned the shelves again, and that was when she saw it.

A long-stemmed black rose stood in a waterless vase that had been tucked behind a stack of towels.

She blinked. The vase and the rose looked exactly like what she'd seen down in the hatch at the asylum, next door.

Did Stu bring it here?

Her blood went cold.

Is this a warning of the last woman's death?

Suddenly, Max whirled around and growled.

Chapter Eighty-eight

Tanya stepped up to the door and peeked into the corridor.

She couldn't see anyone, but Max had smelled something. She turned toward the double doors at the end of the hallway. Tapping her dog on his head to let him know they were going to move again, she scuttled along the corridor toward the entrance.

She stopped and listened, but it seemed this wing was as soundproofed as the others. She tried the handle, but it held firm.

Tanya pulled out her pocketknife.

After glancing behind her to check if anyone was watching, she bent down and picked the lock. This time, it took her four full minutes. By the time she was done, a river of sweat was trickling down her back.

She reached for the handle and pushed it open, aiming her Glock through the opening. But no one was on the other side.

At her feet, Max was on guard, his ears pricked and his tail up. Tanya stepped inside the wing and closed the door behind them.

A shiver went through her as the cool air hit her, even though she was wearing a thick vest.

The corridor was stark and cold, a contrast to the luxurious surroundings she'd just left. The concrete floor was naked, the walls were whitewashed, and the strong smell of antiseptic permeated the unwelcoming space.

There were six rooms on either side of the wing. At the far end was a massive steel door with a red exit sign which she presumed opened to the woods in the back.

She surveyed the hallway, wondering what lay behind these closed doors.

"Hey, bud," she whispered to Max. "Is anyone here?"

He turned to her and cocked his head. Tanya sighed. Of course, he couldn't search for something without a basis for it, like a specific odor, a piece of clothing, or anything that might—

Without a warning, Max perked his ears and trotted down the corridor. He stepped up to the second door on the left and sat down, with a pointed look that told her he had found something.

Tanya scurried over and put a hand on the doorknob. With her sidearm aimed forward, she pushed it down. To her surprise, the door swung open.

The overpowering smell of bleach stung her nose. Max trotted inside and sneezed. He circled the elevated hospital bed that was installed in the middle of the room. He didn't seem to notice the horror etched on the occupant's face.

The bank of monitors surrounding the bed beeped loudly, their green screens casting a ghostly hue on the patient's face. On the ceiling above her bed, a single fluorescent bulb buzzed like a vulture hovering over its prey.

Tanya holstered her weapon and shut the door behind her.

The last woman alive.

Chapter Eighty-nine

Heavy plumes of cleaning bleach hung in the air, threatening to burn Tanya's lungs.

Behind her, Max sneezed again. He had taken position by the closed door, on guard, ready to alert her.

She wondered how long the patient had survived in this badly lit, closed room, immersed in this invisible toxic soup.

I need to get her and Max out of here ASAP.

She turned to the woman on the hospital bed and showed her empty palms to indicate she wasn't a threat.

"I'm here to help you," she said.

The woman's face contorted into a scream, but no sound came out.

Tanya took a step toward her.

"It's okay. It's okay. I'm here to get you out."

The woman thrashed back and forth, making the bed sway, her arms and legs jerking violently under her blanket. With a cold chill, Tanya realized she was tied to the bed's railings.

The medical monitors beeped faster. The graphs turned into jagged peaks like those of a mountain range. Tanya glanced at them in alarm, wondering who was watching the woman's vitals.

Is it Carolyn?

Nurse Benson?

Nurse Ana?

The mousy Ana was the last person she'd have suspected as being a killer. She was still reeling from seeing her try to poison Ray's rum.

Is everyone at Silver Serenity in on this?

Either way, she could do without unwanted visitors right now.

"Relax," said Tanya, her own heart racing in tandem with the intensified beeps from the computers. "Or I won't be able to get you out of here. Stay still and let me unhook you from the bed."

The woman stopped fighting and stared at her wide-eyed.

"Who... who...are you?" she whispered hoarsely, like it had been many days since she last spoke.

"I'm a police detective."

The woman's eyes widened. She glanced mutely at Max by the door, then back at Tanya.

"I work for the Black Rock police precinct. My dog's name is Max. He's a trained K9." Tanya cocked her head. "What's your name, hun?"

The woman swallowed hard.

"J... Jane." She pointed her chin at the nightstand. "Wa...wa...water...."

Tanya turned to see a jug filled with a transparent liquid, similar to what she saw in Ray's room. A chill went through her.

"I'll get you clean water once we leave here."

"P... please," croaked the woman. "I'm th... thirsty...."

Tanya lifted the jug to her nose and sniffed, but all she could smell was the overpowering odor of bleach that seeped into every nook and cranny in this room. Ricin was colorless, odorless, and tasteless, anyway.

She placed the jug down and plucked out the small bottle of water she carried for Max in her cargo pocket.

Jane leaned forward while Tanya held the bottle to her lips. The way the woman gulped it down told her she had been dehydrated for hours.

Once the water was gone, Jane looked up and tears welled in her eyes.

"They...they...want... to kill me." She spoke hesitatingly, but her voice wasn't as hoarse as before. "They injected me...with so many things...."

"Do you know who brought you here?"

"I don't remember...."

"Was it a woman? Or a man?"

Jane sighed heavily. "I... just w... want to go h...home."

Tanya tugged the blanket off of her. Her eyes widened to see the black Velcro straps that locked Jane's wrists to the bedrail.

"This is a p...prison," whispered Jane.

Tanya leaned over and ripped the strap off her left hand.

Jane stared at her freed arm. She didn't pull back, like she had been tied for so long, she no longer remembered how to move her limbs.

The monitors beeped fast again.

"Could you try to remain calm while I untie you, hun?" said Tanya, scooting over to the other side of the bed where the bank of computers sat. "If you don't, Carolyn might come in here and make things difficult for us."

Jane peered at her. "Who's Carolyn?"

"The director of Silver Serenity. Middle-aged woman with short hair, dyed blue. She brought you in here against your wishes, didn't she? "

Jane stared at her with a blank look. "Never... seen her."

Chapter Ninety

T anya examined the tubes sticking out of Jane's arms.

Two tubes came from what looked like insulin bags behind the headboard, while the others were connected to the monitors. She bit her lip, knowing if she removed one needle the wrong way, Jane could get injured.

This is harder than defusing a bomb.

"They brought me here b...because of what h...happened to my b....baby b....boy, didn't they?" Tears rolled down Jane's face.

Tanya turned from the computers, back to Jane's arms again.

"I was a good mother." Jane was speaking in a soft voice, almost to herself. "I tried my best. This is my k...karma. I should have never given my baby away."

Tanya half listened as she traced one wire to a monitor.

If I disconnect this, will the computer alert Carolyn? Or whoever is watching Jane?

No one had burst into the room yet, but she couldn't count on that remaining the case. Whatever luck she'd had so far, it wouldn't last long.

"I knew I was going to pay for my sins one day." Jane rocked back and forth, her face a picture of misery. "I wish I were dead!"

She started to shake. The graph lines went haywire and the beeps from the monitors became erratic. Tanya knew if she didn't calm down fast enough, she and Max would have their hands more than full.

Get those ties off.

"Remember to breathe," said Tanya, as she scurried around the bed, ripping off the Velcro straps that held Jane down.

"He tricked me, you know," said Jane, her voice high pitched. "I believed him. I was just a stupid kid living on the streets. I was so lost. That little girl tried to warn me. She knew what was going on, but we never listened."

Tanya looked up. "What little girl?"

But Jane was so enveloped in her sadness, she didn't seem to hear.

Tanya was removing the last strap that tied Jane's leg to the rail when she spotted the yellow tube. It snaked down Jane's thighs and disappeared into a plastic bag at the bottom of the bed.

Tanya's stomach sank.

A catheter.

This was going to take longer than she expected.

"There were seven of us." Jane was babbling to herself. "We were besties ever since we ran away from our homes. We were barely surviving. We gave up our babies for what? The money? The houses? The cars?"

"We're going to get you home soon, hun," said Tanya, as she racked her brain.

"We had nothing," cried Jane. "Nothing, do you understand? We went from sleeping in garbage bags to a huge house with three bathrooms. But none of that was worth what he did to my baby."

Tanya stepped up to her and put a hand on her arm.

"Right now, I need you to help me if you want to get out of here alive. Let's focus on that first. You can tell me everything once we're free, okay?"

Tanya ducked down to figure out how to remove the catheter from the bed.

"He started with Isabella," Jane continued, like she hadn't heard her. "She was the pretty one. She had long black hair and those beautiful Latina eyes—"

Tanya snapped her head back up.

"There was a Latina in your group?"

"She became a movie star," nodded Jane. "He found a Hollywood agent for her too. It was all part of the deal."

What deal?

"Did Isabella use a different name when she was younger?" said Tanya.

"Her agent called her Isabella Rose because it was better for Hollywood."

"What was her original family name?" said Tanya.

"Lopez."

Chapter Ninety-one

Tanya's brain swirled like a violent thunderstorm.

Isabella Lopez.

Could that be Lopez's mother? Did Lopez bring her into Silver Serenity?

The actress. It was her funeral Tanya had crashed only a few days ago.

The pallid face of the young girl in the shallow grave swam to her mind.

Was Esmeralda visiting her grandmother the night she was murdered? Is that why the girl was killed?

The puzzle pieces were slowly coming together, but some were still fuzzy.

"They took our babies and now they're killing us, one by one," whimpered Jane. "I will die here."

"Listen to me." Tanya leaned over the bed. "I will protect you. But I need you to stay completely calm while I figure out how to get you out, okay?"

Jane's chest heaved, but she nodded.

Tanya squeezed her leg. "Now breathe, hun. Breathe for me."

Jane wiped her tears with the back of her hands and took a shaky breath in.

Tanya pulled her phone out and dialed.

"Katy, send backup. At the residence. Third annex in the back, by the woods."

Katy's voice came clearly through the line. "But Jack hasn't—"

"Doesn't matter. Get an ambulance here immediately. I have a dehydrated victim hooked up to a catheter and monitors. She needs emergency care. Tell the teams to gear up. Our suspects may be armed."

Tanya ended the call and brushed the sweat off her brow.

"I should have said no," moaned Jane. "All he wanted was to sell drugs and make lots of money. He told us children were better than testing on animals. He was a monster!"

Tanya's hands froze on her phone.

"Who's that? Hugo Fernando?"

"He thought he was doing the world a favor by finding a cure for an incurable disease. But did he have to test on our babies?"

"The pharmaceutical company used your stolen children as lab rats?"

"That's why he took them." Jane hugged herself tighter. "My boy's father tortured his own son. His own son, I tell you!"

Tanya's heart raced. This was too fantastic to fathom.

"Was your baby's father Hugo Fernando, too?"

Jane let out a sob.

Tanya blinked rapidly.

"The same man who owns the company?"

Jane nodded, too distraught to speak now. Tanya stared at the sobbing woman, speechless.

The owner of the pharma company fathered his own lab rats?

She stepped up to Jane.

"Did your friend Isabella Lopez have a daughter?"

Jane rubbed her face and dropped her head, like she was exhausted. "A baby girl. Big brown eyes."

"What was her name?"

"Carmen."

Tanya felt sick to her stomach. There couldn't be many Carmen Lopez's around.

"So Hugo Fernando fathered Isabella's child?"

Jane didn't know the hurricane whipping through Tanya's head. She merely nodded and sighed heavily.

"He tricked all of us."

A shiver went down Tanya's spine.

Does Lopez know who her father was? Is that what her mother told her?

"Poor Carmen disappeared, just like my boy." Jane sniffed and wiped her nose. "I guess we'll never find out what happened to our babies."

Carmen Lopez is alive. She works with me.

The wedding photo in Lopez's living room jumped to Tanya's mind.

Santiago Fernando and Carmen Lopez.

Her mind spun.

Did Lopez unknowingly marry her own half-brother? Is this why she had this nervous breakdown?

Max scrambled to his feet and barked at the door. Tanya spun around, her Glock in her hand, her heart pounding.

The sound of someone grabbing the door handle came from the other side.

"Heel, Max," called out Tanya.

He dashed toward her.

Tanya stepped in front of him to shield him. She aimed her gun straight ahead.

Chapter Ninety-two

The door banged open.

Carolyn glared at Tanya.

"You don't have permission to come in here!"

Tanya stared down the barrel of Carolyn's gun. The director's face was flushed. Her eyes twitched and her hands shook.

If Carolyn Pennett-Staresinic had been a corrections officer in her former life, she would have been comfortable with her sidearm and with controlling people, but something about this situation had unsettled her.

"Where's Ray Jackson?" snapped Tanya.

Carolyn frowned. "In his room, like he's supposed to be."

"Not when I checked half an hour ago."

"He's snooping again. That man's a troublemaker. Just like you." Carolyn glowered at Tanya. "Wait till the world hears about you trespassing and intimidating us. I'll be lodging a complaint with the mayor, the city, the state. By tomorrow morning, you'll be on the street."

"Go ahead," said Tanya. "Then, maybe everything that's going on in this place will come to light."

Carolyn jerked her head back, as if in surprise.

"I manage a perfectly legitimate business."

Tanya gestured around the room. "You call this legitimate? It smells like you've disinfected this room to death. What are you hiding?"

"This is a ward for the terminally ill." Carolyn glowered. "We maintain it to industry standards."

Tanya pointed at her gun. "I didn't realize industry standards also included armed security."

"It's licensed." Carolyn's voice wavered slightly, and a pink flush crept up her neck. "It makes me feel safe."

"Safe from what?"

Carolyn didn't answer, but her hands shook even more.

"So, tell me, Carolyn," said Tanya. "How much did you get paid for taking in these supposedly terminally ill patients in your storage wing?"

Carolyn blinked and averted her eyes.

"It's an extra service. I'm helping them spend their last days in peace. It's perfectly legal."

"Is it?"

Tanya took a discreet step closer, keeping her steely eyes on the director.

"If you're not engaged in anything illegal, you wouldn't be pointing a gun at an officer of the law."

"Someone's sending me death threats!"

Tanya raised a brow at her outburst.

"I'm being blackmailed," cried Carolyn. "They said if I tell the cops, they'd kill me!"

"Who's blackmailing you?"

Carolyn's face darkened. "You're the detective. Find out who it is and stop them from harassing me."

"Why are they blackmailing you?" said Tanya, clenching her jaws.

Carolyn turned her face away.

"Is it because you recruited a bunch of untrained ex-convicts to manage a retirement residence?" said Tanya.

"Everyone deserves to make a living wage." Carolyn lowered her weapon, like she had forgotten she'd been pointing it at Tanya all along.

"Did you hire them because they're cheap labor? So, you can siphon off your human resources budget for your gambling addiction?"

"I've done nothing wrong!"

"You look guilty to me, Carolyn."

Carolyn shook her head, like she was trying to shake off a bad dream.

"Look, I borrowed a lot of money. I lost a lot of money. Someone found out about my, er, hobby. That's how I got fired from my last job. I barely make ends meet. I have a ton of debts to pay."

Tanya watched her hand with the gun rise and fall with jerky movements. It was like she had forgotten she was brandishing a weapon.

"I went bankrupt once, okay? Is that a crime? I couldn't find a job to save my life. I just can't go through all that again." Carolyn turned to Tanya, her face dark and pinched. "There. You know all my secrets. So, arrest me!"

Tanya watched her closely as she flapped her arms and spluttered her words.

Either Carolyn was the best actor north of Hollywood, or the real killer was still lurking in the shadows, plotting their next kill.

Chapter Ninety-three

Tanya took a step closer to Carolyn.

"How do you explain the sudden deaths of six women over the past year?"

"They had serious preexisting health conditions."

Tanya kept a close eye on Carolyn's body language and listened to the tone of her voice.

"How do you know their medical histories?"

Carolyn frowned.

"I... I followed the doctor's orders to a T. He comes every week. He pays more attention to them than to our residents." She shrugged. "He's following instructions just like I am. We did nothing wrong."

It's not her.

Carolyn's not the killer.

"The fact they dropped like flies didn't raise a red flag?"

"Wait." Carolyn gasped. "Are you accusing me of *murder*?"

Tanya didn't answer.

"If you think I brought these women here to kill them off," spluttered Carolyn, "you're out of your mind."

Tanya kept quiet, knowing sometimes silence was the best way to glean information.

"They... they died of causes directly related to their addictions. The doctor diagnosed them as terminal within weeks of their arrival. My job was to provide end-of-life care."

Tanya pointed at Jane cowering on the bed behind them.

"That's your version of end-of-life care? You medicate them and tie them to their beds like medieval prisoners?"

Carolyn glanced at Jane with a startled look like she had just seen her.

"I... I just do as I'm told...." A trail of sweat trickled down Carolyn's face. She wiped it away hastily. "The doctor told me if we didn't put the straps on, they'd fall out and hurt themselves."

Sounds like I need to check up on this doctor.

Tanya straightened up.

"Who owns Silver Serenity?"

"Richard James." Carolyn said the name like Tanya should have known it.

"Where's Richard James right now?"

"How on earth would I know?"

"He's your boss."

"He lives on a yacht in the Caribbean in the summer, and skis in Switzerland in the winter. He's one of those super rich men. You can bet your bottom dollar he doesn't spend any time around here."

"Have you met him?"

"Not in real life." Carolyn shrugged. "He interviewed me for this job, but it was via video conference."

Tanya narrowed her eyes. Since when did a yachting and skiing moneyed man interview regular staff? Someone like that would have staff to hire staff to hire staff, and then some.

"What does the owner look like?"

Carolyn's brow furrowed.

"Bald. Round glasses. A bit fat. Not someone I'd expect to see living the high life on a yacht, but what do I know about the rich?"

A bald, plump man with round glasses?

That wasn't how anyone would have described Santiago Fernando. It sounded more like someone else she had met on the hill.

"Do you know the day manager at the hospital next door?"

Carolyn gave her a startled look.

"Paul?" She wrinkled her forehead. "Come to think of it...." But Paul's fat, bald, and ugly, while Richard had this charming debonair air about him."

Funny how money can make the most unattractive man appealing.

"Are you certain there's no other resemblance?"

"The video wasn't clear." Carolyn frowned. "It was fuzzy and his voice was robotic. The Internet in the Caribbean isn't so good. He said it's worse when he's at sea, so all comms was via email and text messages after that. Hey, he's the boss."

Paul Hammerston's shifty eyes and cobweb tattoo sprang to mind. Tanya had had suspicions about the day manager from the minute she'd met him.

Did Santiago Fernando pay the hospital's day manager to kill those women?

Chapter Ninety-four

"Have you seen the young victim we found on the hill before?"

Carolyn's eyes widened.

"Never met her. And I certainly didn't give any kids permission to walk in here." She glowered at Tanya. "I've got enough intruders to worry about."

"Whoever killed the girl," said Tanya, speaking slowly, "also killed the six women whom you thought were terminal."

She watched the director carefully.

"And they also tried to poison your newest resident, Ray Jackson."

"Why would anyone do that?" said Carolyn, whipping her face up, like she couldn't believe what she'd heard. "They're our golden geese. Without them, we couldn't keep this place open. Everyone would lose their jobs, including me."

"I saw Nurse Ana drop something from a vial into Ray Jackson's drink today."

"Vitamins," said Carolyn. "We add supplements to the food and water. She was probably making sure he got his daily dose."

"Vitamins don't make you vomit or faint, and supplements don't lead to your stomach getting pumped. Ask me how I know."

Carolyn's jaw dropped.

"If Max hadn't got help in time," said Tanya, "I wouldn't be standing here."

"But...but..." Carolyn spluttered. "Ana wouldn't hurt a fly. She's the sweetest.... I hired her because of her qualifications, but I kept her because of the way she treats people. The others can be rough. I have to keep reminding them they're not in prison anymore, but once in a while, one of them gets snappy."

"Your Nurse Ana is moonlighting," said Tanya. "She's working for someone else, and I think I know who it is."

"That girl's a registered nurse and came with glowing references."

"Easily faked."

"Everyone loves her."

"Ted Bundy was known to be charming."

Max growled. Tanya whipped around. The door was still closed.

"You're insane," Carolyn was saying. "Why would Ana do anything like that? She's a kind person—"

"She's also loyal, isn't she?" said Tanya, one eye on the door. "She's the meek and subservient person that manipulators and narcissists love to push around, am I right?"

Carolyn's brow furrowed. "What are you implying?"

"Ana is undoubtedly involved, but she's doing this for someone she cares for or respects."

Carolyn scoffed. "You think it's me?"

"No, but I think you know who might be manipulating her."

Carolyn spluttered. "Why would I—"

Max howled, making her jump. She twirled around and stared at him.

"What is it, bud?" said Tanya.

That was when the door opened an inch, followed by a muffled bang.

A second shot rang out from within the room. Tanya slammed to the floor.

That was when Max pushed through the opening and raced out of the room, barking at the top of his lungs.

"Max!" hollered Tanya as she leaped toward the entrance. "Come back!"

The door slammed shut on her face.

Chapter Ninety-five

T anya yanked the door handle.

It didn't budge.

"Max!"

She banged on the surface with her fists, her heart pounding.

"Don't you dare touch my dog!"

She felt the entrance for latches or knobs with her shaking hands, but the door was smooth. There wasn't even a hairline gap between the door and the frame to pick the lock.

"Carolyn?" she called out, as she checked the door. "How do we unlock this from the inside?"

The director had fallen eerily silent.

Tanya spun around. Carolyn was leaning against the foot of Jane's bed, gripping the railing, her face etched in terror. By her feet was her gun.

Tanya clenched her jaws.

That second shot.

"You almost killed me!"

"I...I..." stammered Carolyn. "I was aiming at the...."

Tanya marched up to her. "We'll sort that out later. We have to leave immediately!"

Carolyn shook her head but still didn't speak.

"Unlock that door!" bellowed Tanya, almost spitting in the director's face.

"These r...rooms can only o...o...open from the outside," she whispered. She stared at Tanya, her eyes helpless and filled in pain.

That was when Tanya noticed she was leaning at an odd angle. Carolyn was holding her stomach and blood was seeping through her hand.

Tanya broke into a cold sweat.

"That bang at the door," she whispered, more to herself than to Carolyn. "It was a gun with a silencer."

She reached over to her, but Carolyn turned away with a shudder.

"Please don't touch."

Her hand slipped from the railing but Tanya caught her before she dropped to the ground. Carolyn started shaking uncontrollably.

"Let me see the wound," said Tanya, bringing her gently to the ground. "Remove your hand."

Carolyn took a raspy breath in. "It hurts."

"We need to stop the bleeding."

Tanya glanced around for a first-aid kit, but the room was sparse. There wasn't even a chair or a cot to get Carolyn on.

"T...take this."

She looked up to see Jane, her face still white in terror, kicking a pillow toward her. Tanya yanked it down and ripped out the case.

Carolyn closed her eyes.

"Who did this to me?" she whispered.

"I...I didn't see...." stammered Jane from on top of the bed.

Tanya didn't have time to discuss who she thought fired the shot. Right now, each and every person on this hill was at the top of her list.

Maybe they're all in this together.

She pried Carolyn's bloodied hand from her stomach. The injury was worse than she thought.

"It's not that bad," she lied. "We're going to patch you up in no time."

She wrapped the ripped pillow cloth around Carolyn's stomach, applying pressure with one hand.

Then she pulled her phone out of her pocket and hit the last number she dialed, her throat clinching to even imagine what was going on with Max outside.

"Where's the ambulance?" she hollered, keeping her eyes on Carolyn. The director was still breathing, but they were raw, raspy breaths.

"They're parked on the driveway," came Katy's voice. "The recon team has to sweep the buildings before the medics are allowed inside."

Tanya gritted her teeth.

"We don't have time for procedure. I have two serious medical emergencies on my hands now. Where's Dr. Chen?"

Katy went silent for a second.

"Are you still there?"

"Dr. Chen's disappeared."

Tanya stared at her mobile.

"What do you mean disappeared?"

"She went to Lopez's home to check up on her. I've been calling her, but she's not picking up. I was going to go—"

"No!" Tanya shouted at the phone. "Don't go anywhere near Lopez's house!"

She had one hand on Carolyn's stomach, but the blood was oozing through the cloth and onto her hand. Carolyn sat hunched, her eyes closed, and her head hung to the side like she had no energy to hold it up any more.

She's not going to last long.

"I've got to go," said Tanya, her heart thumping hard. "Promise me. Don't go near Lopez's house until I come down, got it?"

"Why?"

"Trust me on this!"

She hung up and wiped the sweat running down her face.

Where's Max?

Her heart sank.

She ripped another piece of the pillowcase with her teeth when she heard the sound. Someone was at the door. Her heart leaped as she heard Max baying in the distance.

He's alive!

"Hey!" she hollered. "Who is it? I need medical—"

That was when she noticed the black barrel of a gun. It was slipping through the narrow gap in the doorway.

Chapter Ninety-six

"Lie down, Jane!" hollered Tanya, as she dragged Carolyn behind the bed frame.

Carolyn screeched in pain as her injured stomach grazed the floor.

"No!" screamed Jane from the top of the bed, still tied to the monitors and her catheter. She yanked at the wires on her arms.

"Don't shoot me! I wanna get out of here! Let me go!"

"Keep your head down!" hollered Tanya, as she wrapped her arms around Carolyn and pushed her behind the bed frame.

"We're all gonna die," garbled Carolyn.

Tanya's heart pounded.

No, we're going to get out of here.

Alive.

The shooter hadn't fired yet. Whoever it was, they didn't want to be seen.

From behind the bed, Tanya watched the barrel as it moved up and down the doorframe, like they were searching for their target. Jane was screeching on the bed, in plain view, but she hadn't been shot.

If the shooter had decided everyone in the room would die, they wouldn't care about showing their face. This was a targeted hit.

They're after Carolyn.

They've come back to finish the job.

Tanya let go of Carolyn and scrambled to the corner of the bed frame, wielding her Glock. She didn't notice Carolyn slip to the floor, her face falling into a pool of her own blood.

With her eyes on the door, Tanya aimed her Glock and pulled the trigger. The rapid echoes of gunfire boomeranged in the small room, drowning out Jane's screams of terror.

The black barrel disappeared from view, and the door closed shut.

Tanya waited, her heart hammering. She knew this relief would be temporary. The shooter would be back.

I need a better vantage point.

Saying a silent prayer to her dead mother and touching the sunflower pendant on her neck for good luck, Tanya scrambled out from behind the bed and dashed toward the far wall. She was more exposed here, but she had a better chance of getting the shooter.

She reached the wall precisely when the door opened and the black barrel was thrust through the gap again.

Tanya raised her hand and fired. The muffled thud of the silencer came, and a bullet slammed into the wall behind her head.

Tanya dropped to the floor.

More muffled shots came erratically through the opening. Jane flailed and wailed, unable to get off the bed. On the floor, Carolyn groaned in pain. Bullets flew through the air, hitting everything but the three women inside.

Tanya slammed herself against the wall, her chest heaving, her mind spinning.

Something didn't add up.

TIKIRI HERATH

A silencer suggested experience in weaponry, but the stray bullets meant they weren't trained on how to aim. If this had been a professional, all three would be dead by now.

Tanya turned to fire once more, when something slammed into her chest. She flew across the room. A blinding pain flashed through her head.

She tried to blink but her eyes remained shut. All she could hear was Carolyn's agonizing moans mixed with Jane's horrified screams.

Then the world went black.

Chapter Ninety-seven

T he sound of barking came from the distance.

Max?

Tanya squeezed her eyes and winced.

Her ribs ached like a giant rhino had rammed into her. Her throat was parched and her chest hurt. Her head pounded like a construction worker had started a jackhammer inside her brain.

Where am I?

She pried her eyelids open and looked up, trying to see through the muggy haze of a migraine. A single fluorescent bulb glared down on her.

The pungent odor of cleaning bleach wafted into her nose, making her gag. The sickly smell of kerosene or diesel was mixed in with the smell of the bleach.

Tanya struggled to recall what had happened moments before she had blacked out.

Jane had been on her bed struggling to get out, Carolyn had been on the floor, bleeding, and the perpetrator had been firing through the door.

I got shot.

A chill went through her.

Is this what it feels like to be dead?

She remembered she had her Kevlar vest on. She lifted her head and twisted her chin down.

There was no blood, as far as she could see. Peeking out from underneath her jacket was her bullet-proofed vest, but she wasn't sure whether the liquid drenching her stomach was sweat or blood.

She closed her eyes and tried to concentrate. If the bullet had smashed through her skin and bone or ripped through her organs, she wouldn't have been able to breathe or feel the pounding of her heart.

My lungs are working.

My heart's okay.

The vest. It saved me.

Her breath came fast.

Why can't I move?

She lifted her head and glanced around. She jerked as she spotted the prone figure on the floor.

Carolyn.

The director was lying in a pool of blood, her hand resting on her wounded stomach. Her head was turned upward and her eyes were wide open, gazing to the heavens in a soulless stare. Her face was etched in terror of her imminent death.

Carolyn's dead.

Mixed with her red blood on the cold concrete floor was a slick and oily substance Tanya hadn't noticed before.

What is that?

She swallowed hard and stayed still for a moment, trying to come to terms with what had just happened.

Max's barks had receded as quickly as she'd heard them, and all that was left was the eerie hum of the fluorescent light above her.

Is Jane dead too?

Did they take her?

Max's barks had been an illusion her distressed mind had conjured up. This room was soundproofed, which meant she couldn't hear him or anything else outside.

Where's my gun?

She distinctly remembered her sidearm flying out of her hand when she crashed against the wall. She scanned the room but her weapon was nowhere to be seen.

The strong acrid smell of bleach came back, but the odor of fuel was new.

Fuel!

Tanya's heart raced.

The oily slick that surrounded Carolyn's body meant only one thing.

She struggled to sit up, but it felt like a truck was pinning her down. She jerked her head from side to side, the only body part that seemed to be free.

She yanked her right arm, but didn't get far. She kicked her legs, making the bed rattle against the concrete floor. A wave of panic rolled through her body.

I'm strapped down.

Just like Jane was.

Chapter Ninety-eight

Tanya let out a roar.

She thrashed back and forth.

But the straps held tight.

Her heart pumped on overdrive and her body shook in fury. The jackhammer inside her head was getting louder and louder, asking the same questions over and over.

How did I get into this position?

How did I not save Carolyn's life?

Her heart dropped as she remembered how Max had raced out of the room. Anyone who would shoot Carolyn in cold blood wouldn't think twice of killing her dog.

If they have harmed even one hair on him, I swear I'll—

She gritted her teeth.

Max! Where are you?

Tanya screamed until her throat was hoarse. She struggled until the straps bruised her hands and feet. But a wiser part of her knew fighting was only sapping her strength, the little she had to escape this hell.

She stopped moving and lay still, her chest heaving.

Breathe, girl, breathe.

It took ten uneven raspy breaths to get her heart down to a level where she wasn't panicking like a trapped animal. What she needed was a cold and clear head to find a way out of here.

Think, girl, think.

She was tied up inside a soundproofed room that could only be opened from the outside. That is, if the shooter hadn't taken the key or made it impossible to open the door.

The backup teams were on the hill, doing a sweep of the buildings. They should be here soon. But would they be able to get inside?

My phone. Where's my phone?

She wiggled her legs, trying to feel the contents of her pockets. As much as she twisted herself like a pretzel, she couldn't reach inside of them.

She stared at the single light bulb on the ceiling, her face drenched in sweat, wishing it could tell her what had happened in this room from the moment she had blacked out.

She went through the facts.

Carolyn, her primary suspect was dead. That left Nurse Ana, but she couldn't have moved Jane out and transferred her to the bed alone. She had to have had help. That meant there had been at least two or more people on the other side of this door.

Benson.

Nurse Benson.

He carried people onto and off beds for a living. The memory of him feigning fear in Ray Jackson's room swirled through her mind.

If anyone had the strength to kill Esmeralda and bury her in a shallow grave, it would have to be him. It was all an act. He was part of this racket.

Wait.

Benson had left Ray's room hastily when Nurse Ana had walked in. He hadn't warned the nurse of Tanya and Max's presence in the bathroom.

Why would he have done that if he was working with her?

A sting of pain shot through Tanya's head. She scrunched her eyes as the throbbing intensified and receded, but she knew the next pain cycle would come again soon.

She popped her eyes open as a terrifying thought came to mind.

Why didn't they kill me?

There's a reason they didn't. And it can't be a good one.

A bolt of rage flashed through her. She lifted her head up and slammed it down, wincing as her neck hit something hard under the pillow.

What's that?

She craned her neck. Using her shoulder as a crutch, she turned and grabbed the pillow by her teeth. She pushed it to the edge of the bed inch by inch. That was when she saw it.

An electronic device had been hidden under the pillow.

Using all the energy she had, she yanked the pillow with her teeth and pushed it over the side.

It was a digital clock.

It was one of those outmoded timekeepers with oversized numbers in an eye-straining red color. Intertwined black and red wires protruded from the side of the device and ran the length of the headboard before disappearing under the bed.

Tanya stared at it, frozen.

She was certain she hadn't seen it when she was trying to untie Jane. The strong smell of fuel made sense now.

This is why they left me alive.

The numbers on the clock were ticking down.

In nine minutes and fifty-eight seconds, this room would explode in flames.

Chapter Ninety-nine

A loud bang came from the outside.

Tanya jumped, startled.

The bang came again, this time rattling the walls.

Her heart raced, and her mind lifted with hope. It sounded like a battering ram was being used to break down the door.

Backup.

She stopped fighting the straps and took deep breaths in.

Thank you, Katy.

Thank you, Jack.

The door crashed open. Tanya lifted her head. A ball of brown fur rocketed through the doorway and leaped onto the bed. She jerked back in alarm.

"No, Max!" she shouted as he jumped on top of her chest, licking her face, his tail wagging a million miles a second. "Get out! Get out, Max!"

Her heart pounded. An eighty-pound dog rambling on the bed could have easily triggered the explosive device.

Max whined, as if to ask why she wasn't getting up. Tanya felt like her heart would burst open. Tears rolled down her cheeks.

"Get out, Max!" she cried.

Max pawed at her chest.

"Bomb!"

The frightened cry came from an unfamiliar male voice.

Tanya nudged Max to the side with her head and peered. Two heavily geared police officers were backing out of the room. They were staring, their horrified eyes not on her, but on something underneath the bed.

"Cut me loose!" hollered Tanya, but the men backed into the corridor.

"Hey!" she hollered. "Get my dog out of here!"

The men whirled away, their attention on someone in the corridor.

"Sir!"

"IED, sir!"

"We need BSO now!"

All of a sudden, a cacophony of shouts and the sound of running boots broke outside. She glimpsed officers in riot gear, helmets, and batons running through the corridor. A man in a sheriff's hat and badge rushed over, pushing through the melee.

He took one look at Carolyn's immobile body on the floor, then bent down to scrutinize something under the bed. Without even acknowledging Tanya, he spun on his heels and bellowed on his radio for the bomb squad.

"Hey, get me out of here!" hollered Tanya.

He didn't even look her way, but Tanya could see the sweat streaming down his face. She watched him walk away in disbelief. It was like she was invisible.

Do you people even see me?

Chapter One Hundred

Tanya turned her attention to Max.

He was standing on top of her stomach, huffing with happiness to be reunited.

Her mind spun as she tried to figure out her next steps.

Most local county precincts didn't have experts on explosives. This meant they would have to first contact, then hang around for the trained professionals to arrive from the state department with the right equipment.

She glanced behind her.

Six minutes and forty seconds.

Her throat went dry.

I can't wait for these small-town cops to get their act together.

"Max?" She tapped the bed rail with her fingers on her right hand to get his attention. "Help me, bud."

He turned and sniffed the strap. Tanya banged her hand on the railing.

"Get it off me."

Max growled at it.

"That's it," said Tanya, jerking her hand even more. "Grab it."

He clamped his powerful jaws around her hand. Tanya knew she had to trust her pup. He would never hurt her, but he was still a dog.

He curled his lips back and bit into the strap.

"Yes!"

He clamped his jaws tighter, growling fiercely like he had caught a live animal.

"Good boy!"

He shook his head violently, making the whole bed sway.

"Easy there, bud."

A trickle of sweat ran down Tanya's back. She had no idea what their jerky movements were doing to the explosive device. She twisted her neck and glanced at the clock behind her.

Five minutes and ten seconds.

It was counting down normally, and so far, hadn't seemed to have been impacted. At least, so it seemed.

Better to die fighting, than wait helplessly for death to arrive.

"One more time, bud."

Max tugged at the strap with his teeth.

Tanya heard the rip of the Velcro come loose. In one swift movement, she snapped her hand out and relief flooded through her veins.

"Freedom!"

Max whirled around and licked her face, kneading her stomach with his paws, excited to see her excited.

Tanya pushed him away with her freed hand. "Out, Max! Go!"

He whined and gave her another lick, as if to say, *Nope, I'm good here.*

Tanya ducked under his massive head to reach over and wrench the strap off her other hand.

"Get out, Max!" she cried, pushing him forcefully with both hands. "Out of the room! Now!"

He scampered to the side of the bed, his tail down, looking hurt.

Tanya bent down and reached for the leg straps. She ripped them off swiftly, her heart racing.

Outside in the corridor, the bedlam had ceased. She wondered if they had left them alone to die.

She glanced back at the clock.

Four minutes and thirty seconds.

Chapter One Hundred and One

Tanya grabbed Max's collar.

"We're going to get out together, got it?"

A loud gasp came from the open doorway.

"Thank goodness, you're okay."

Tanya whipped her head up to see Ray's face pop through the side of the door.

"Ray!" called out Tanya.

"Max came to get me—"

"Step away, sir!"

Ray turned around. "Wait a minute, Officer, I'm the one who called—"

"This is a major crime scene. Move out!"

The officer grabbed Ray's arm and shoved him back.

"I said evacuate the building!" roared the squad leader, beating his baton on his shield. "Get him outta here now!"

Tanya turned to Max who had his head cocked, like he was wondering what was going on.

"We're going to move really slow, bud."

He thumped his tail, as if to say *Sure*. Tanya stretched her legs out, ignoring the cramps in her muscles. Pulling Max with her, she slid to the bottom of the bed.

"What do you think you're doing?" came an angry yell from the doorway. "Don't move."

Tanya didn't even look up.

Like hell, I will.

She fastened her hands on the bed's railing and peeked underneath the mattress. The wires from the clock disappeared into a black box on the floor. That was what had terrified everyone.

The box was sitting two feet underneath the bed exactly below where her head had been, only moments ago.

Tanya's stomach twisted into a knot. She pulled Max in closer. She wouldn't have felt this sick if it had only been her.

"I said, remain still!" hollered an authoritative voice. "We're gonna get you out of there."

Yeah, right.

Tanya glanced at the man hollering at her from behind a police ballistic shield from where he thought was a safe distance. She could hardly see his eyes behind the thick bulletproof glass visor that covered his entire face and neck.

That's not going to save you from an explosion, mister.

"Get out of the way," she yelled as she gripped Max's collar. "We're coming out."

"Stay where you are," he shouted. "Bomb squad's on their way."

Tanya glanced back at the clock by the pillow.

"I have three minutes before I blow up into pieces."

"You could blow it, if you get off the bed."

Tanya pointed at Carolyn's body.

"They poured kerosene all over her. This means this entire room will be engulfed in fire in seconds."

The officers stared at her, mutely.

"My choices are to get blown up or get burned to death." Tanya swung her legs over the bed. "And I have decided which one I prefer."

She glared at the men.

"So back off!"

Chapter One Hundred and Two

"On the count of three," said Tanya to Max, speaking more to herself than to him.

Max thumped his tail.

The officers had backed off to the farthest point of the corridor where they could still see her.

"Take cover, boys," she hollered. "We're coming out now."

To her relief, they scampered off, but their furious curses echoed through the hallway.

"Ready, Max?" said Tanya.

Another thump of the tail.

"One, two, go!"

She leaped from the bed, pulling him down with her.

"Run, Max!"

She stumbled for a split second, but found her footing and raced out of the room after her dog. She turned toward the exit door at the end of the wing, but it was closed.

"This way!"

"Hurry!"

She spun around to see the officers had fled to the other side of the double doors. They gestured to her from behind their shields.

"That's locked!" shouted one of them.

Jane? Where's Jane?

Tanya's eyes swiveled around the corridor. "Did you see a woman in a hospital gown?"

"Negative!" roared the squad leader. "We need to get out now!"

"Go, Max, go!" yelled Tanya.

Max darted through the double doors. Tanya raced after him, her heart in her mouth, bracing for the explosion that would tear them into blood and bone.

She shot past the men. They turned and followed, moving slower, encumbered by their heavy gear.

Max galloped down the main corridor, his ears back and his tongue out, leading the way. He was heading straight to the front entrance.

Tanya sprinted for her life, trying to keep up with his four strong legs.

Max bolted out of the main entrance and into the residence's grounds. She leaped down the front steps after him, her heart hammering like mad.

Max stopped and turned for a split second to check if she was following. With an encouraging bark, he turned back and dashed toward the crowd that had gathered on the driveway.

A fleet of police cars and emergency vehicles were parked at the end, their lights flashing. The residents of Silver Serenity were huddled behind them, shocked expressions on their faces. They were all staring at Max shooting across the lawn toward them.

I hope they got everyone, thought Tanya as she scrambled over, panting.

Nurse Benson was huddled in a corner with Ocean and Sahara. The kitchen and cleaning staff, nurses, and nurses' aides were scattered among the crowd, but she didn't see the one person she was looking for.

The three officers with the shields were making a beeline toward an armored police truck that was parked in the middle of the grounds.

"Tanya!"

She turned.

Ray Jackson was hunkering behind a squad car.

"This way!" he shouted. He waved his arms. "Max! Here, boy! Get behind here!"

Max did a forty-five-degree turn and zoomed toward him. He leaped into Ray's arms, bowling him over.

"Everyone down!" hollered an officer.

Ray flattened himself on the ground.

Tanya slammed down next to Ray. She put an arm around her dog and pressed him to the ground, her heart pounding. She was still in wonder they got out in one piece.

Ray turned his head to her.

"You need to get—"

He didn't finish.

Silver Serenity exploded into a ball of fire.

Chapter One Hundred and Three

Something buzzed in Tanya's pocket.

It had been buzzing for a while, but she had been so focused on getting herself and Max to safety, she had forgotten about her phone and her gun.

She pulled her mobile out and patted her other pockets.

Where's my Glock?

"Tanya?" came Katy's panicked voice through the speakerphone. "Are you okay, hun?"

Tanya's heart was hammering nonstop. She swallowed the thick saliva that had gathered in her mouth.

"Sounds like a war zone." Katy's voice rose in pitch. "I told you to wait for backup."

"I'm good," said Tanya, finding her voice. "And Max is fine."

"I've been trying to reach you. We have the warrants."

Tanya turned toward the burning building.

A little too late for that.

Flames were spreading through the wings, sending plumes of black smoke in the air. Wooden beams cracked and walls crumbled, sounding like a battle was waging among the inferno.

The residents and the officers at the end of the driveway were gaping at the fire, like they couldn't take their eyes off the scene. From behind them, came the wail of a fleet of firetrucks, their gears screaming, as they climbed the steep incline up the hill.

Katy was saying something.

Tanya turned away from the building and stuck a finger in her free ear.

"Santiago Fernando's not it," came Katy's voice.

Tanya raised a brow.

"He's been at the summit all week, except for that brief heli ride to Black Rock," said Katy. "Jack paid two bellhops to follow him around and confirmed that he never left the hotel's premises after that."

"Santiago would get others to do his dirty work." Tanya pinched her lips together. "Do we have a team watching the hospital?"

"Six officers. They're sweeping the building as we speak."

"Tell them not to let anyone out of their sight."

"Got it," said Katy. "You need to talk to Carolyn. She has a shady past. She got fired from correctional services for chronic gambling. She filed for bankruptcy a month before she got the job at the residence."

Tanya cleared the sweat from her brow. "I know."

"Is she finally talking?"

"She's dead." Tanya sighed heavily. "If she was involved in this, it was unwittingly."

A low whistle made her look up. Ray, who was crouched with Max behind the police car, was gesturing to her.

Tanya mouthed, *Just a sec.*

"I found histories on all the nurses, except for one," Katy was saying.

"Let me guess. Nurse Ana."

"She appeared out of nowhere. She's never even had a parking ticket. I couldn't find any employment, college, high school, or prison record. She isn't registered with the national nurses' union either."

Tanya scrunched her forehead. "How big was the immediate Fernando family?"

"There was the father, Hugo Fernando, his wife who died from cancer, and two children."

"Tell me about the kids," said Tanya.

"Must be in their mid-thirties or early forties now. We know about Santiago, the son, but there's no record of the daughter."

"Do we have a name?"

More clicking came from the other end.

"If I believe this old tabloid, it's Angelica."

"Angelica," said Tanya quietly. "Ana would be an easy contraction, a name she could answer to without attracting suspicion."

"You think *she's* behind all this?"

"We don't know Nurse Ana's real identity yet," said Tanya, frowning. "Her actions in Ray's room were highly suspicious."

"I'll keep digging, but Jack will have to ask for more access to information."

The sirens got louder, and it was harder to hear Katy.

The fire trucks had arrived, and were preparing to douse the flames. Uniformed officers were taping off the grounds to keep the residents and the few local reporters at bay.

Tanya scanned the crowd, searching their faces for signs of guilt, disdain, or pride, but it seemed like everyone was staring at the remnants of the residence, riveted by the fire.

Silver Serenity hadn't been just an institution for these residents. This had been their oasis, a welcome escape from their pasts. A pang of sympathy went through Tanya to see them watch their beloved home burn to the ground.

"Stone?" called Ray, his face grave.

Tanya nodded and put a hand up. She turned back to the phone.

"Katy, tell the officers at Lopez's house to be extra vigilant."

"Don't tell me she's a suspect too."

"I don't think all those kids were taken across the border after testing," said Tanya. "Carmen Lopez was left behind."

"Carmen? *Our* Carmen?"

Tanya didn't have time to explain.

Ray was gesturing even more urgently to her now.

"Have to go," said Tanya. "I need to find Ana."

Chapter One Hundred and Four

R ay glowered as Tanya hung up.

"Find and arrest Nurse Ana already."

"We need justification," said Tanya, "or a bunch of high-priced lawyers will unravel this case faster than a cat with a knitted top."

Ray brought out a navy booklet from his pocket. "I was on my recon mission in the staff quarters. Guess what I found at the bottom of the closet in Ana's room?"

Tanya took the passport, flipped to the main page and scratched the photo and signature.

"Is this real?"

"I know a fake when I see it. This is the real deal." Ray jabbed at the black-and-white photo. "Her last name is Fernando. Angelica Fernando."

Tanya frowned. "If Ana was planning a series of murders, why would she carry an official government issued—"

She stopped as a piece of paper fell from the booklet and landed by Max's paws. She bent down and picked it up.

"An e-ticket to Buenos Aires." Her eyes widened. "She was going to fly to Argentina on the same flight as Carmen Lopez."

"They were planning their escape." Ray hissed in disgust. "Dirty, rotten scoundrels. All of them. What do you expect from the family who owns a private pharmaceutical company that used children as test subjects?"

A sting went through Tanya's heart.

Was Lopez involved in these murders? Right under our noses? Was this a family feud gone horribly wrong?

"I can't believe I thought Ana was innocent," Ray muttered. "I protected her from Carolyn. I was a foolish man. That saccharin sweet personality was all fake."

His eyes flashed.

"That woman tried to *poison* me. You saw her. She's the devil in disguise, masquerading as an angel of light."

"Santiago has to be the mastermind." Tanya narrowed her eyes.

"We need Ana to open up, so we can pin down the bigger criminal. Santiago Fernando could get on the next flight to Venezuela or whichever country we don't have an extradition treaty with, and all our efforts will have been in vain."

"I don't care how you do it," Ray whispered hoarsely. "Arrest them all and bring justice to those dead women."

Tanya peered over the squad cars.

Most of the residents were crying and hugging each other for comfort, while others were sitting in the backs of the police cars, glazed looks in their eyes. The officers' attention was on a fire truck that was lifting a bucket with a firefighter and a hose.

Ray jabbed Tanya's arm with his finger.

"The squad leader sent a search party into the woods. A bunch of fresh-faced, two-bit cadets. She's too cunning for them. She's going to get away."

Tanya bit her lip. "If Ana's in the woods, so is Jane."

"They have vehicles parked along the road," said Ray, pointing at the officers. "As the crime scene response team, they control the area now. Not you. And certainly not me. Those guys aren't going to let you through their perimeter."

Tanya turned to him.

"Can you distract them?"

"Happy to be the sacrificial lamb again."

"Do you have a sidearm?"

"I don't go anywhere without my gun."

Ray slipped his hand into his pocket and pulled out a small pistol. He plonked it on her palm.

"Keep Max close. I was in Ana's room when he ran up and grabbed my sleeve. He wouldn't let go until I came with him. He deserves a medal."

Max barked a soft bark and thumped his tail, like he knew they were talking about him.

"Go," said Ray, waving Tanya off. "I'm about to get another heart attack, but I can't have these clowns take me away in their death buses to the morgue. Hurry up and get Ana!"

With another glance at the officers by the yellow tape, Tanya crouched low and scurried toward the woods, using the vehicles as a shield. Max followed her movements, his eyes bright and his ears pricked.

Tanya straightened up only when they were concealed behind the tree line.

Chapter One Hundred and Five

T anya could hear the search party thrashing through the woods.

They weren't being stealthy, and that was a good thing. Nudging Max, she turned in the opposite direction.

It took her a few minutes to find the path they took earlier. As soon as they landed on it, Max trotted in front of her, like he knew their destination.

Tanya treaded after him, deeper into the forest with Ray's gun in her hand, her head swiveling back and forth, alert for strange shadows.

It took them ten minutes to get to Stu's cabin by the small lake on top of the hill.

Max stopped at the tree line and barked a muffled bark. His tail was stiff and his eyes were on the crooked cabin. The door was closed and there didn't seem to be anyone inside at first glance.

All of a sudden, the sound of a shovel hitting dirt came from beyond the structure.

Tanya's heart missed a beat.

Someone's digging.

"This way," she whispered to Max as she slunk back into the woods.

Tanya stepped in between the trees, trying her best to avoid the dried twigs on the forest floor. She slipped around the house and walked past the fire pit where she had chatted with Ocean and Sahara.

The backyard was empty.

She had passed the cabin by several yards when she heard the sobs. It was like someone was struggling to stifle their crying.

Jane?

The noise was coming from farther down, closer to where the cemetery was. Tanya kept moving, thankful she had a weapon on her.

The sound of the shovel got louder. When they got close, Tanya tapped Max on the back to tell him to halt. She stepped behind a large pine tree and peered out.

Stu.

He was digging in a clearing by the cemetery, using an old wooden shovel. He was dragging the tool and had barely dug a few inches deep.

Stu hadn't noticed her or Max. He scraped at the dirt, panting and sighing. He stopped to wipe the sweat glistening on his brow, then shot a furtive glance at the woods, before scraping the soil again.

Collapsed on the cold, hard ground behind him, was Jane.

Her face was pallid and her body was shaking. She had a hand over her mouth like she was forcing herself not to cry out.

She's alive.

But Tanya knew she wouldn't last long in this environment.

Jane had been taken violently from a room where she had been hooked up to saline, a catheter, and drugs, and thrown on the cold forest floor in her flimsy hospital gown.

Stu was digging the grave for her.

Even from where she was, Tanya could see the fear in the man's eyes. His shoulders were taut and his head was bowed low. He worked slowly, dragging the spade, stopping every once in a while to let out a heavy sigh.

He isn't doing this on his own volition.

Is he buying time? Who's making him do this?

Tanya glanced around her.

With a jerk, she realized Max was no longer by her feet. Her mouth turned dry.

Max?

She whirled around. That was when she spotted his furry outline in a clearing, deeper in the woods.

What are you doing?

She couldn't call out to him without warning Stu of her presence, so she stepped away from the tree and crept toward Max.

He turned around and wagged his tail as she approached, but remained in his spot.

He's found something.

Tanya's heart was heavy with guilt for abandoning Jane, but it would be a while before that grave was deep enough to bury an adult body. Right now, her priority was to neutralize Ana and her companion or companions.

Tanya stepped in between two fir trees and squinted to see what Max wanted to show her.

A body lay at the edge of the clearing.

Tanya stopped and stared at her dog's discovery.
Nurse Ana.

Chapter One Hundred and Six

Ana lay on her side, her arms extended like she had been pleading for her life.

There was no mistaking the splatter of blood soaking through her top.

Tanya bent over and was about to check her pulse when Ana snapped her eyes open.

Tanya fell back in shock.

"You're alive!"

Max whined and nudged Ana's arm with his snout. Ana opened her mouth as if to speak, but closed it again. She was breathing heavily.

Tanya leaned toward her, her heart racing.

"Don't move."

Ana opened her mouth and whispered something incomprehensible.

"Stay completely still." Tanya scrutinized the blood on her shirt, then surveyed the rest of her body to gage the extent of her injuries. "Did you get shot?"

"Y... yes."

Ana's voice was reedy, like she was using the last reserves of her energy.

Tanya reached over to her blouse and gently rolled it up. Ana didn't object, but lay still, her chest heaving.

Max was watching Tanya, his head cocked to the side.

"You did a good job, bud," whispered Tanya, nodding to him. "Now guard. Guard the perimeter."

Max whirled around the clearing and sniffed the surrounding trees. Then, he sat back on his haunches, his ears straight up, his eyes peering into the woods.

Tanya plucked her flashlight from her pocket and shone it on Ana's chest.

The bullet had entered through the bottom part of her left flank. She was bleeding heavily. If the blood flow didn't stop, Ana's chances of surviving were slim.

"I... t... tried to...." Ana spoke haltingly and in a raspy voice, her eyes not wavering from Tanya. "H...h... help...Jane...."

"Did you say *help Jane*?"

Ana nodded, but it was so imperceptible Tanya wasn't sure if she had misread the gesture. She slipped off her jacket, her mind whirling a million miles a second.

I was so sure you wanted her dead.

Behind her, she could still hear Stu. He was working like a mechanized but reluctant robot. The slap of the steel against the soil, the scraping of the blade, then a long pause followed by the sound of soil being thrown onto the ground.

Tanya rolled her jacket and turned to Ana.

"I'm going to put this on your side. You're going to feel some pressure, okay?"

Ana nodded mutely, her face white, like she was draining of blood fast. Tanya rolled her to the side and nudged the jacket under the open wound. She pressed on it to stop the bleeding.

Using her free hand, Tanya pulled out her phone and typed a message.

"Parameds ASAP. Cemetery. 2 vics."

She hit send to Ray's number, but she was sure his mobile was a mangled mess in the ruins of the fire by now. She copied the text and sent it to Dr. Chen's number, and then to Katy's.

She glanced down at her phone, biting her lips, praying for someone to answer, but it remained silent. Normally, Katy would have replied within seconds.

She clicked on Katy's office number and hit call. An unfamiliar male voice came on the line.

"Black Rock police precinct."

"Get me Katy."

"Pardon?" came the young man's high-pitched voice.

"Tanya Stone, here," she spoke firmly. "I need to speak with Katy McCafferty."

"She's gone, ma'am."

"Where?"

"She went to Deputy Lopez's house five minutes ago. Said something about Dr. Chen gone missing."

Tanya hissed in frustration.

"Are the officers at Lopez's premises still there?"

"Affirmative."

"Call the team on the hill ASAP. I have two vics in severe medical condition near the cemetery. One with a gunshot wound."

"Er... aren't the teams already up there?"

Tanya gritted her teeth.

"Backups are at the building grounds. I need help at the cemetery in the woods. Send paramedics now."

"Yes, ma'am."

Tanya wiped the sweat dripping down her neck, wondering what her friend and the doctor were up to.

This case was so convoluted, every time she thought she'd figured out the perpetrator, they sent her a curveball. If Santiago was behind these incidents, he was the most organized, resourceful, and clever criminal she knew.

"Th...thank... thank you."

Thank you?

Tanya looked down at Ana with a frown.

"Who shot you?"

Chapter One Hundred and Seven

Ana opened her mouth, then shut it.

"It was your brother, wasn't it?" said Tanya. "Or whoever works for him."

Ana's face scrunched like she was about to burst out crying. Tanya wondered how much of those tears were due to remorse and how much came from the guilt and shame of being ferreted out.

"Were you assisting him? Or were you calling the shots before your brother turned on you?"

Ana shut her eyes, like those words stabbed her like daggers.

Tanya glanced around the darkened woods. The sun was setting. It was getting harder to see, but Max hadn't budged from his sentry duty. Behind him, Stu was still digging, but Jane's sobs had diminished.

Is she still alive?

Where are the medics?

She turned her focus back to Ana.

"I will save your life but you won't get much sympathy from me. You and your brother were willing to kill to protect your family's reputation and your company's profits."

Ana shuddered.

"You pretended to be a nurse and signed up as staff, knowing fully well Carolyn was embroiled in her own issues."

Ana gasped. "Sto...stop."

But Tanya couldn't stop herself.

"You blackmailed her to confuse and distract her. You sent the memo instructing her to set up the rehabilitation center. You and your brother lured those women in."

"No..."

"You got the residence's doctor to sign off on those death certificates, didn't you? Your family has enough money to bribe an entire nation's worth of corrupt physicians."

"I n... never—"

"I saw the gun barrel you stuck through the doorway. Carolyn suspected your scheme but was too afraid to speak up, given her maligned past. You killed her to silence her."

Tanya felt her blood come to boiling point.

"Those women were victims, Ana. They were victims of a madman, your abusive father. You eliminated them, one by one. Then, you killed the only witness, a young girl whom you murdered in cold blood, and forced Stu to bury on the hill."

Tanya knew she shouldn't be goading the injured woman. She wanted to stop talking, but Esmeralda's innocent face kept spiraling through her mind.

"You thought these were your perfect murders. I have news for you. Be prepared to spend the rest of your life in a jail cell, Angelica Fernando."

Ana shuddered and closed her eyes.

"I heard... heard... them," she whispered, blinking through her tears. "I r... remem....their s... screams... n.... nightmares. They asked me to h.... help... but I c...couldn't."

Her tears came down in a cascade.

Tanya narrowed her eyes. "You heard the women screaming before they died?"

"The kids..." Ana swallowed hard. "Father... took... me.... I saw... I saw them l... locked... in... the... lab...."

Tanya suddenly realized she was reliving a memory from a long time ago.

"You saw the children your father tested on?"

Ana nodded.

"They were... so ... scared. They c... cried... I was s... scared too...."

She scrunched her eyes like she couldn't bear the memory.

"Why did you lure their mothers and kill them, then?"

Ana blinked and stared at Tanya.

"It...was...m... my... b... brother...." Her chest heaved. "I tried...to s...stop....him...."

Chapter One Hundred and Eight

T anya scrutinized Ana's face.

It was hard to believe someone in her condition would have the foresight or the energy to lie.

"I...f...found his p...plans....," stammered Ana in a low voice, wincing like it hurt to speak. "I c...came here...to save....them...."

Tanya frowned.

Are these the words of a dying woman seeking absolution?

She recalled the helicopter in the parking lot behind the precinct building. Other than his brief foray into Black Rock, Santiago Fernando had been at the Seattle summit. Jack had kept a sharp eye on him. That meant whoever killed the most recent women and Esmeralda was from the hill.

She leaned close to Ana.

"Why did you try to poison Ray Jackson?"

Ana's eyelids fluttered.

"He... he's a s... spy... s...sent by... my... brother..."

Tanya raised a brow.

"Ray's working for your brother?"

Ana nodded, with more vigor this time.

Tanya's body went cold. She shook her head.

No. It can't be. Ray wouldn't be helping me if he was involved.

She noticed Ana was clenching and unclenching her hands, like she was trying to control the pain. The pressure from the jacket was helping, but she needed proper medical attention soon.

"You're the one who sent the anonymous letter to the FBI HQ."

"I t... tried to...to warn them...."

"You did the right thing," whispered Tanya. She softened her voice. "Please tell me who killed those women."

Ana swallowed. "My...my brother...."

"Who's your brother's accomplice inside the residence?"

"He.... k...killed them him..self...."

Tanya stared at her, wondering if Ana was in so much pain, she was hallucinating. Santiago couldn't have been in two places at the same time.

"Was Stu involved?"

Ana shook her head. "S...Stu never...hurt...anyone...he...he warned me...with rose...."

"The rose?" said Tanya, sitting up. "The black rose was Stu's way of saying someone's going to die?"

Ana nodded.

"He was... s...scared...m...my brother...would find out...and kill him....," she whispered.

"How did he know when someone was about to get—" Tanya stopped as she realized the answer. "He found the death ledger."

Ana gave another feeble nod.

Tanya was sure she had the final puzzle pieces now, but they were slowly converging to form an image she hadn't anticipated.

"Where did he find the ledger?"

"In my b... brother...my brother's room...."

Wait. When did Stu meet Santiago Fernando, the elusive pharmaceutical tycoon from Seattle?

Tanya's eyes widened as the last puzzle pieces clicked into place.

With a shaking hand, she pulled her phone out and swiped through the photographs and images related to this case that Katy had curated for her. She clicked on one photo and turned the screen toward Ana.

"Do you recognize this man?"

Ana squinted.

Tanya brought the phone closer to her face.

"This is Santiago Fernando," said Tanya.

Ana lifted her eyes.

"That's ....not my b.... brother."

Her voice was thin, like she was barely holding on to the vestiges of her life, but Tanya pressed on.

"Have you seen him before?"

Ana nodded and closed her eyes.

"He...w...works for m....my brother...."

Chapter One Hundred and Nine

M ax whirled around and bayed into the dark woods.

Tanya jumped to her feet and whipped out Ray's pistol, aiming it in the direction he was barking at.

She grabbed him by the collar as she had no idea if the intruder was armed. Max lunged forward, wheezing as he struggled to get out of her grasp and attack the intruder.

"Heel, bud."

He stopped fighting her and stood in place, his angry howls echoing through the forest.

Tanya could feel a dark presence behind the trees, watching her. On the ground, by her feet, Ana moaned in pain.

"H... help... me..."

Tanya kept her eyes on the foliage in front of her, her heart racing. There was only one reason for anyone to remain a shadow behind those trees. She, Ana, and Max now made easy targets.

"Come out," hollered Tanya.

Her palms were wet with sweat and her heart was thudding like a drum.

"Show your face," she roared, "or I'm going to unleash my K9 on you. He'll tear you to pieces in seconds."

Max let out a volley of barks as if to say, *That's right.*

That was a bluff. There was no way she would let Max head into danger without knowing who it was.

"Come out!" she hollered. "You coward!"

That was when the muffled shot ran out.

Ana screamed.

Tanya whipped around.

Ana had collapsed to her side and had fallen completely still. Her arms were extended like before, but this time there was a gaping bullet hole in her forehead.

Tanya's heart jumped to her mouth.

A loud rustle made her whirl around, but she was a second too late. Max lunged toward the clump of trees from where the shot had fired.

"Max! Get back!"

He disappeared into the bushes, barking.

"Max!"

Tanya leaped toward the tree line after her dog. It sounded like a herd of elephants was crashing through the underbrush now. She ran through the woods using Max's barks to guide her, dodging the low branches overhead.

From somewhere on the hill came the wail of a police siren. She cursed under her breath as a thorny branch slapped against her forehead.

Where's backup when I need you?

Max's barks were getting closer. He seemed to have stopped running.

Tanya dashed in his direction, sweat dripping down her face, hoping whoever it was wasn't about to attack her dog.

She burst into the clearing and halted.

The darkening woods had disoriented her. She hadn't realized she had done a full circle. She had ended at the corner of the cemetery where Stu had been digging the shallow grave.

Max was in front of a small group, barking his head off.

Stu was standing stock still, clutching his old shovel to his chest. His raging eyes weren't on Max or her, but on the newcomer pointing a sidearm at Jane's head.

Tanya's eyes widened.

That's my Glock.

The man had a second weapon in his left hand. She recognized it instantly. It was the gun with the silencer, the one she'd spotted through the narrow doorway in Jane's wardroom. It was the gun that had killed Carolyn.

And now Ana.

Tanya raised her hands and aimed her pistol at the killer.

Chapter One Hundred and Ten

"You're the real Santiago Fernando," snarled Tanya.

Paul Hammerston's face was flushed but his hand was steady. He was holding her own weapon against Jane's temple. He had Tanya where he wanted.

Checkmate.

A ball of rage flared inside Tanya. She finally saw the puppet master who had been orchestrating the murderous show on the hill.

"It was you. *You* arranged the multiple homicides of those innocent women." Tanya gritted her teeth. "And you just murdered your own sister."

Paul glowered.

"You switched identities with your buddy and sent him to the Seattle summit as the CEO of your firm. Since there are no public photos of you, no one knew. You planned this all along. You're a cold-blooded murderer."

"Seems like you have a few more brain cells than the average cop," said Paul.

Jane whimpered and placed her hands together in prayer, silently pleading with him to spare her life. Tears rolled down her mottled face.

"Let her go," said Tanya, not wavering her aim at his head. "She's gone through enough."

"If Ana hadn't meddled, I would have put her out of her misery sooner," growled Paul.

So Ana was telling the truth.

Tanya's stomach turned. She recalled the harsh accusations she had lobbed at her during her last moments on earth. That would haunt her for the rest of her life.

"She didn't have the brains to plan," said Paul, "but she had help."

Tanya frowned. "Ana had a partner?"

"That snooping Ray Jackson from the residence. She hired him to spy on me."

Tanya's eyebrows shot up.

They both thought Ray Jackson worked for each other. Ray's innocent. He was just trying to solve the case like she was.

Tanya swallowed hard.

"Why did you kill your own sister?"

"She was the dumb twin. We called her DT for short." A smirk crossed Paul's face. "Father and I used to laugh at her stupidity. She was always trying to save the world and interfere with our business decisions. She was a thorn in our side, and what did that get her? A bullet in the head."

Tanya stared at him.

You're a psychopath.

"I came here to finish the job my father started," said Paul, "but she thought she could stop me."

He spat on the ground. Jane jerked her head back like he had slapped her.

"What the hell was she thinking? That she's Mother Theresa? I was protecting our family and our company. The moron deserved to die."

Tanya listened to him silently, her body still, but her brain whirling in a tornado.

How do I get his attention off Jane? How do I stop him from shooting us all before I take him down?

From the corner of her eyes, she caught a movement.

It was Stu.

His attention was on Paul, his eyes mixed with fear and fury, the twisted scar on his face making him look like a monster.

She could see how every word Paul uttered boiled a rage inside of him. She could only imagine how Paul Hammerston had manipulated him.

Stu was still hugging his shovel, but he had stepped away from the dugout.

Chapter One Hundred and Eleven

Tanya turned her attention to Paul.

"You killed Esmeralda, didn't you? And you made Stu bury her in the shallow grave on the hill."

"The idiot tried to hide her from me in the storage room." Paul shot an angry look at the man with the scar. "This deformed retard thought he could outwit *me*?"

Stu didn't respond, but his scowl darkened.

Paul glared at Tanya. "You small-town idiots don't know who you're up against."

"I may be a small-town cop," said Tanya, "but I know what your father did to these women when they were vulnerable girls."

"We took them off the streets. We gave them homes and cars."

"In exchange for ripping their children from their arms?" Tanya glowered at him. "Except for one. One of those kids was left behind."

A flicker went through Paul's eyes.

"Carmen Lopez," said Tanya. "She was one of the children your company used as lab rats, wasn't she? Just like Jane's child here was."

Jane broke into sobs. She beat her chest, crying.

"They stole my son! They tortured him."

Paul glowered at Tanya, but his face had turned a shade paler. Tanya maintained her steely gaze, knowing she had hit a nerve. He hadn't realized she knew as much as she did.

She sent a silent note of thanks to her friend for all the research she'd burrowed through.

Thank you, Katy.

"Carmen's mother was Isabella Lopez, one of the seven women your father abused. Esmeralda was visiting her at the residence when she witnessed you murder her."

Tanya had no idea how Esmeralda had found out about her grandmother or how she had entered the residence that forbade children. All she knew was she had to keep talking until backup came. Otherwise Jane would be as dead as Ana.

Paul laughed out loud. It was the hollow mirth of a man who knew he was being checkmated, but didn't want to show it.

"You can't prove any of it." He smirked. "I have a building full of lawyers who will protect me and my company. All you have is a bunch of fairy tales you can't back up. If you think you'll find any evidence, let me remind you, it's all gone up in flames."

Tanya noticed another movement from the side.

Stu had moved a few steps closer to Paul.

Tanya's heart ticked faster. Her body broke into a sweat, as she realized what he was planning.

Stu was about to make the biggest mistake of his life.

Chapter One Hundred and Twelve

Tanya knew Paul would fire at Stu without remorse.

She took a step forward, maintaining her aim.

"Let Jane go. She's already in bad shape."

Paul slammed the Glock on Jane's neck, making her head snap. Tanya's heart leaped into her mouth.

"Come one inch closer and she's a dead dodo," growled Paul. "Just like the others."

"Please...please don't kill me," cried Jane, shaking like she was consumed by fever. A trickle of blood ran down her forehead.

"Don't think I won't put a bullet through you in return," snarled Tanya. "I've killed bigger men than you."

Paul laughed an uncanny laugh. It was like he was certain of his freedom.

Max started to bark again.

"This woman is my insurance," said Paul. "Here's the deal. You're going to get me a helicopter with a civilian pilot. Land it on the grounds of Silver Serenity. You have two hours."

A warm flush crept up Tanya's neck.

"Call your head honcho," snarled Paul, "and tell them my request is non-negotiable."

Tanya knew this wasn't the time to act superior. One wrong move and Jane could die. Stu as well, if he didn't run fast enough.

The police sirens had turned off, but she could hear faint hollers from somewhere in the woods.

Backup.

Hope rose in her chest. They couldn't have heard the muffled shot that killed Ana, but they would be hearing Max's barks.

As if he knew what she was thinking, Max bayed louder, jumping on his hind legs, like he was itching to have a go at the man in front of him.

"Keep that mutt under control," growled Paul.

"Stay, bud," said Tanya, her heart hammering inside of her.

Paul was a cold-hearted killer who wouldn't think twice about shooting a dog. She had to talk, and talk fast, until she could think of a way out for all of them.

"I didn't realize you bought the private hospital and the retirement residence a year ago," she said, forcing her voice to stay calm. "I have to admit that was a pretty solid plan."

Paul smirked. "I could have bought the entire town of Black Rock if I wanted to."

Tanya narrowed her eyes.

I don't think so.

It was corrupt men like him Jack was trying to keep at bay at the summit. She wondered whether the chief had figured out the

Santiago he was watching was an actor, doing the bidding of the real owner.

"You hired Carolyn to manage the residence, and you encouraged her to recruit ex-convicts," continued Tanya, holding his gaze. "You knew they were easy to manipulate because none of them wanted to lose their cushy jobs and end up back in jail."

Paul didn't respond, but Tanya could see the smugness in his eyes.

"As a cherry on top, you blackmailed Carolyn and hiked the fear factor."

Paul furrowed his brow.

"I didn't need to blackmail that woman. With her track record, no one would hire her for the rest of her life. She would've done anything I asked."

It was Tanya's turn to frown. Paul may have been a killer, but something told her he was telling the truth.

Who was blackmailing Carolyn, then?

Jane turned a tear-stained face at Tanya and whimpered. She was hugging herself, trembling like every nerve inside her was falling apart.

Behind Paul, Stu took another step closer.

Chapter One Hundred and Thirteen

S tu raised the shovel in the air.

Paul's attention was split between Jane and Tanya, so he didn't notice who was behind him.

"Let Jane go!" cried Tanya, her heart racing, talking fast.

"No one's going to agree to a helicopter and an escape plan. Not after what you've done. If you want to live, your best bet is to drop your weapons and surrender. You're cornered, Paul Hammerston."

"She dies before I die."

"You've already got your quota of deaths. Spare her."

Paul cocked his gun. "What's one more?"

Stu smashed the shovel on his head.

Paul crashed to the ground with a shocked scream, his weapons flying from his hands. Tanya leaped down to grab both guns.

When she spun around, Stu was pounding Paul's head in a merciless frenzy. Paul was curled into a fetal position, his blood-curdling screams reverberating through the woods.

Stu hit the man with such ferociousness that it even shocked Tanya.

"Stu!" she shouted, jumping toward him. "Stop it!"

Stu slammed his shovel down. With a final shriek, Paul lurched into the shallow grave.

Tanya yanked the spade from Stu and glared.

"Are you trying to end up in jail?"

Stu didn't reply, hyperventilating from his exertion.

He stared down at the prone figure of the real Santiago Fernando. The pharmaceutical company's owner was lying immobile in the very grave he had commissioned for his victim, his head a bloodied mess of flesh and bone.

He wasn't moving.

Tanya kneeled next to the pit, her heart thudding. She leaned over to check Paul's pulse when she saw his mouth was contorted into a terrified scream, permanently.

She pulled back and looked up.

Stu was staring mutely at the dead man, his arms hanging by his sides. His eyes were wide in shock like he couldn't believe what he had done.

He looked at Tanya, his face a picture of horror.

"He... he... killed... Es...Esmeralda...."

Tanya could hear the hollering of the backup teams somewhere in the woods. They were getting close.

"He k...killed...I...I...Isabella..." stammered Stu, his eyes filling with tears. "I s...s...saw...him...."

She got to her feet and put a hand on his shoulder.

"Listen to me. You need to get out of here now. Do you understand?"

His eyes widened even more, but he stood frozen in the spot.

Tanya turned her head. Max was still barking. The cemetery would soon be filled with law enforcement.

"Leave," she hissed. "Get out of here."

Stu stared at her, his feet seemingly rooted to the ground. She shook him by the shoulders violently.

"Run. Run, Stu, run!"

He jerked back. Tanya let go of his shoulders and pushed him toward the bushes.

The crashing through the woods was getting louder.

"Go!"

Without a word, Stu slid into the forest.

Tanya let out a breath. She knew she would have a lot to answer for.

Soon, three officers blasted into view, their weapons drawn.

Tanya put her hands up.

"Tanya Stone from the Black Rock precinct."

The officers stopped as they spotted the bloodied body in the dugout. Their shocked eyes went from the three guns lying at Tanya's feet to Jane sobbing on the ground, then to Paul in the shallow grave.

"What the hell happened here?"

Tanya looked up to see the squad leader, the same officer who had ignored her while she was strapped to the hospital bed with an explosive ready to go off.

A steel coil of anger rolled up her spine.

"What's happened here," said Tanya, "is justice."

At Lopez's Home

Chapter One Hundred and Fourteen

K aty turned to Tanya.

"She's holding Dr. Chen hostage."

Her face was lined with fatigue. Next to her was one of the junior officers dispatched to guard Lopez's home.

"We've been trying to communicate," he said, "but she's got a gun."

"Her service weapon?" said Tanya.

"Couldn't say for sure, ma'am." The officer gave a doleful shrug. "Either way, she's not co-operating."

"Where are your partners?" said Tanya, scanning the front yard of Lopez's home.

"Watching the back and side doors. More guys from up the hill said they'll back us up soon."

"Good." Tanya nodded.

She had left the squad leader and his team up on the hill twenty minutes ago. They were cordoning off the crime scenes, securing the bodies, and photographing the evidence, while they waited for the forensics teams to arrive.

Jane was inside an ambulance, on her way to the nearest hospital.

Stu had disappeared in a flash, and Tanya hoped he wouldn't return to confess to his crime.

The squad leader had taken her statement, but she wasn't sure he believed her story.

Paul Hammerston had two guns. She had no choice but to kill him to save Jane's life, then hers, using the only weapon she could find. The shovel that had belonged to the local handyman.

Who was digging the grave? Paul Hammerston, of course.

The squad leader hadn't known Tanya had Ray's pistol in her pocket. Jack would have questions and so would the forensics investigators, but she pushed that worry for another day.

Right now, she needed to get Dr. Chen out safely and deal with Lopez.

"I've called her. I've screamed through the window." Katy rubbed her face. "I've been banging on the door ever since I got here. It's been hours."

"We've got a battering ram in the truck," said the officer. "We can crash in."

"Not with our doctor in potential peril," said Tanya.

"I've tried diplomacy, and it hasn't worked," said Katy with a tired shrug. "How could she do this? She even came to Dr. Chen's birthday party last week."

A loud thud came from inside the house. All three swiveled their heads around.

"What was that?" whispered the officer.

Tanya stepped up and banged her fist on the front door.

"Lopez!" she called out. "It's me, Tanya. Open up. I know what happened to your mother and your daughter."

Silence.

"I know why you ran away from Santiago Fernando."

Another thud came from the inside, like something fell. Katy pushed Tanya to the side and beat her palms on the door.

"Carmen! It's Katy. For heaven's sake, we're your friends. We want to help you. Let us in. Let Dr. Chen go!"

Tanya surveyed the windows on the first floor. The curtains were drawn, but the one closest to the front door had a sliver of an inch open in the middle.

"Do me a favor and keep banging on the door," she said. "Ask her questions and keep her occupied."

Tanya bounded down the front steps and hunkered under the window.

"If she sees you, she's going to shoot you," whispered the officer through the railing.

"I'll take my chances."

While Katy and the officer shouted to Lopez through the closed door, she peeked through the narrow opening between the curtains.

It was dark inside the living room.

Two chairs lay on their sides, like a scuffle had broken out in the room.

Tanya let her eyes adjust. She saw the outline of a diminutive woman on the sofa, sitting next to Deputy Lopez.

Dr. Chen.

The doctor was leaning close to the deputy, talking to her. Lopez sat with her head in her hands. On her lap was her service Glock.

What's the doctor saying? Trying to convince her to let her go?

A movement behind the sofa caught Tanya's eyes.

There's someone else inside the house.

Tanya pressed her nose on the glass and shifted her gaze to the rest of the living room.

Her eyes widened.

A child was sitting on the floor, behind the upturned chairs.

Chapter One Hundred and Fifteen

T he boy was thin and lanky, six or seven years old at the most.

He was playing with a rope on the floor, but his hands moved listlessly like he was bored.

Is that who I think it is?

The kid lifted his head as if he felt Tanya's presence.

Tanya ducked and crouched under the window, her heart thumping. Keeping her head low, she scurried toward the front door and tapped the officer's shoulder.

"There's a child inside. Get the battering ram."

He raced to his truck, yelling to his partner through his shoulder radio.

Tanya turned to Katy.

"Lopez has a son."

"Oh, my goodness." Katy put a hand on her heart. "Austin Lopez. That's him, isn't it?"

"It would explain the second mattress in the storage room," said Tanya. "Stu was hiding both kids, protecting them from Paul."

"Did Carmen ask him to?"

"She's the only one who can tell us how and why that happened. If I have to bet, she got Stu to hide her kids temporarily while Ana did her bit to save the mother, which all ultimately failed...."

Katy shook her head like she couldn't believe it. "Carmen wasn't trying to run out of the country with Santiago. She was running from him."

She whirled around to Tanya.

"I can't believe she had two children. I wish she'd told us about them and asked us for help. Why didn't she?"

Tanya turned back to the door. "Let's give her one more chance before we break this down."

She pounded her palm on the wood.

"Lopez? Your husband, the Santiago Fernando you know, isn't who you think he is. He's an impostor."

They waited quietly, but all they heard was silence.

"You're safe now. Your son is safe. Let Dr. Chen go."

More silence.

"Your real half-brother's been manipulating you. He's the one who killed Esmeralda, your mom, and all those other women. Please let us come in so we can talk."

No answer.

Pangs of guilt crossed Tanya's heart.

Esmeralda and Ana's deaths hung heavily on her mind. If only she had figured this out sooner, she may have saved them both, but there was no going back.

"She's too rattled to listen to us," said Katy, hanging her head in disappointment. "Imagine finding out the man you had kids with was your half-sibling. It was a lie, but she didn't know that. No wonder she's had a nervous breakdown."

Tanya banged on the door once more.

"Lopez, I'm sorry to say Ana was shot dead today—"

"Ready, ma'am!" called a male voice from behind her.

Tanya pivoted around to see three officers at the bottom of the steps. They had their battering ram. They had also changed into full riot gear, with helmets, shields, batons, guns, and Kevlar vests, looking like they were prepared to take down an international terrorist.

"Step aside," hollered one officer as they pounded up the steps and took position in front of the door.

"We got this, ma'am," said the second officer. "She's armed. You need to move to safety."

With a resigned sigh, Tanya took a step down.

The men hunched low and swung the ram back. That was when Tanya heard the click of the bolt.

"Stop!" she cried.

The men froze.

The front door flew open. Lopez stood on the threshold, her Glock in her limp hand. The barrel was pointed to the floor. She stared at the officers with a glazed look, like she was seeing ghosts.

"Stand back!" called out Tanya.

Katy pushed through the men, rushed toward Lopez, and threw her arms around her shoulders.

"Oh, honey. You're safe now, sweetie. Austin, too."

Lopez's shoulders drooped and her grip on her gun loosened. Tanya pried it out before it fell to the floor.

The face of a small boy popped out from the side of the door. His eyes widened as he spotted the officers and their heavy equipment.

Tanya got on her knees in front of him.

"You okay, sweetie?"

The child pointed at the armored men who had hustled down to the bottom of the steps. "Are those daddy's friends?"

"No, honey," said Tanya, reaching out to him. "They're the police."

He looked at her with his big brown eyes. "Mommy said Daddy and his friends were going to kill us."

Tanya's heart broke to hear his young voice utter those words. She squeezed his shoulders.

"You're safe now. No one's going to hurt you or your mommy, okay?"

"Esmeralda," cried Lopez, tears streaming down her cheeks. "Esmeralda paid because of me."

Katy pulled her in closer.

"You were only trying to protect your children. You can't blame yourself, hun."

Lopez fell into Katy's shoulders, sobbing.

Day Four

Chapter One Hundred and Sixteen

"**M**y whole life was built on a lie."

Carmen Lopez's eyes were lined and her face was haggard. She sat sandwiched in between Katy and Tanya at the café table, a shell of her former self.

Across from her, Austin was slurping an iced tea from a straw, one hand stroking Max's ear. Chantal, Katy's ten-year-old daughter, sat next to him with her coloring book.

Max had taken a strategic position in between the two children. He didn't flinch as Austin twisted his ears or Chantal stroked his fur the wrong way. But Tanya knew she had to keep a sharp eye for suspicious little hands with food being slipped under the table.

The heavenly smell of warm baked goodies came from Lulu's kitchen. Ray, Jack, and Katy's husband, Peace, were on their way to join them at the café, but Tanya had decided to order, anyway.

It had been a trying morning. They had just buried Esmeralda and Ana at the Black Rock cemetery, and given Lopez's mother a proper burial. Emotions were still raw.

Paul Hammerston was awaiting trial for multiple premeditated homicides, the most severe charge he could have received.

The fake Santiago Fernando was in custody. He had quickly agreed to tell all in exchange for leniency. His first helpful tip was the name of the corrupt physician Paul had hired to medicate and eventually kill the seven women.

Tanya's eyes were red with exhaustion.

She had stayed up for three days in a row, working with Jack and the forensics team and officers sent from the other counties. After sloughing through evidence and interrogating suspects and witnesses with little sleep, she was beginning to see double. But the loose threads were finally coming together.

After all that hard work, a quiet coffee chat with her good friends was exactly what Tanya needed.

A young man with baggy pants and a hip-hop T-shirt stumbled out of the kitchen. Perched precariously in his hands was a tray filled with hot drinks.

Troy West.

Tanya rustled up a tired smile.

"Good to see you, Troy," she said. "Seems like you've found yourself a good job."

The teen blushed and looked down. He set the drinks on the table, rattling the tea and coffee cups with the jerky movements of a newbie.

"I told you he'd turn around," said Lulu, bursting from the kitchen with a wicker basket full of muffins. She shot Tanya a stern look. "A sound talk from me was all that was needed."

Tanya smiled but didn't reply.

After all that had happened on the hill, her encounter with the gun-toting Lulu and her delinquent nephew seemed a lifetime ago. Whatever the café owner thought, Tanya was sure her fake gun had scared Troy into submission, more than anything else.

"He's going to learn to be on time, work hard, clean up after himself, and become responsible." Lulu huffed. "He's going to turn into a good man, just you wait. You'll see."

Troy grimaced.

"I'm right here, Aunt Lulu. I can hear you."

"Good. Then you'll know what's expected from you, young man."

Lulu turned her focus on the kids at the table. She placed a muffin each in front of Austin and Chantal, and leaned over to them.

"I made these just for you," she whispered. "Don't tell your moms, but you can have two each."

Chantal giggled. Austin's face brightened. He placed his drink down and reached for his muffin, a happy smile of anticipation crossing his young face.

Tanya watched the boy, her heart filling with sorrow at the memory of the sister he had lost.

He'll survive this. He'll be fine.

Lulu spun around to Troy, who was dawdling toward the café counter.

"Didn't I tell you not to touch your phone until your shift is done?"

"Come on. It's just for a minute."

"One minute, my foot. Where's Max's bowl of water? Do you want the poor dog to die of thirst?"

With a sigh, Troy turned and shuffled toward the kitchen.

"Kids these days," said Lulu, pulling a chair next to Austin. She looked at Lopez and tilted her head. "How are you holding up, honey?"

Lopez shrugged but didn't speak.

We'll need time to heal, thought Tanya. *All of us.*

Katy turned to Lopez, her eyes narrowed.

"I say this with a lot of love, but I'm really, really mad at you. I want to shake you."

Lopez shot her a surprised look.

"Why didn't you ask us for help?" said Katy, unable to conceal her annoyance. "Why didn't you trust us?"

Chapter One Hundred and Seventeen

L opez opened her mouth and shut it.

She placed her hands on the table and shook her head, like she had lost her voice.

Lulu turned to the children.

"Why don't you two join Troy in the kitchen? Tell him the sugar cookies I baked this morning are for you."

The kids spun around to her, eyes wide. Chantal whipped around to her mom. Katy nodded and mouthed, *You can go*.

Chantal took Austin by the arm and stepped down.

"Cookies are better than muffins," she said as she led the boy away from the table. She craned her neck and gestured at the dog. "Hey, come on, Max."

Max didn't ask for permission. He twirled around and trotted toward them, sniffing the air and licking his lips.

"No cookies for Max!" called out Tanya, but the trio had already vanished through the kitchen door.

Lopez was still staring at her hands.

"The Fernandos are...were a powerful family. I was scared for my kids. I couldn't risk anything." She spoke in a low voice. "I didn't know who was working for Santiago. I didn't even know who the real Santiago *was*."

She looked up at Katy, her face filled with misery.

"I didn't mean to hold Dr. Chen. I thought if she was with me, no one would hurt us. I was so desperate. My life was exploding in front of my eyes...."

"Dr. Chen's forgiven you, but you'll have to be on your best behavior around her now." Katy pursed her lips. "Good thing her bark is worse than her bite."

Tanya leaned over to Lopez. "How did you find out your mother was at Silver Serenity?"

Lopez sighed heavily.

"Ana tracked me down last year. She left her family at eighteen to teach English in Thailand, so she didn't know anything about my marriage. It was only when she returned to the US for her father's funeral, she learned what her brother had planned for the seven women."

Lopez clasped and unclasped her hands.

"She was the one who told me my birth mother had been trying to find me all these years."

"Is that why you transferred to Black Rock's precinct from San Diego?" said Tanya. "To find your mother?"

Lopez nodded silently.

"You trusted Ana even though she was from the family that tortured you?"

"Ana and I met when we were kids. I didn't recognize her after all these years, but I believed her. She was the little girl who stared at me through the glass windows of the laboratory. Her father brought her and Santiago down to showcase us like we were circus freaks."

Tanya shuddered in horror.

Tears welled in Katy's eyes. "No one should ever have to go through that, let alone a child."

Lopez shrugged like she had come to terms with her past.

"Ana used to cry every time she saw us. I heard her scream to her dad to let us out. But her brother always had this gleam in his eye, like watching us suffer was a power trip for him."

"Like father, like son." Lulu shook her head. "May they burn in hell."

Tanya frowned as the faces of Ana and Paul swirled through her mind. "Were the two Fernando children really twins?"

"Not identical," said Lopez, wiping her nose. "Didn't look like siblings, even when they were kids."

"What about your husband?" said Tanya. "When did you meet the fake Santiago?"

"My first year in college. He said he was a vice president at a Fortune 500 company. He swept me off my feet. After being in foster care for so long, I dreamed of a real family. He was my knight in shining armor." She sighed. "He was sweet when we dated but became a monster after we married."

"Men, I tell you." Lulu scowled. "They change their colors as soon as they have you in their den."

Lopez drew in a trembling breath.

"He told me his name was Jim Jones. He used to beat me. I endured it, because I didn't want the kids to grow up in a broken family. The first day he took his belt to Esmeralda was the day I tried to get out."

She swallowed hard.

"That's when he blackmailed me."

"How?" said Katy.

"He said he'd tell the world my mother was a child trafficker who sold her kid to a pharma company for testing. She'd end up in prison for life. That's when I realized he knew more about my past than I did...."

Tears rolled down Lopez's face.

"I'd repressed those memories, but they came back in full force. I remembered being locked up in the lab. We were medicated, prodded, and poked all day and night. It was horrible."

Tanya frowned. "Do you know what drugs they were testing you on?"

"Hugo Fernando was looking for a cure for the Stoneman syndrome."

Katy gasped.

Tanya gaped.

"I saw an episode about that on TV. Isn't that a bone cancer where you turn into a living fossil?" Lulu shuddered. "Imagine being trapped in your own body, not being able to move? That would be true hell on earth."

She scrunched her eyes. "I thought they hadn't found a cure for it."

Lopez didn't look up, but her shoulders drooped.

"We sacrificed our childhoods," she whispered, "for nothing."

Tanya sat back, shaking her head. "Hugo Fernando's wife was battling this same rare cancer."

She spoke in a quiet voice as she unraveled the history of this bizarre case that had been consuming her.

"His response was to impregnate a group of vulnerable girls, manipulate them into giving up their babies, and experiment on the kids to find an illusory cure...which ultimately resulted in abject failure."

"Not to mention the cold-blooded murder of almost all the mothers," said Katy, "and that of a young girl who was an innocent bystander."

Lulu's face darkened.

"All I can wish for, right now, is that the devil is making him pay for his devious sins."

Chapter One Hundred and Eighteen

L opez put her head in her hands.

"Santiago sent that man to seduce me and hold me prisoner. How could I have been so naïve?"

"Santiago Fernando met your husband in prison well before you met him," said Tanya. "There's no way you could have known what they were scheming."

"What happened to the other children they tested on?" said Lulu. "Were they taken to Mexico?"

"The Mexico story was a red herring," said Tanya. "They were quietly fostered into families in different states. Their birth mothers never knew."

Lopez took a raspy breath in.

"My mom was the most vocal of the group. She's the one who hired a lawyer to find us. That's why she was targeted. The money meant nothing to her. She just wanted to find me."

"Hugo Fernando was a cunning man." Tanya's mind went over the documents she'd read into the late hours. "To stop your mother once and for all, he told her you had married his son. Your half-brother. That must have stunned her into silence."

Lulu tsked. "The Fernandos had no humanity."

"Except for Ana," said Lopez, looking up.

"She never forgot us and never stopped trying to help us. She was planning an escape for the women, but Carolyn worked her to the bone and watched her like a hawk. When that failed, Ana tried to get us out of the country, and now she's...."

Lopez took a shuddering breath in.

"She's dead."

Katy reached over to Lopez and wrapped her arm around her shoulder.

The image of Ana's prone figure by the cemetery slammed into Tanya's mind. A pang of guilt shot through her like a lightning strike.

"Did you meet your mother in the end, honey?" she asked in a soft voice.

Lopez turned a tear-streaked face to her.

"Two weeks ago. Carolyn put my mom in one of the nicer resident rooms up front. Maybe the third wing was full. Good thing because that's always locked down tight. Either way, Ana got me inside so I could meet her, while Stu kept watch. That was the night my mom told me I was married to my half-brother."

Lopez's voice cracked.

"She started drinking the day Hugo told her the lie. He told her I wanted nothing to do with her. She was broken."

"That's why you went to San Diego," said Tanya. "To rescue your kids from their father?"

"I never felt so sick in my life," said Lopez. "I knew he'd retaliate, but I had to get Austin and Esmeralda away from him. If I had just stopped to show a picture of my husband to Ana, she could have told me it wasn't her brother."

Lopez beat her fists on her forehead.

"How could I have been so stupid?"

"You can't blame yourself, honey," said Lulu, shaking her head. "Everyone was fed a different story."

Katy held Lopez tightly. "I'm still trying to figure all their lies out, too, hun."

"Esmeralda and Austin were so excited to meet their grandmother," said Lopez, her face pale. "Stu said he'd help them get inside without Carolyn seeing. I shouldn't have said yes."

"We're still trying to put Esmeralda's final movements together," said Tanya. "Stu took her to visit her grandmother at the residence the night she was killed. It seems like she witnessed the murder, so she was next."

Tanya took a deep breath in.

"Stu blames himself for both of their deaths. He's beyond devastated."

Katy turned to Tanya, her brow furrowed. "Who owned the death ledger?"

"Paul Hammerston, the real Santiago, kept a record of his victims," said Tanya. "Stu discovered it and tried to warn Ana, by placing a black rose in the towel room. It was the only way he could communicate. When she kept failing to save the women, he stole the ledger and brought it to the residence, but Carolyn found it and confiscated it."

She paused.

"I don't think the director ever knew what that book signified. She was occupied by her own problems."

"Why did Esmeralda have to pay for it all?" Lopez broke into sobs.

The three women leaned across the table and held her. There was nothing they could say or do that would unburden the grief of a mother who lost her child.

Lopez looked up and wiped her face.

"Stu's an angel," she whispered. "He hid Esmeralda and Austin for me, because I was so scared their father would come looking for them. Like Ana, Stu has a heart of gold."

The image of Stu bludgeoning Paul Hammerston flashed to Tanya's mind. Jack had asked her questions about the incident, and so had the squad leader at the crime scene. There would be more inquiries to come.

Tanya clenched her jaws.

Jack can arrest me if he wants, but I'm not letting Stu suffer any more than he has.

The jingle of bells by the front door made them all turn.

It was Black Rock's police chief, Jack Bold.

He stepped inside, his face dark.

Chapter One Hundred and Nineteen

R ay Jackson and Katy's husband, Peace, trooped into the café behind Jack.

Ray slapped his hat down on the table and plopped on the chair by Lulu.

Jack took the chair next to Tanya and reached for a muffin. Tanya sat back and watched him peel the wrapper back.

I guess I'm free, at least for another day.

Peace walked over and kissed Katy on the cheek.

"I've got my first pro bono case in Black Rock," he announced as he took his seat. "I promise you the Fernandos will pay for their sins."

Katy furrowed her brow.

"But babe, you're not a *criminal* lawyer."

"I'm bringing a civil case against the Fernandos in court."

"But they're all dead. The father, the mother, the son. Even Ana, who was completely innocent."

"My main argument," said Peace, "will be for the company to be dissolved and for the mothers and the children to be duly compensated."

Ray nodded. "Justice will be served finally. That's what matters in the end."

Jack turned to Tanya.

"You're a trooper. You did good work, Stone."

Tanya twirled her coffee cup, trying not to make eye contact.

Stu is the unsung hero here. Not me. He watched from the shadows and found out what was going on. He tried to warn us.

"Thanks, Jack," she said in a quiet voice.

Jack nodded. "I only wish I could have been here with you."

Tanya picked up her cup and took a sip to hide her expression.

"Katy did the important research work. She deserves a raise."

Jack turned to Katy and touched his cap. "I'll have to ask the mayor for a bigger budget."

Tanya noticed Ray was watching her with a twinkle in his eyes. No one around the table, except for Katy, knew his real identity. The others considered him an engaged citizen who had risen to the occasion and helped Tanya out during a crisis.

"You look smug," she said to him, hoping to divert Jack's attention away from her. "Anything you want to share?"

Ray grinned. "Guess who's going on a nice getaway?"

"Who would that be now?" said Lulu. "You?"

"Yes, ma'am. I'm taking two lovely ladies for a well-deserved beach vacation." He rubbed his hands. "Hawaii, here I come."

Tanya raised a brow. "You're going on a holiday with Ocean and Sahara?"

"Are those even their real names?" huffed Lulu. "I swear they're on a witness protection program or something."

Ray's grin grew. "My girls and I will have a real romantic time."

Lulu's eyes widened. "They're your girlfriends now?"

"They call him their boy toy," said Tanya to Lulu. "Though, sometimes, I'm not sure who's toying with whom, to be honest."

"At your age?" Lulu turned to Ray, mouth open. "Here I thought you were a respectable man with principles and....and scruples."

Ray shrugged. "I like feisty, smart, older women. What's wrong with that?"

Lulu scoffed.

"Life just got interesting again." Ray stretched his legs and leaned back in his chair. "If there's one thing I've learned, it's you're never too old. You only *think* you're too old. Well, I refuse to sit out in the pasture anymore."

Tanya suddenly realized why he had been so adamant to be part of the Silver Serenity case.

You were worried about becoming irrelevant. That's why you twisted Director Cross's arm. And mine.

As if Ray could read her mind, he turned to her and winked.

"My heavens." Lulu scraped her chair back and got to her feet. "Two girlfriends? I have no words. What has the world come to?"

Ray snickered as Lulu shuffled toward the kitchen, shaking her head.

A buzz in her pockets startled Tanya. She fished her phone out and checked the screen. It was a text message from Ocean.

Speaking of the devils.

She clicked on it and read the note twice to make sure she understood it correctly.

We know who blackmailed Carolyn. But she's dead now. PLEASE stop that investigation.

Tanya stared at the text for several seconds. Around her, the conversation had drifted onto something more benign. Something about arranging play dates for young Austin so he could adjust to a normal life again.

Tanya typed a quick response.

Who blackmailed Carolyn? Why?

Her phone went silent for a minute, before pinging again. Tanya stared at the screen.

If we tell you, you must promise not to pursue it any further.

With a heavy sigh, Tanya slipped her mobile back into her pocket and got up. Everyone turned to her.

"I, er, have to take Max out for his walk."

Jack looked at her, disappointment in his eyes, like he wished she'd stay with the group.

"See you back at the office, then?"

Tanya nodded and stepped away from the table. She walked toward the kitchen, wondering how many cookies Max had eaten.

The phone buzzed in her pocket again. She didn't pick it up, but she was sure it was another panicked note from Ocean and Sahara.

Time to find out what those two feisty women were up to.

To be continued...

◆━━━◆

I hope you enjoyed this story. Our detective team has done their job and the villain(s) have got their just desserts.

But would you like to know what Ocean and Sahara are up to? I have written a very short story about these two sassy characters and their shenanigans, and also how Stu fared at the end. Read the twist to this story that no one, not even Tanya, expected....

Download your bonus gift here.

Ocean and Sahara Twist:

https://tikiriherath.com/oceansaharatwist

Start Reading

Dive into the next spine-tingling, pulse-pounding thriller in this series.

HER GRISLY GRAVE

Don't miss out on another fast-paced murder mystery thriller with Special Agent Tanya Stone, K9 Max, Chief Jack Bold, and the eccentric characters of this small seaside town, each of whom holds a secret they'd rather you not find out.

Will Tanya find out who ANON is and if her brother is truly alive?

Find out in HER GRISLY GRAVE next.

https://tikiriherath.com/hergrislygrave

A Note from Tikiri

Dear friend,

Thank you for reading this book. Did you enjoy the story?

Would you like to help other readers meet Tanya and Max, and follow their adventures on the West Coast? If you do, tell your reader friends about this book and share on social media. Leave an honest review on Goodreads, Bookbub, or your favorite online bookstore.

Just one sentence would do. Thank you so much.

Would you like to know more about Tanya? I didn't get too much into her background in this book, because I wanted to sweep you away in the intrigue and mystery. You can read Tanya's origin story in my earlier book, *The Girl Who Made Them Pay*, a Red Heeled Rebel international crime thriller.

Learn how Tanya fought her way out of Russian-occupied Ukraine, only to land in a worse fate in central Europe. Read how she met Asha and Katy, and how they created their own found family. The Girl Who Made Them Pay is written in Asha's first voice and will take you on a wild ride from London to Brussels, to Luxembourg, and finally to Marseilles.

Have you heard of the Rebel Reader Club?

This is my exclusive reader club where you will get early access to my new mystery thrillers before they're published. You can also receive bonus content and reader stickers, bookmarks, personalized paperbacks and even a postcard from K9 Max himself, sent to your home.

If you'd like to learn more, join the wait list to get an invitation when the club opens to new members next. You'll find the secret entrance to the club on my **website**

https://tikiriherath.com/thrillers

You might have to sleuth a bit to find the door, but by now, you've become a good detective, haven't you?

My very best wishes,
Tikiri
Vancouver, Canada

❖———❖

PS/ Don't forget! Download the twisty bonus story here.

I enjoyed writing the two sassy characters, Ocean and Sahara, so much that I wanted to spend more time with them. Here's what happens when Tanya ferrets them out. You'll also learn how Stu fared at the end. Download your bonus here.

Ocean and Sahara Twist:
https://tikiriherath.com/oceansaharatwist

Start Reading

PPS/ If you didn't enjoy the story or spotted typos, would you drop a line and let me know? Or just write to say hello. I would love to hear from you and personally reply to every email I receive.

My email address is: <u>Tikiri@TikiriHerath.com</u>

Continue the adventure

Continue the story with HER GRISLY GRAVE –
https://tikiriherath.com/THRILLERS

Don't miss out on another fast-paced murder mystery thriller with Special Agent Tanya Stone, K9 Max, Chief Jack Bold, and the eccentric characters of this small seaside town, each of whom holds a secret they'd rather you not find out.

Will Tanya find out who ANON is and if her brother is truly alive?

Find out in HER GRISLY GRAVE next.

https://tikiriherath.com/hergrislygrave

◆━━━━━◆

HER GRISLY GRAVE: A gripping Tanya Stone FBI K9 crime thriller with a jaw-dropping twist.

A dangerous killer on the loose. A small town gripped by terror.

411

The victims are discovered in unusual places, eyes blindfolded and heads crowned with sunflower garlands. A chilling calling card from a twisted mind who enjoys psychological games.

With Max, her faithful police dog by her side, FBI Agent Tanya Stone is on the case. They race against time, on the hunt for a cold-blooded criminal.

But the devious psychopath is always one step ahead, taunting the detective with a riddle sent to a true crime podcaster an hour before each murder.

Deadly lies converge and the body count rises. Tanya fights to unravel the clues and uncover the dark secrets of this town.

She doesn't realize the shocking truth is connected to her haunted family and her painful past. The stakes are personal as well as deadly. And the clock is ticking.

Can Tanya and Max unmask the serial killer before the next victim dies?

Or will Tanya pay the ultimate price for her family's tragedy fourteen years ago?

Pick up HER GRISLY GRAVE and get your thriller fix today!
HER GRISLY GRAVE:
https://tikiriherath.com/hergrislygrave

❖———••———❖

There is no graphic violence, heavy cursing, or explicit sex in these books. No dog is harmed in this story, but the villains are.

❖———••———❖

My books are available in e-book, paperback, and hardback editions on all good bookstores. Also available for free in libraries everywhere. Just ask your friendly local librarian to order a copy via Ingram Spark.

Debate This Dozen

Twelve (plus one) **Book Club Questions**

1. Who was your favorite character?
2. Which characters did you dislike?
3. Which scene has stuck with you the most? Why?
4. What scenes surprised you?
5. Did you catch the sentence that had the title?
6. What was your favorite part of the book?
7. What was your least favorite part?
8. Did any part of this book strike a particular emotion in you? Which part and what emotion did the book make you feel?
9. Did you know the author has written an underlying message in this story? What theme or life lesson do you think this story tells?
10. What did you think of the author's writing?
11. How would you adapt this book into a movie? Who would you cast in the leading roles?
12. On a scale of one to ten, how would you rate this story?
13. Would you read another book by this author?

The Reading List

T he Red Heeled Rebels universe of mystery thrillers, featuring your favorite kick-ass female characters.

Tanya Stone FBI K9 Mystery Thrillers
www.TikiriHerath.com/Thrillers
An FBI K9 thriller series starring Tetyana from the Red Heeled Rebels as Special Agent Tanya Stone, and Max, as her loyal German Shepherd. These are serial killer thrillers set

in Black Rock, a small upscale resort town on the coast of
Washington state.

Her Deadly End
Her Cold Blood
Her Last Lie
Her Secret Crime
Her Dead Girl
Her Perfect Murder
Her Grisly Grave

Asha Kade Private Detective Murder Mysteries
www.TikiriHerath.com/Mysteries
**Each book is a standalone murder mystery thriller,
featuring the Red Heeled Rebels, Asha Kade and Katy
McCafferty. Asha and Katy receive one million dollars for
their favorite children's charity from a secret benefactor's
estate every time they solve a cold case.**

Merciless Legacy
Merciless Games
Merciless Crimes
Merciless Lies
Merciless Past
Merciless Deaths

**Red Heeled Rebels International Mystery & Crime - The
Origin Story**
www.TikiriHerath.com/RedHeeledRebels

The award-winning origin story of the Red Heeled Rebels characters. Learn how a rag-tag group of trafficked orphans from different places united to fight for their freedom and their lives, and became a found family.

The Girl Who Crossed the Line
The Girl Who Ran Away
The Girl Who Made Them Pay
The Girl Who Fought to Kill
The Girl Who Broke Free
The Girl Who Knew Their Names
The Girl Who Never Forgot

◆—––—◆

The Accidental Traveler
www.TikiriHerath.com
An anthology of personal short stories based on the author's sojourns around the world.

◆—––—◆

The Rebel Diva Nonfiction Series
www.TikiriHerath.com/Nonfiction
Your Rebel Dreams: 6 simple steps to take back control of your life in uncertain times.

Your Rebel Plans: 4 simple steps to getting unstuck and making progress today.

Your Rebel Life: Easy habit hacks to enhance happiness in the 10 key areas of your life.

Bust Your Fears: 3 simple tools to crush your anxieties and squash your stress.

Collaborations
The Boss Chick's Bodacious Destiny Nonfiction Bundle
Dark Shadows 2: Voodoo and Black Magic of New Orleans

Tikiri's novels and nonfiction books are available on all good bookstores around the world.

These books are also available in libraries everywhere. Just ask your friendly local librarian or your local bookstore to order a copy via Ingram Spark.

www.TikiriHerath.com

Happy reading.

Tanya Stone FBI K9 Mystery Thrillers

S ome small-town secrets will haunt your nightmares. Escape if
you can...

The Books:

Her Deadly End

Her Cold Blood

Her Last Lie

Her Secret Crime

Her Perfect Murder

Her Grisly Grave

An FBI K9 serial killer thriller series for a pulse-pounding, bone-chilling adventure from the comfort and warmth of your favorite reading chair at home.

Can you find the killer before Agent Tanya Stone?
www.TikiriHerath.com/thrillers

FBI Special Agent Tanya Stone has a new assignment. Hunt down the serial killers prowling the idyllic West Coast resort towns.

An unspeakable and bone-chilling darkness seethes underneath these picturesque seaside suburbs. A string of violent abductions and gruesome murders wreak hysteria among the perfect lives of the towns' families.

But nothing is what it seems. The monsters wear masks and mingle with the townsfolk, spreading vicious lies.

With her K9 German Shepherd, Agent Stone goes on the warpath. She will fight her own demons as a trafficked survivor to make the perverted psychopaths pay.

But now, they're after her.

__Small towns have dark deceptions and sealed lips. If they know you know the truth, they'll never let you leave...__

<hr/>

Each book is a standalone murder mystery thriller, featuring Tetyana from the Red Heeled Rebels as Agent Tanya Stone, and Max, her loyal German Shepherd. Red Heeled Rebels Asha Kade and Katy McCafferty and their found family make guest appearances when Tanya needs help.

There is no graphic violence, heavy cursing, or explicit sex in these books.

The dogs featured in this series are never harmed, but the villains are.

<hr/>

__To learn more about this exciting new series and find out how to get early access to all the books in the Tanya Stone FBI K9 series, go to www.TikiriHerath.com/thrillers__

Sign up to Tikiri's Rebel Reader Club to get the chance to win personalized paperback books, chat with the author and more.

<hr/>

Available in e-book, paperback, and hardback editions on all good bookstores around the world. Print books are available for free in libraries everywhere. Just ask your friendly local librarian or your local bookstore to order a copy via Ingram Spark.

Asha Kade Private Detective Murder Mysteries

How far would you go for a million-dollar payout?

The Books:

Merciless Legacy

Merciless Games

Merciless Crimes

Merciless Lies

Merciless Past

Merciless Deaths

◆────────◆

Each book is a standalone murder mystery thriller featuring the Red Heeled Rebel, Asha Kade, and her best friend Katy

McCafferty, as private detectives on the hunt for serial killers in small towns USA.

There is no graphic violence, heavy cursing, or explicit sex in these books. What you will find are a series of suspicious deaths, a closed circle of suspects, twists and turns, fast-paced action, and nail-biting suspense.

www.TikiriHerath.com/mysteries

A newly minted private investigator, Asha Kade, gets a million dollars from an eccentric client's estate every time she solves a cold case. Asha Kade accepts this bizarre challenge, but what she doesn't bargain for is to be drawn into the dark underworld of her past again.

The only thing that propels her forward now is a burning desire for justice.

What readers are saying on Amazon and Goodreads:

"My new favorite series!"

"Thrilling twists, unputdownable!"

"I was hooked right from the start!"

"A twisted whodunnit! Edge of your seat thriller that kept me up late, to finish it, unputdownable!! More, please!"

"Buckle up for a roller coaster of a ride. This one will keep you on the edge of your seat."

"A must read! A macabre start to an excellent book. It had me totally gripped from the start and just got better!""

✦━━━✦

A brand-new murder mystery series for a pulse-pounding, bone-chilling adventure from the comfort and warmth of your favorite reading chair at home.

Can you find the killer before Asha Kade does?

✦━━━✦

To learn more about this exciting series, go to www.TikiriHerath.com/mysteries.

Sign up to Tikiri's Rebel Reader Club to get the chance to win personalized paperback books, chat with the author and more.

✦━━━✦

Available in e-book, paperback, and hardback editions on all good bookstores around the world. Print books are available for free in libraries everywhere. Just ask your friendly local librarian or your local bookstore to order a copy via Ingram Spark.

The Red Heeled Rebels International Mystery & Crime

The Origin Story

Would you like to know the origin story of your favorite characters in the Tanya Stone FBI K9 mystery thrillers and the Asha Kade Merciless murder mysteries?

In the award-winning Red Heeled Rebels international mystery & crime series—the origin story—you'll find out how Asha, Katy, and Tetyana (Tanya) banded together in their troubled youths to fight for freedom against all odds.

＊—————＊

The complete Red Heeled Rebels international crime collection:

Prequel Novella: The Girl Who Crossed the Line

Book One: The Girl Who Ran Away
Book Two: The Girl Who Made Them Pay
Book Three: The Girl Who Fought to Kill
Book Four: The Girl Who Broke Free
Book Five: The Girl Who Knew Their Names
Book Six: The Girl Who Never Forgot
The series is now complete.

———✦———

An epic, pulse-pounding, international crime thriller series that spans four continents featuring a group of spunky, sassy young misfits who have only each other for family.

A multiple-award-winning series which would be best read in order. There is no graphic violence, heavy cursing, or explicit sex in these books.

www.TikiriHerath.com/RedHeeledRebels

———✦———

In a world where justice no longer prevails, six iron-willed young women rally to seek vengeance on those who stole their humanity.

If you like gripping thrillers with flawed but strong female leads, vigilante action in exotic locales and twists that leave you at the edge of your seat, you'll love these books by multiple award-winning Canadian novelist, Tikiri Herath.

Go on a heart-pounding international adventure without having to get a passport or even buy an airline ticket!

———✦———

What readers are saying on Amazon and Goodreads:

"Fast-paced and exciting!"
"An exciting and thought-provoking book."
"A wonderful story! I didn't want to leave the characters."
"I couldn't put down this exciting road trip adventure with a powerful message."
"Another award-worthy adventure novel that keeps you on the edge of your seat."
"A heart-stopping adventure. I just couldn't put the book down till I finished reading it."

Literary Awards & Praise for The Red Heeled Rebels books:

- Grand Prize Award Finalist - 2019 Eric Hoffer Award, USA

- First Horizon Award Finalist - 2019 Eric Hoffer Award, USA

- Honorable Mention General Fiction - 2019 Eric Hoffer Award, USA

- Winner First-In-Category - 2019 Chanticleer Somerset Award, USA

- Semi-Finalist - 2020 Chanticleer Somerset Award, USA

- Winner in 2019 Readers' Favorite Book Awards, USA

- Winner of 2019 Silver Medal - Excellence E-Lit Award, USA

- Winner in Suspense Category - 2018 New York Big Book

Award, USA

* Finalist in Suspense Category - 2018 & 2019 Silver Falchion Awards, USA

* Honorable Mention - 2018-19 Reader Views Literary Classics Award, USA

* Publisher's Weekly Booklife Prize - 2018, USA

To learn more about this addictive series, go to **www.TikiriHerath.com/RedHeeledRebels** and receive the prequel novella - **The Girl Who Crossed The Line** - as a gift.

Sign up to Tikiri's Rebel Reader club and get bonus stories, exotic recipes, the chance to win paperbacks, chat with the author and more.

Available in e-book, paperback, and hardback editions on all good bookstores around the world. Print books are available for free in libraries everywhere. Just ask your friendly local librarian or your local bookstore to order a copy via Ingram Spark.

Acknowledgments

To my amazing, talented, superstar editor, Stephanie Parent (United States of America), thank you, as always, for coming on this literary journey with me and for helping make these books the best they can be.

To Forensic Identification Examiner, Chantelle Foster of the Royal Canadian Mounted Police of British Columbia. Many thanks go for her detailed and patient explanations on collecting and examining forensics evidence at crime scenes. If I got anything wrong, it's all on me!

To my international club of beta readers who gave me their frank feedback, thank you. I truly value your thoughts.
Michele Kapugi, United States of America
Kim Schup, United States of America.

✦———•—•✦

To my special Rebel Reader club member, Carolyn
Pennett-Staresinic (Canada), who now has a character named after
her.
   For the record, the real Carolyn is nothing like the character
in this novel. The real Carolyn is an absolutely lovely, generous,
friendly, smart, and good-hearted soul with a very pleasant
personality. She literally beams with kindness. Anyone would be
lucky to meet her.

✦———•—•✦

To my special Rebel Reader club member, Denise A Monroe
(United States of America), who mentioned her lovely ladies' cigar
smoking group at church in a comment, inspiring the creation of
Sahara and Ocean, the two cigar-smoking, feisty women in this
story.

✦———•—•✦

To the kind and generous readers who take the time to review my
novels and share their frank feedback, thank you so much. Your
support is invaluable.

✦———•—•✦

I'm immensely grateful to you all for your kind and generous
support, and would love to invite you for a glass of British
Columbian wine or a cup of Ceylon tea with chocolates when you
come to Vancouver next.

About the Author

T ikiri Herath is the multiple-award-winning author of international thriller and mystery novels.

◆───────◆

Tikiri has a bachelor's degree from the University of Victoria, Canada, and a master's degree from the Solvay Business School in Brussels, Belgium. For almost two decades, she worked in risk management in the intelligence and defense sectors, including in the Canadian Federal Government and at NATO in Europe and North America.

Tikiri's an adrenaline junkie who has rock climbed, bungee jumped, rode on the back of a motorcycle across Quebec, flown in an acrobatic airplane upside down, and parachuted solo.

When she's not plotting another thriller scene or planning an adrenaline-filled trip, you'll find her baking in her kitchen with a glass of red Shiraz and vintage jazz playing in the background.

An international nomad and fifth-culture kid, she now calls Canada home.

＊━━━━━＊

To say hello and get travel stories from around the world, go to
www.TikiriHerath.com

Made in the USA
Middletown, DE
12 October 2024

62489233R00265